> "JUST BECAUSE YOU'RE BECOMING
> A STAR DOESN'T MEAN YOU FORGET
> WHERE YOU CAME FROM."

Veronica froze in the middle of the room. "Why did you say what you did?" she asked.

"No reason, except that I've seen it too many times before. Local girl makes good, rises to the top, and forgets the names of her friends when they come backstage."

"And you think that's happening to me? That's absurd. You're crazy, Craig."

He came off the bed and struck her across the side of her head with the back of his hand. The blow sent her reeling against a wall. She watched as he quickly dressed and walked to the bedroom door.

"Why?" she asked . . .

THE "GIRLS" IN THE NEWS-ROOM

MARJORIE MARGOLIES

CHARTER BOOKS, NEW YORK

THE "GIRLS" IN THE NEWSROOM

A Charter Book / published by arrangement with
the author

PRINTING HISTORY
Charter edition / July 1983

All rights reserved.
Copyright © 1983 by Marjorie Margolies and Donald Bain
This book may not be reproduced in whole
or in part, by mimeograph or any other means,
without permission. For information address:
Charter Books, 200 Madison Avenue,
New York, New York 10016

ISBN: 0-441-28929-0

Charter Books are published by Charter Communications, Inc.,
200 Madison Avenue, New York, N.Y. 10016.
PRINTED IN THE UNITED STATES OF AMERICA

THE "GIRLS" IN THE NEWSROOM

July, 1982

Howard Monroe, vice-president of news for the Empire Broadcasting System, left the office of EBS's president, Morgan Rachoff. He walked briskly down a long carpeted hall, paused before entering the newsroom, then went to a door on which a sign read Renée Ballantyne. She was executive producer of EBS's nightly network newscast.

"Buy you a drink?" he asked.

She looked up, checked her watch, said, "It's only four-thirty."

"I don't care what time it is, I'd like to buy you a drink. In fact, I insist. It'll be a quick one; we'll be back in a half hour."

She realized it was not a frivolous invitation. It was an order, and since he was her boss she decided not to argue the point. They went downstairs to a bar where an assortment of executives and workingmen were getting an early jump on the evening's relaxation. Monroe placed their order, paid, and they carried their drinks to a table at the rear of the establishment, behind a jukebox.

"Here's to you," he said, raising his glass. She clicked the rim of her glass against it.

After he'd downed most of his bourbon, he leaned across the table and said, "They've done it, Renée."

1

"Done what?"

"Turned over a revamping of News to the clowns in Entertainment."

She sat back and processed what he'd said. There had been rumors that Rachoff was considering a total shake-up of the News Division because of consistently falling ratings against the three network competitors, NBC, ABC, and CBS. But she hadn't considered the possibility of his crossing the line between News and Entertainment. It was unthinkable, violated every canon of the business. She leaned forward and asked, "Are you sure?"

"Damn sure," Monroe said, finishing his drink. "I'd like another. You?"

"No."

She watched him go to the bar and order a second drink over the shoulders of those in front of him. He returned, sat heavily, and said, almost to no one, "Can you believe it, bringing in people like Jenkins Drew and Herb Machlin to tell us what to do with News?" His laugh was bitter, sardonic. "It represents a milestone in journalism, doesn't it?"

"More a low point."

"Worse," he muttered.

"When does this take place?" she asked.

"It's effective right now. Rachoff didn't get very specific, but one thing he did say was that Drew and Machlin wanted a new face, a new anchor."

"That's not too upsetting," Renée said. "We've been talking about it for a long time."

"Yeah, except that they insist it be a woman."

"Hooray," Renée said. She saw that her attempt at humor was not going over, and said seriously, "Any candidates?"

"I wouldn't know, Renée. Rachoff said that Drew and Machlin would go out and find one."

"Good God," she said.

"There is no God, Renée, not in television news, unless his name is Nielsen."

Ten minutes later they were back in their offices, and although the pressure of once again seeing that a nation received a half-hour of news every night occupied most of Renée's thoughts, what Monroe had told her kept bobbing to the surface.

September, 1982

Herb Machlin waved good-bye to his wife, Marcie, boarded the 7:12 commuter train, and found a seat. He stretched and crossed one leg over the other. That was when he noticed his socks. One was royal blue, the other black. "Damn it," he said. Usually, he took time in the morning to see that they matched but he'd been rushed this particular morning. He'd returned home last night after having been on the road for two weeks.

It hadn't been a warm reunion with Marcie. She refused to make love with him because, as she put it, "While you were flitting around the country, I was here running a god-damn car pool and short-order kitchen and clinic and . . . I'm tired, Herbie. Get your hands off me."

He hadn't complained too strenuously, because he'd not been without female companionship on the road, and he was just as happy to roll over and go to sleep.

Herb Machlin's office at the Empire Broadcasting System was on the twenty-sixth floor. A large gold-leaf sign outside the main reception area said Program and Talent Development. Because he'd recently been promoted to second in command, his new office was the second largest in the P-and-T Division. Originally, he'd been disap-pointed that his windows faced west instead of east. He wanted a view of the river, but that was reserved for the largest office, which belonged to his boss, Jenkins Drew.

He settled in behind his desk, emptied the contents of his briefcase, and sorted papers into piles. One of his secretaries, a short bubbly blond named Chris who lived with her parents in Corona, Queens, poked her head into his office and said, "Good morning, Mr. Machlin, welcome back."

Herb looked up and grinned. "Thanks," he said, "but I'd rather be in Cincinnati."

She giggled. "It's supposed to be Philadelphia," she said.

"Not once you've been to Cincinnati. Besides, Cincinnati is a funny word, *and* I had a good time once in Philadelphia."

His other secretary arrived. Her name was Waldine, Wally for short, and she lived with her boyfriend in SoHo. Tall, slender, and brunette, Wally claimed that her boyfriend was an artist. Herb had seen some of his work and had suggested that the kid get out of the business.

"Coffee?" Wally asked.

"Yeah, and I need a favor."

"What is it?" Wally asked.

"After you bring the coffee, run out and buy me a pair of socks."

"Socks?"

"Yeah, black over-the-calf-ones. Here, this should cover it." He slid a ten-dollar bill across the desk.

She picked up the money and asked, "Where will I get them?"

"Jesus, Wally, you get them where everybody gets socks, in a store." He was sorry he sounded so annoyed and added, "Sorry, I'm still on California time."

She brought the coffee, then returned a half-hour later with a pair of Esquire socks, which he changed into once she was gone. He checked his watch. He had almost an hour until a meeting he'd scheduled for the day of his return. He propped his feet up on the desk and carefully went over some of the notes he'd made while traveling. He segregated three sets of pages from the pile and considered, for a moment, having them typed before the meeting; then he decided against it, not only because of the lack of time but because he didn't want to circulate them to others who'd be at the meeting.

Each set of notes he'd pulled from the pile began with a woman's name. The first read:

CINDY LEWIS . . . pert, blond, cute figure. Bubbles, gushes a little too much, a little too cutesy but it could be toned down. Lots of enthusiasm . . . "golly-gee," probably a cheerleader in high school. Sincere as hell, no gloss . . . male population probably in love with her . . . that's it, love, no carnal thoughts . . . maybe not . . . Would look better with slightly longer hair. More sure of herself since last tape. Would pair up okay with a slick male . . . an "in town with the egg money" act . . . good interviewer . . . who the hell would say no to her? Nice rapport with other on-air types. Good Middle America dimension . . . nice rep around town, good local vibes. Not a classic anchorwoman but that could be a plus.

The second set of notes read:

VERONICA FRAZIER . . . dynamite-looking black woman. Smooth as silk, cultured voice, probably worked hard at it. Looks like a high-fashion model . . . tall (like the way she stands around the set and talks to other on-air types) . . . could be considered uppity by some . . . maybe a little too refined . . . too cool? ? ? Could be shaped . . . not much in the chest department but might be the clothing . . . why do black broads always have such dynamite teeth? Contrast with dark skin? ? ? Moves like a cat . . . problem is, doesn't have the look of someone who would roam the streets after a story . . . can't

type her that way, hard-nosed reporter come inside
. . . glad the stock bio gets to her poor background in
Detroit . . . adds dimension. Make a good on-air
match with a blond type . . . male, female? ? ? Probably wouldn't matter. If the racial thing holds up,
she's a definite.

Finally:

MAUREEN O'DWYER . . . remind Sid to include some soft stuff she did on tape to balance the
war-correspondent image . . . push up the audience
tests . . . we all know she's an old pro and that people in News would probably like to see her end up on
the network. For me, she's a bust, does nothing to get
the juices flowing . . . she has that same image that
the rest of them have, serious, concerned about world
events, trying to be a Walter Cronkite with boobs
. . . frankly, she turns me off, has no sex appeal and
won't cause a single male viewer to turn to us.

He used a paper clip to fasten the three sets of notes
together. There were others, each describing a female
newscaster he'd monitored during his trip, but those were
placed in a pile of papers he would not carry to the
meeting.

He again checked his watch, then turned his attention to
a pile of receipts from his trip. Many of them were blank,
and he busily filled in amounts, depending on the type of
restaurant from which he'd taken them. He often joked
with Marcie that filling out his expense account after a trip
was the most creative thing he did in life, and although
there were times he suffered pangs of conscience, his discomfort never lasted any longer than did acid indigestion
after he'd taken a Tums. He considered whatever profit he
made on expenses just compensation for being away from
his family.

It was time to go to the meeting. He gathered up his
papers, checked his appearance in a full-length mirror that
hung on one of his closet doors, and walked briskly

through the secretarial area. Wally tried to say something to him but he ignored her and continued out the door and down a freshly carpeted hallway leading to a large conference room. He paused in front of the door to Jenkins Drew's suite of offices. A man from The Itkins was measuring the area occupied by one of Drew's secretaries, and Machlin felt resentment well up inside him. All the executive offices in Program and Talent Development were being renovated, but Drew was the only one to have his office redesigned by the prestigious Itkins organization. Other executives, including Herbie, were given a modest budget and told to use it the best way they could to spruce up their surroundings.

He entered the conference room, where a dozen chairs were neatly positioned around a large oval oak table. In front of each chair was a fresh pad of lined paper, two pencils on top of each pad, an empty paper coffee cup in a red plastic holder, and a file folder in which certain documents applicable to the meeting had been placed by Wally and Chris.

Ordinarily, Herbie would sit one chair removed from the head of the table, and to Jenkins Drew's right. Today, he went directly to the head because Drew would not be present. Herbie enjoyed chairing meetings after attending a seminar conducted by the American Management Associations in which techniques of running a meeting had been taught.

The room quickly filled and he looked up over half-glasses to give each arriving staff member a quick, professional greeting. Both his assistants arrived and took chairs flanking him. One, Sanford London, was a Harvard M.B.A. who had come up through a management development program. Machlin didn't like him but had had little choice in accepting him on his staff. That was the way it was done at EBS, and he'd learned early in the game that there was no sense in fighting the system.

His other assistant, Rick Simmons, took a chair two removed from the head of the table. Herb motioned for him to move closer. He wanted those two chairs reserved for representatives of the News Division.

Eventually, the people from News arrived. One of them was a wiry little man who wore wire spectacles and heavy dark suits, no matter what the season. His name was Carl Schwartz. He was known as a supreme and dedicated cynic, and his face mirrored it. He'd been around the TV news business a long time, starting as a field producer for a Chicago station, then moving to New York after working in that same capacity at a rival network until being summoned to produce segments of an EBS morning program, *This Day*. He'd done a good job and was quickly elevated through the ranks until recently being named vice-president for network news operations. His appointment had come as a surprise within the industry, and many people claimed that the Peter Principle had reared its ugly head. Machlin had been surprised, too, although in some ways he'd welcomed the news. Schwartz, with his wry, unassuming manner, made Herb feel more at home than did some of the more self-possessed heavy hitters from News.

The other person from News was one of them: Renée Ballantyne, executive producer of EBS's nightly network newscast, *This Night*. She was taller than Carl Schwartz and seemed to stretch for every additional inch she could garner. No one was quite sure of the route she'd taken to reach her position at EBS, although there was much speculation, some of it salacious. She'd established a reputation years ago as an aggressive, effective journalist. After starting in a nonreportorial position with one of the network's owned-and-operated stations in the Southwest, she'd suddenly found herself propelled into the public eye by being in the right place at the right time.

She'd been assigned to cover a feminist convention in Houston, Texas, and had just arrived with a camera crew when one of the most vicious hurricanes in years struck the Gulf Coast. For two days and nights the American television viewing public watched her stand in the midst of the storm, water dripping down her aquiline nose, fierce winds whipping her long blond hair into a wet and stringy mess, her voice filled with urgency as she detailed the storm's devastation. The drama and public identification with her was heightened even more when, during a feed, a piece of roofing landed on her and knocked her to the ground. But as the camera zoomed in on her prone figure half-covered with water, she looked up, held the microphone close to her lips, and continued the story.

From that point forward it was all upward and onward for Renée Ballantyne. She was brought in to coanchor the weekend news, then found herself on *This Night* as a reporter and occasional anchor. Suddenly, in a move no one expected, she abandoned the performer's role and took over the job of associate producer for the nightly news. Six months later she was named executive producer.

She flashed a cursory smile at Herbie as she sat in a chair next to Schwartz and crossed long, slender legs in Herb's direction. She wore a beige linen suit over a lime-green blouse, blond hair pulled back into a loose chignon. There was something of the predator in her features: a pinched nose that threatened to flare at any moment, large green eyes that seemed to be constantly demanding further explanation of everything happening around her, and a full, sensuous set of lips that when pulled back exposed teeth that would be the envy of any cosmetic dentist.

Sandy London asked Schwartz whether he'd caught *60 Minutes* last night, referring specifically to a piece on a government farm loan program riddled with scandal.

Schwartz laughed. "No, I cheated, watched channel thirteen all night."

"Traitor," Machlin said over his glasses. He was about to mention that Marcie had recently donated one hundred dollars to public television and had received, in return, a handsome tote bag and a subscription to *The Dial*, but thought better of it.

Renée Ballantyne glanced at her watch and said, "Could we get on with this? I have another meeting in twenty minutes."

Her request annoyed Machlin. It was, after all, his meeting. He stifled his urge to respond, cleared his throat, and looked down the length of the table, avoiding her eyes. "You all know that I just returned from a trip around the country. I had a chance to monitor some of the candidates firsthand, and I've come up with some definite conclusions about those who should be in the running. I haven't had a chance to write up my notes from the trips, but I can give you a verbal rundown." He waited for some reply from Schwartz and Ballantyne. When there wasn't any, he started to read from the paper with Cindy Lewis's name on it.

"I'm not sure this is necessary," Renée said. "It would make more sense to to wait for the written report from Corsan."

"When are they supposed to give us their recommendations?" Schwartz asked.

"Next week, Carl," she said. She looked at Machlin and smiled. "I'm not suggesting that your opinions from your trip shouldn't be included in the final analysis, but we are investing a great deal of money in Corsan. Maybe it's better to keep your opinions and their findings separate and apart, then see how they match up. I'd rather double-blind it."

It took Machlin a moment to realize she was referring to a classic method of scientific research. He scribbled the word "Corsan" on the legal pad in front of him. Corsan was an independent personality evaluating firm consisting of six psychologists and a battery of trained interviewers. It claimed it could come up with a qualitative analysis of an individual's appeal to others, and had offered EBS a study of candidates for a new female anchor spot. Machlin thought it was a waste of money, and had told Jenkins Drew how he felt, but was told, in turn, that if the News Division wanted to squander its money, it was entitled to. That didn't make any sense to Herb because, according to directives from the highest echelons of the network, the Program and Talent Development Division was to be squarely in the middle of the search for a new female anchor, no matter how distasteful it was to News. Besides, Herb considered all psychological testing nonsense. He'd once been involved in a series of tests in which viewers taken off the street were exposed to different series ideas. Their saliva was evaluated for its salt content, the theory being that the saltier the spit, the more positive the viewer's reaction to what he or she was seeing. The same sort of testing had also been done on their eye movements. None of this made any sense to him, because he believed that decisions about what went on the air should be left to the instincts of professionals in the business, not tainted by a bunch of outside shrinks who were probably too crazy to make valid judgments. But like so many things in the corporate structure, he was powerless to fight it, and had learned long ago to go along with network absurdities while pursuing his own climb toward the top.

He asked Renée Ballantyne how much weight News would assign to the Corsan study, and she indicated it would play a major role.

"I still think it's a waste of money," Herb said.

"Maybe not, Herb," Schwartz said with a thin smile. "Look at it this way. Using Corsan is like taking a physical examination. You feel good, but it takes a doctor's negative findings to prove it to you."

Herb's secretary, Chris, who was taking notes, asked, "Shouldn't it be the other way around? Wouldn't it be better for us if it were positive?"

Machlin tried to disguise his impatience but failed. "It doesn't matter, Chris," he said. "Positive, negative, just write down what you want."

"I was only asking, Mr. Machlin. I want the notes to be correct."

"Put 'positive,'" Herbie said.

"'Negative,'" Schwartz said. "If you want to be correct, young lady, a negative finding is . . ." He bit his lower lip, sat back in his chair, and closed his eyes.

"It doesn't matter, is my point," Herbie said. "Look,

choosing the new anchor is going to end up a matter of subjective judgment anyway. I'll put in my—"

"*I'll?*" Ballantyne asked. "You make it sound terribly dictatorial."

"*Whatever,*" Herbie said. He glanced down at the notes he'd carried with him about the three finalists. "If you don't want a verbal rundown on these people I've focused on, we might as well end this meeting. If you feel better having the Corsan study completed, then that's the way it will have to be."

Carl Schwartz leaned forward, twirled a pencil in his thin fingers, and said, "We're here, Herb. You might as well give us some indication of what you thought about the people you monitored on the trip. What about Veronica Frazier in San Francisco?"

Herb was pleased at Schwartz's interest. He quickly said, "She's definitely a finalist. The same goes for Cindy Lewis in Amarillo."

"Maureen O'Dwyer was up here the other day," Schwartz said.

"I heard," Herbie said. "If it were entirely up to you, she'd be a hands-down favorite, wouldn't she?"

Renée's nose flared as she said, "Maureen is well known and has a solid journalistic reputation. She also has the highest viewer familiarity ratio on the network."

"Would you repeat what you just said?" Chris asked.

"They said she has a familiar face," Sandy London said.

Machlin said, "We've been convinced all along that a new personality would do better, an unknown, someone fresh and provocative."

"Exactly," Rick Simmons said, looking to Herb for approval.

"That might work for game shows and sitcoms," Renée said, "but news is a different ball game. People like their newscasters to be familiar. It makes them comfortable. It gives them security when the rest of the world is falling apart around them. They hear Cronkite's voice or Chancellor's, Harry Reasoner or Howard K. Smith, and somehow they feel they'll make it through the night.''

"Those names might cure insomnia," London said, "but ratings were never built on comfort. Besides, we're talking about females. Name me a female who ever accomplished what you just said about Cronkite.''

Machlin sighed and leaned back. He thrust his hand into the air and said, ''The female half of an anchor team doesn't have to comfort viewers about war or famine or Washington fuck-ups. The woman who coanchors is there to add color and glamour and sex appeal, that's all.''

"That's a little cynical, isn't it?" Schwartz asked.

Herb laughed. "Cynical? For you?"

"Yeah, even for me," Schwartz said. His eyes narrowed, and Herbie realized that he'd gone too far in downgrading what the role of the female anchor would be. He'd denigrated the general role of television news, and no matter how caustic and jaded Carl Schwartz might be, he was a newsman through and through, something his demeanor often caused people to forget.

Renée stood and asked, "I have to go. Maybe we can do this again after Corsan has reported.''

Sandy London said, "We still haven't ruled out raiding a competitor.''

Herbie realized he'd shifted his attention to Renée's body beneath the beige suit. All professional considerations aside, she was a hell of a good-looking woman.

Schwartz seemed unsure whether to respond to London or to get up and leave with Renée. He stood, told her he'd be with her in a moment, then turned and said to London, "Going outside is a mistake, and I've said that from the beginning. There's only one way to build a ball club, and that's through a solid farm system. Buying up free agents might win games for a few years, but it can only be temporary.''

"This isn't a ball game, Carl," Machlin said, "this is network television.''

Schwartz's expression said many things. He said in a weary voice, "I know."

There was a moment of silence, which was broken by Renée's laugh. She'd stood at the door taking in the exchange, but now she returned to the table, placed her hands flat on it, looked Machlin in the eye, and said, "I want you to know, Herb, that not only do I resent the cavalier approach to choosing someone to report the news to millions of people every night, but I especially resent what you said before about a female coanchor being nothing more than window dressing."

The directness of her words and hard stare made him very uncomfortable. He glanced at Sandy London but received nothing in the way of support. Carl Schwartz leaned against the wall of the conference room and methodically tamped tobacco into a pipe. Chris looked up, her pencil poised over her legal pad. Rick Simmons seemed interested in coming to his boss's defense but couldn't find the words.

"I didn't mean anything by it," Machlin said, and he was immediately sorry he did. She'd put him on the defensive, and he hated being in that position.

"People shouldn't say what they don't mean," she said. She stood, and her face softened as a smile emerged. Obviously, she was savoring having backed him down, and any discomfort he was feeling only enhanced her satisfaction.

Rick Simmons said, "I've heard the rumor that Mr. Monroe is still interested in going after Sue Patton from channel eleven."

"The rumor I heard is that he's had a crush on her for years," Sandy London said.

"It wouldn't work," Machlin said.

"I have to go," Schwartz said as he held a match close to the tobacco and drew with gusto. "I have to see Mike Ackerman up in Legal."

Herbie shuffled his papers together and asked, "About the equal-time thing?"

"No, about his boat. He's selling it. I want to make him an offer. '

"Well, thanks for coming," Herb said. Schwartz nodded and went through the door, followed closely by Renée. Sandy London asked Herb whether he had time to discuss something.

"Not now, Sandy. I have some appointments. Catch me after lunch."

He had lunch with an airline stewardess he'd met on a flight a number of months ago. He tried to convince her to go to her apartment but she refused, which took the edge off the lunch they shared at Peng's, his favorite Chinese restaurant. He returned to the office, where he finished creating his expense account and gave Wally the forms to type, along with the notes he'd made on his trip around the country. He called Marcie, who informed him that one of the children had been acting up in school and that the teacher requested they make an appointment to see her.

"When the hell am I supposed to do that?" he snapped into the phone.

"He's your son, Herbie," she said.

"Yeah, but dealing with teachers is your problem. I don't have time. What's for dinner?"

"I don't know. What train are you catching?"

"I haven't figured that out yet."

He caught the 7:06 after a couple of drinks in a commuter bar at Grand Central. He'd seen a few familiar faces but chose to drink alone. It usually took two drinks before he could put behind him the frustrations of the day and reflect on anything, especially his own life. All in all it had been an unsatisfactory day, beginning with the mix-up with socks and ending with an unpleasant exchange at five-thirty with his boss, Jenkins Drew, who subtly questioned whether Herbie had a handle on the delicate matter of intruding into the News Division in search of a female coanchor. Drew had said in his tight Ivy League manner, "We've been given this challenge from the very top, Herb, and how well we perform could determine not only the direction of individual careers in this division, but the future of the division as well."

All Herbie could do was agree with Drew, although he resented the implication. "How'd a nice guy like me end up like this?" he asked himself.

"What?" a gray-suited executive sitting next to him asked.

"Oh, nothing," Herbie said, cupping his glass with both hands and looking into the shimmering clear gin. He fell into a pleasant, introspective state, and thought back to his beginnings in broadcasting. It had started in his hometown of Pittsburgh, where he'd studied communications at college, had gone on to be a disc jockey on two small stations in Pennsylvania before returning to Pittsburgh, where he became a management trainee at EBS's Pittsburgh O-and-O, one of five stations wholly owned by the network. Most stations carrying network programming were independently owned and chose to be EBS affiliates. He rose to the position of general manager at that station, and after an impressive year in which billings and profits increased dramatically, he was summoned to New York for a job in network radio programming.

He became friends with the vice-president of radio O-and-O's, and when it was decided that something drastic had to be done to beef up the New York outlet to make it more than simply a conduit for network programming, Herbie's advice was sought. He had lunch with his friend and suggested that the only real way to make the change was to fire everybody and hire the best talent in the country. "Of course," he'd added, "that'll take megabucks."

"No problem," his friend told him. "They've just come down with a million-and-a-half budget for talent to get the job done. I've suggested that you spearhead the project. How's that sound to you?"

That was the way it had started. He jumped into the project with zeal and scoured the nation for the best emerging on-air talent. After three months in a succession of motel and hotel rooms with his ear glued to a portable radio, he returned with a briefcase bulging with notes and a clear idea of whom he wanted to bring to New York. He cleared his choices with his friend, then fired the existing management of the New York outlet and replaced it with friends from other stations whom he considered loyal to him. Once he had the new management team together, he dangled lucrative offers in front of the talent he'd decided on. He knew, of course, that the biggest carrot of all was the chance to come to the Big Apple, where being on the air screamed of making it.

It had worked. The station's new talent and management, aided by a million-dollar advertising campaign, paid off in significantly higher ratings. It also brought Herbie to the attention of network brass on the television side. He'd become known as someone who had his finger on listener and viewer pulses, someone with an inherent, almost mystical ability to evaluate talent. Soon, he was firmly ensconced in the Program and Talent Development Division, second in command only to Jenkins Drew, and a shiny new nameplate that read Herbert N. Machlin—the *N* standing for Nance—was affixed outside the second biggest office on the floor.

"You want another?" the bartender asked. Herb checked his watch. There wasn't time. Besides, they poured stiff drinks in the bar and he was feeling them. He paid his bill, slapped an old friend on the back, and caught his train.

AMARILLO, TEXAS

Cindy Lewis pulled into the driveway of her home on Amarillo's southwest side and pushed the button on the garage door opener. The door groaned and slid up against the ceiling. She pulled her dusky-rose Lincoln in next to her husband's blue one, turned off the ignition, and went inside. The house smelled of onions, testimony to what the family had had for dinner. The Carson show could be heard coming from a den at the rear of the house. She stopped to pet the family dog, a mutt they'd picked up four years ago, flipped through a pile of mail on a Spanish table in the foyer, and went to the den. Her husband, Hal, was asleep in a black vinyl recliner, the TV blaring in front of him. She turned down the volume and sat on the arm of the chair. "Hi," she said, touching his cheek.

He awoke with a start. "Oh, I . . . you're home. Hi." He kissed her.

"You had onions for dinner."

"Onions? Oh, right, Maria made a beef dish with them. How are you?"

"Good." She went to a matching chair a few feet away, kicked off her shoes, and massaged one foot with the other.

"How did it go?" she asked.

"What?"

"The newscast."

"Oh, fine. It's always good. You know that."

She knew he'd fallen asleep five minutes into the news, just as he always did. It bothered her, yet she was appreciative that he at least made the effort night after night to stay up to see her. There had been a time when she would question him about specific portions of the news to catch him in a lie, but she'd given up the practice. It wasn't fair. He worked hard all day and had to be given *A* for effort.

"Want a drink?" he asked.

"I'd love one. A little bourbon and ice, light, please."

She leaned back in the recliner and closed her eyes. The fatigue of having put in a long, arduous, and productive day at the station was so different from the fatigue she used to experience after a day at home with the kids. Then, her days had been spent busying herself around the house preparing for Hal's return from the insurance agency that bore his name. He'd come home, they'd have a drink before dinner, and a wave of fatigue would settle in on her, as though someone had released it through the air-conditioning ducts.

This was different. Any physical and mental exhaustion after a day at the station was mitigated by a rush of un-defined, welcome exhilaration.

Hal handed her the drink.

"Aren't you having one?"

"No. I had lunch with Arnie and Billy. We had a few. Enough's enough."

"To us," Cindy said, raising her glass.

"I'll drink to that," he said, an imaginary glass in his hand.

"Me, too," she said.

"Me, too."

It was a ritual between them. Years ago, when they were courting, she'd called him at the house of his best friend and told him on the phone that she loved him. He was embarrassed to reply in front of his friend and simply said, "Me, too." It had caused his friend and his wife to laugh. "Me, too," they parroted. "She must have said she loved you."

Hal and Cindy had been saying it to each other ever since, and she closed every newscast with it.

The dog, whose name was Jesse, nuzzled his snout beneath her knee and whined. She asked Hal, "Everybody's asleep?"

He shook his head. "Johnny's still awake. I think he's working on that model I bought him."

"That's nice. Any calls?"

"No. There's mail."

"I saw it. Junk."

"Hmmmm." He knelt in front of her chair and ran his hand over her foot. "I miss you."

"I miss you, too."

His hand went up her leg until it came to rest between her thighs. "Let's go to bed."

"I'm too wound up."

"The drink will relax you."

"I know. In a minute."

Hal got up from his knees and motioned for Jesse to follow him. "Come on, boy, let's take a walk."

They left the den and Cindy was overwhelmed with a rush of sadness. She sipped her drink and gazed absently at the television screen while she tried to identify the source of her feelings.

There was guilt, certainly, contributing to her melancholy, an emotional guilt that was at constant odds with her intellect. She knew cognitively that returning to work had not betrayed her commitment to Hal and to the kids. She'd managed to shelve her journalistic aspirations when their first child, John, was born, and had contented herself with being the linchpin that held the Lewis family to the wheel. They'd been blessed with two other fine, healthy, and handsome children. Hal had built his insurance agency into the most successful one in town, and Cindy had guided the development of the Lewis brood, taking immense satisfaction from seeing the positive results of her efforts. It was a good family made up of good people, and she often acknowledged, at least to herself and sometimes to Hal, how blessed she'd been.

Two years ago she'd broached the subject of returning to work. Hal wasn't pleased at the contemplation but didn't stand in the way of her reentering the field for which she'd trained at the University of Texas, and that she found inherently fascinating and rewarding.

The *Amarillo Globe Times,* where Cindy had worked as a reporter prior to meeting and falling in love with Hal, enthusiastically offered her a job, which didn't surprise anyone. She'd proved herself a dedicated, hardworking, and aggressive reporter during her days at the *Globe Times,* and had been instrumental in uncovering a story of gross malfeasance in office involving two wealthy and powerful members of local government. The exposé that resulted had won the paper numerous journalistic accolades and awards.

She would have taken the job at the newspaper had a client of Hal's not intervened. He was station manager for a local owned-and-operated station, and persuaded her to try television. It proved to be a good move. The money was twice what the newspaper job would have paid, and the exposure she gained by being part of the nightly news, first as a reporter, then as coanchor, provided a pleasant notoriety. She and Hal became a highly visible couple in Amarillo and, despite the conflicts in their schedules that left them a limited amount of time together, the arrangement had worked.

Hal returned to the house with Jesse, turned off the television, and smiled at his wife. "It's been a long day, Miss Anchorwoman, let's hit the sack." He took her hand and pulled her to her feet. She looked up into his gray eyes. He was considerably taller than she was, and kept in good shape by jogging, playing tennis, and swimming at the local YMCA. He was a handsome man by any standards and had grown even more so as the hair at his temples silvered and the lines in his face gave added definition to his features. There were times—and this was one of them—when Cindy responded passionately to his masculinity.

They embraced, and he slid his hand down to cup her buttocks beneath the silky fabric of her yellow dress. "I love you," he whispered into her ear.

"Me, too," she said, aware of his emerging hardness. "Let me say good night to Johnny."

"See you in bed," he said, an exaggerated leer in his voice.

Johnny had fallen asleep on his bed with his clothes on. A half-completed airplane model was strewn all over his desk. Cindy woke him, urged him to change into pajamas and to go to bed. He said he would, returned her kiss, and pulled the pillow over his head.

"Now," she said.

"Okay, Mom." He got up and hunted for his pajamas in a drawer. "Good night, Ma."

"Good night, honey. Sweet dreams."

Hal was in bed when Cindy reached the bedroom. She knew he was naked beneath the covers and waiting for her. She was tired, and despite the vague yearnings she felt in her groin, she could easily have postponed lovemaking. But she wouldn't, not this night. She would satisfy him and feel less guilty than she'd felt in the den.

Quietly, in moonlight filtering through partially closed venetian blinds, she undressed and placed her clothing on a chair. Hal watched, his head propped up on a pillow.

"Damn," Cindy said when she was naked. She pinched a tiny roll of fat on her belly. "I'd better get out there and jog with you."

"Don't you dare," he said, extending his arms to her. "You know I love every inch of you, including—no, especially—your belly."

"I'll be back in a minute."

She returned from the bathroom and slipped beneath the

cool sheets. The feel of him against her, his hands stroking, thigh against thigh, lips and tongues caressing, sent a spasm of pleasure through her body. He kissed her nose, then her eyelid.

"You feel good," she said, finding him with her hand.

He came over on top of her, leaned on his elbows, the tip of his penis brushing against her vulva. He looked down into her eyes and said, "I miss you, damn it."

"Don't say that," she said, her voice breathless as he slowly stroked the exterior of her with his maleness. "We're here now." She didn't want to hear his complaints about how little time they seemed to find for each other since she'd returned to work. Although a tension had been growing, she preferred to ignore it, to put her head in the sand and to deal with only the good between them. "Kiss me," she said.

He moved lower so that he could kiss her breasts, his fingers probing between her legs as he did. Her breathing became deeper and she emitted a low guttural moan. He resumed his position on top of her and slowly, deliberately, penetrated. She gasped at the sudden sensation of being filled with him and they began to move easily, in concert, their mutual pleasure slowly building.

The sound of the phone at the side of the bed was deafening in the dark, passionate stillness of the room. It was one of two phones in the bedroom, a special one installed at the TV station's expense that was to be kept clear in case some late-breaking important event occurred that would involve Cindy.

"Jesus," Hal muttered as he continued moving.

"Damn it," she said. Her movement ceased.

"Let it ring," he said.

"Hal, I . . ."

The ringing continued. Hal raised himself up, took a deep breath, and withdrew. He fell on his back, his head on the pillow, his teeth clenched. Cindy picked up the phone.

"Cindy?" a male voice asked.

"Yes."

"This is Sammy at the station. Bob called me."

"What is it?" she asked.

"That Klan rally tomorrow morning. He wants you to cover it."

"I thought Ricky was assigned to it."

"He was, but the network wants a feed from here tomorrow night. Bob wants you to do it personally."

"I . . . the network? Why are they interested?"

"Who knows, who cares? Hey, Cindy, don't knock it. A network feed is a network feed. Anyway, the boss says cover it and I'm passing it along like a dutiful, loyal employee."

Cindy glanced over at Hal, who had turned his back to her. She said into the phone, "All right, Sammy, have a crew pick me up at the house."

"Sure. Nine?"

"Who's working with me?"

"Jack Jicklin, for sure. I don't know about sound, maybe Chip."

"That's great, a black sound man covering a Ku Klux Klan rally."

"Might be fun. Pleasant dreams. Hope I didn't disturb anything."

She hung up. The irony of the call's timing struck her. Early in her career that phone had rung with annoying regularity. That was when she was a reporter spending her days, and too many nights, covering stories around town. But once she'd been named to coanchor the news, there had been a distinct drop-off in emergency calls. They went to others who toiled in the reporter role.

She sat up against the headboard and thought of what to say to Hal. If it had happened a few years ago, she would have tried to initiate lovemaking again, but she knew such an attempt would fail now. Her demanding role as a career woman had become an increasing bone of contention between them, although Hal tried very hard not to express his feelings about it. He wanted to be a supportive husband in her quest for self-fulfillment, but there were times his resentment got the better of him. Unfortunately, it had been allowed to crawl into the marriage bed with them and was sometimes expressed, however, subtly, in that most intimate of settings.

She touched his bare shoulder. "Hal, I'm sorry. I should have taken it off the hook."

He said, without moving, "You can't take it off the hook, Cindy. Who knows when you might be needed to cover a great national disaster?" He didn't try to disguise the bitterness in his voice.

They were silent for a few moments until she said, "Hal, I promise I'll figure out a way to find more time for us. We have a vacation coming up in a month."

"Do we?" He did not turn to face her. "Have you arranged for it? It wouldn't be the first time that a vacation plan had to be changed because of the demands of your profession."

"Nothing will get in the way of this, Hal, I promise. It's all set."

Now, he turned. She took his hand and they sat next to each other, their eyes fixed straight ahead at a pattern of light filtering through a window and dancing on the far wall. "What did they want?" he asked.

"I have to cover that Klan rally in the morning. I hadn't planned to go in tomorrow until two. I wanted to spend the morning with the kids."

He turned his head slightly. "Why didn't you refuse, then?"

"I don't know. I'll be on the network tomorrow night."

"Good."

"Hal."

"What?"

"It is my job."

He squeezed her hand, got up and slipped into pajamas, then returned to bed and turned on his side. "Have a good sleep, Cindy."

"You, too. And me, too." She kissed the back of his head.

She heard him drift off into sleep, an occasional snore confirming it. As tired as she was, she didn't fall asleep for an hour, and her final thought was that she must call her sister in St. Louis in the morning to tell her to be sure to watch the network news that night.

Chapter 4

SAN FRANCISCO, CALIFORNIA

Veronica Frazier climbed behind the wheel of a new taupe Porsche she'd taken delivery on a week ago, waved to an employee-parking-lot guard, and headed into town. The eleven o'clock news had gone smoothly except for when, as she began a news item about the Iranian hostages, the rear-screen projection behind her flashed a picture of San Francisco Giants star Jackie Clark. She'd covered the goof easily, quipping that other teams in the National League would like to see the streaking Clark taken captive. The moment the newscast was over she laced into the director for allowing the mistake. He apologized, as he always did when there was a miscue, then muttered to his assistant when she was out of earshot, "They ought to send that black bitch back to the Mandingos."

She cut in front of a cable car on Hyde, stopped to allow a wino to stumble across the street, and proceeded to Leavenworth, then to the crest of Lombard Street, the world's most crooked street. She eased down the narrow winding road until she reached a short break in the hill that served as a driveway to her rented house. She'd fallen in love with it the moment the real estate agent had shown it to her. The rent was steep—fourteen hundred a month—

but it seemed worth it. Lately, the constant stream of tourists had begun to bother her, but not enough to consider moving. The house represented a dream come true, a jewel in the middle of a city she loved.

She left the Porsche in the driveway, climbed the steps, pulled mail from the box, and leaned down to pet Sugar, one of two Siamese cats—the other was, of course, named Spice. The door was unlocked, as she knew it would be. She'd seen his Mercedes parked on Leavenworth, at the top of Lombard, had heard the faint strains of recorded music from her stereo as she approached the front door.

"Craig?" she called from the foyer.

"In here."

Spice rubbed against her leg as she flipped through the mail before tossing it on a red-lacquered reproduction of a Chinese antique table. She kicked her shoes into a corner and went to the living room, where Craig Stanton stood next to the fireplace. She kissed him lightly on the mouth, then allowed him to pull her close and to increase the intensity of the kiss.

"I need a drink," she said. "I see you're ahead of me."

Stanton laughed and sipped his scotch. "You looked good tonight," he said, referring to her newscast.

"Thanks, but did you see the foul-up on the hostage story? Stupid bastard does it all the time. He's so hung up on that little blond bitch he hired as a production assistant that he can't keep anything straight."

"Go easy on Morris. He's a good director."

"I'm heading for the shower. Where's my drink?"

"Jesus, you are a tiger tonight, aren't you?" he said as he went to the bar in the corner of the room and made her a kir.

"Thanks," she said, taking the glass and heading for the bathroom. "Only a minute."

"I only have a minute," he called after her.

Stanton sat in a leather-and-chrome sling chair and put

29

his feet up on an ottoman. He checked his watch. It was getting late. He'd told his wife he was entertaining out-of-town media buyers and would be stuck with them well into the evening. She wouldn't question him, but there was no sense in pushing things.

Craig Stanton had been having an affair with Veronica Frazier for over a year, ever since his efforts to launch her on a broadcast journalism career had borne fruit. Veronica was his discovery.

He'd first become aware of her when she was a senior in communications at Berkeley, and he'd been a guest lecturer. There wasn't any debate on his part—she was the most beautiful female he'd ever seen, and he'd left the classroom determined to get to know her.

Which was easy. He contacted her prior to graduation, took her to dinner, and offered to pave the way with some of his broadcasting colleagues in the city. The first job through his connections was with a small radio station that played acid rock, where Veronica did hourly five-minute newscasts. Stanton's friend hadn't even bothered auditioning her. If the general manager of San Francisco's biggest television station wanted her in the slot, that was the way it would be.

Veronica was openly appreciative of what Stanton had done for her and frequently demonstrated it, but not in the way he'd hoped for—in bed.

Six months after she'd begun work at the rock outlet, Stanton arranged an audition for her at a larger radio station that was news and public affairs oriented. She was hired, which meant significantly more money and prestige. By this time, they'd started sleeping together, usually once a week in an apartment he'd found for her in North Beach, and on which he contributed to the rent. He never questioned the equity of the arrangement. She was everything he'd anticipated, a warm, imaginative, and loving sexual partner.

Often, he would lie in bed and simply stare at her, the

dusky, burned quality of her skin, the fine nose and almond eyes, breasts that were surprisingly full and firm when freed, a belly curving seductively above a dark rich patch of gleaming sexual hair. She moved in bed as she did out of it, with consummate grace and assurance, touching him at precisely the right time and in the right place, *knowing* his needs and desires, *anticipating* them so that he never needed to express them.

Six months ago he'd hired her to work for him. It was not a popular move within the ranks of those already employed by him. She didn't join the working reporters who chased stories around the city, but became a coanchor right from the start. Stanton defended his decision to his critics. The addition of a black, and a black *woman* to boot, was a smart move, he preached. Besides, she was good, no doubt about that. He'd never seen anyone her age possessing so much presence, and she was a good *reader,* as good as the best the network had to offer.

There was, of course, a period of tension while Stanton waited for a tangible display of viewer reaction and, by extension, advertiser response. His decision quickly proved itself. Aside from a few disgruntled written comments from viewers, most of them racist, Veronica was a success. The dissension within the station eventually dissipated, although it remained as an undercurrent of snide comments and an occasional overt display that quickly faded in the hustle and bustle of the daily grind.

Stanton finished his drink, stood, and looked at himself in a smoked mirror on the wall above the fireplace. "You look beat," he told himself. No wonder. He'd risen to his high management position by means of a single-minded dedication to achieving it, putting it above all other considerations, family and friends, hobbies, vacations, everything—except Veronica. He was drawn to her like a moth to a summer candle, couldn't get enough of her.

He went to the bedroom, decorated in pastel silks and dominated by a king-size bed, stripped off his clothes, and carefully placed them over a chair back. A single pin spot focused on a Kandinski print was the room's only illumination. Naked, he used another mirror to evaluate himself. He didn't look bad for fifty, aside from too many rich and expensive lunches and dinners adding pounds around the middle. He'd been blessed with good thick Irish hair that he'd only recently begun to dye to temper creeping white at the temples.

Veronica stood beneath the shower and enjoyed the incessant sting of hot water against her body. At the same time she was disturbed that Stanton was waiting for her outside the door. He seemed always to be there, taking a proprietary interest in the house that she preferred to view as her own. That was the problem, nothing ever seemed to be her own. She was always mortgaged to someone, and Craig Stanton seemed to hold a lease on her life no matter how hard she tried to break it.

Her salary should have been enough to support a good life-style. That was to her one of the wonders of broadcasting, the amount of money paid to on-air personalities for doing so little. But when push came to shove, she couldn't afford the expensive trappings of her new life, and rather than do without those things that were expensive, she found it easier to accept the terms of the relationship with Stanton. She didn't admire herself for it, simply viewed it as another temporary reality leading to her ultimate ambition, total independence in her professional and personal life.

Stanton heard the shower stop and pictured her stepping from it, water dripping onto a fluffy pink rug, fringes of damp hair protruding from beneath her shower cap. It was a provocative image, and he responded physically.

The phone rang. Veronica walked into the bedroom and picked up the receiver. "Hello," she said.

Stanton came up behind her, cupped her breasts, and pressed his pelvis against her buttocks.

"... I'm surprised, that's all," she said into the

mouthpiece. ". . . No, no, that wouldn't be good. I'm . . . I'm busy . . ."

Stanton stepped back and observed her. She obviously was uncomfortable with her caller and wanted to end the conversation, yet wasn't sure how to do it. Finally, she said, "I will, I promise. Yes, of course." She hung up.

"Who was that?" Stanton asked.

"Oh, just an old friend from Detroit. A neighborhood pal. We grew up together."

"What's his name?"

"Roscoe . . . oh, it doesn't matter."

"I don't believe you."

Her laugh was forced. "Why not?" she asked, going to a table and lighting a cigarette.

"Are you seeing somebody else?" he asked as he sat on the edge of the bed.

"Of course not." Her anger flared. She stamped out the cigarette in an ashtray, turned, and said, "What if I were? You don't own me, for Christ's sake. You're married. We have a relationship. That's nice, but who ever said I couldn't see somebody else if I wanted to?"

Stanton reclined, a hand and elbow beneath his head. "*I* said it, Veronica. Who's the guy who called?"

"I told you who he was."

"And I say you're a liar." He sat up and pointed his finger at her. "Don't jerk me around, Ronnie. You owe me too much."

"Oh, God." She took a silk robe from the closet and wrapped herself in it, lighted another cigarette, and said softly, "Please, Craig, I'm very tired. I don't want to fight. How about being a good guy and going home? I need a long, quiet sleep . . . alone."

He got up from the bed and dressed. When he was finished, he came to where she sat in a chair in front of her dressing table, kissed her on the ear, and said, "I meant what I said, Ronnie. Don't ever forget it."

"We'll talk tomorrow. Can you get free after the news?

Maybe we can catch some music, come back here, and . . ."

"I'm tied up, can't get free. Make it Sunday. I'm going tc New York at noon Sunday. I'll come by early with the papers and we can spend a few hours."

"That'll be nice. Thanks for understanding."

"See you tomorrow."

"Okay."

When he was gone, when she was *certain* he was gone, she picked up the phone and dialed a number in Detroit. Her mother answered on the first ring.

"Mama?"

"Ronnie? What's the matter? Is something wrong?"

She laughed. "Why do you always think something's wrong when I call you?"

"It's too much money to call all the way from California."

Veronica didn't argue. They'd been through it before. She said, "I just wondered how you were doing."

"Just fine, honey."

"Did you go to the doctor?"

"I will, don't you worry."

Veronica couldn't help the pique in her voice. "You promised me you'd go last week, remember? You promised you'd see him before you come out here."

"I'll call him first thing in the morning. Now, that's a promise, Ronnie." Her voice was patronizing, soothing, a mother comforting a child.

They talked for a few minutes about mundane things, the conversation peppered with her mother's protestations about how much the call was costing. Finally, bringing up what had been on her mind when she'd picked up the phone, Veronica asked, "Have you seen Roscoe Williams lately?"

There was a pause, but not long enough to be meaningful. Her mother said, "He's been around."

"Why?"

"Asking about you. I told him I wasn't sure where you were."

"Then why did he call me here?"

"He did? I wish he hadn't done that."

"So do I."

She was again the consoling mother. "Well, don't you worry a hair about that man. You have enough to worry about with all your television business. I'm so proud of you I could just scream out the window."

Veronica thought of the window in her mother's bedroom. It was small and looked out over an alley strewn with bottles and other debris. She forced herself to lighten her voice as she said, "Save your screams for the dinner, Mama. I'll be so happy to have you here."

"Did you find out yet whether you won somethin'?"

"No. They don't announce the winners until the night of the awards. I might not win, you know."

"It doesn't matter. Every day I'm alive I realize how much I've won by having a daughter like my Ronnie."

Veronica fought back tears. "We'll have a nice time together no matter who wins, Mama. You'll love San Francisco."

She laughed. "I don't know if I will. I've never been on an airplane before. I don't like it, flyin' around up in the sky like a bird."

Veronica laughed, too. "You'll enjoy every minute of it."

"You're sure I won't be a nuisance staying with you?"

"You, a nuisance? You're my mother. I just wish you could stay longer."

Her mother cleaned house for a woman in Grosse Pointe and was afraid she'd lose the job if she was away too long. No matter how much money Veronica sent her each month, her mother hung on to the job, and the checks were deposited in a savings account bearing both their names.

After they'd hung up, Veronica went to the living room

and shut off the lights and the stereo. She returned to the bedroom, got on the bed, and huddled against the headboard, her legs drawn up tightly beneath her, the knuckles of her right hand pressed against her mouth. She wanted to cry, yet knew she would not. The crying had ended long ago.

She remained on the bed in that position for almost an hour, until fatigue washed over her and she allowed herself to stretch out and to drift into a dream-riddled sleep that caused her to toss and turn all night and to awaken in the morning in a tangled heap of bedclothes.

_____CHAPTER 5

Maureen O'Dwyer arrived at Washington's National Airport and was met by an aide to Congressman Jack Maitland. Maureen had been seeing Maitland socially ever since his divorce six months ago. They had dinner together on the average of once a week, and spent occasional weekends at his Virginia home. He'd told her the last time they were together that he thought he might be falling in love with her.

And she'd replied, "When you're sure, let me know."

It was typical of her. Maureen had a reputation for possessing an acid tongue, which, although it occasionally got in the way socially, served her well in her profession. She was known as the toughest interviewer in the business, a no-nonsense journalist who kept up with current affairs and who wasn't afraid to stick someone with an embarrassing, revealing question, no matter how lofty his position.

She'd traveled with the First Lady, had exposed a scandal involving the misappropriation of refugee funds, and had spent two days with a mass murderer who'd said the only person he'd speak to was Maureen O'Dwyer. Visiting despots requested interviews with her, wives of politicians in trouble easily confided in her, and a President of the

United States had once quipped, "Maureen O'Dwyer scares the hell out of me."

"How was New York?" Congressman Maitland's aide asked as the limo headed for town.

"Vibrant and alive, a melting pot," Maureen replied as she pulled a pocket mirror from her purse and played with her hair. "And dirty. How's Mr. Maitland?"

The aide smiled. Maureen always called his boss "Mr." Ordinarily, one might have taken it as an attempt to disguise the affair between them. With Maureen, however, there was another meaning that escaped few people, including the congressman's aide. She said "Mr." with a finely honed hint of scorn, as one might say "Your Majesty" or "Msssssss."

"Jack is fine," said the aide. "He's looking forward to seeing you."

"It'll have to wait."

"Pardon?"

"I didn't get a chance to call before getting on the plane. I'll have to cancel dinner with him tonight because I have a business appointment." The aide was obviously perplexed by what she'd said. She added, to minimize his discomfort, "Maybe I can catch up with him later in the evening."

"He was planning on it."

"The best-laid plans of mice and men. . . . Tell him I'm sorry, but this came up as I was leaving New York. It's very important."

"I'll tell him."

She leaned forward and said to the uniformed driver, "The Jockey Club, please, at Massachusetts and Twenty-first." She touched Maitland's aide on the arm and said sweetly, "You don't mind, do you? I appreciate the ride."

"Sure. You will call him?"

"Tell him I'll call before ten. And please apologize for me. It couldn't be helped."

"Good evening, Miss O'Dwyer," the maitre d' at the Jockey Club said, "Mr. Coughlin is waiting inside."

"Thanks," she said, "but I need the john first."

She lingered for a few minutes in front of the ladies' room mirror. Looking back at her was a thirty-five-year-old redhead with green eyes. It had been a long and arduous day and she knew she reflected it. The crow's-feet around her eyes and the lines in her forehead seemed especially pronounced. She ran her tongue beneath her upper lip and squinted at her mirror image.

"Are you Maureen O'Dwyer?" a woman asked as she exited the inner recesses of the facility.

"Yes."

"I love you on TV."

"Thank you."

"I don't like Mr. Poulson, though," said the woman. "I don't trust him." She laughed. "But I never did trust men whose eyes are too close together. My former husband had eyes like that."

"I'll be sure to tell Mr. Poulson," Maureen said, inwardly smiling at the reaction that was sure to come from her coanchor on the evening newscast.

"Oh, don't tell him. I mean, I like him, but those eyes are . . ."

"I know, so close together. Have a nice evening."

"Thank you. You, too."

The woman left, and Maureen returned her attention to the mirror. Her father, who was now dead, had told her repeatedly, "Honey, you look better getting up in the morning than most women do on their way out to a ball." She seldom forgot his words, especially when the mirror said otherwise. She ran a hand around the waistband of her skirt to straighten out wrinkles in a pale-green-and-white-striped cotton button-down blouse she wore beneath a tan blazer, applied an added touch of lipstick, and headed for the dark-paneled dining room where Joe Coughlin was waiting.

"Hello, gorgeous," he said, standing and pulling out a chair.

"Hello, Joe. Sorry I'm late."

"I didn't notice. Drink?"

"God, yes, I need one after spending the day with the sharks."

Coughlin laughed, motioned for a waiter, and ordered extra-dry martinis for both of them. "I'm ahead," he said, indicating an empty glass.

"You usually are, Joe. Have you noticed what's happened to airline stewardesses?"

"No."

"They've become ugly, ill mannered, and every goddamn one of them has the mind of a mole."

"That bad?"

"Worse. I saw one of them actually picking her nose. Speaking of that, what's new here in the nation's capital?"

"Speaking of *that*?"

The waiter brought the drinks and she took a long, sustained, and satisfying swig. "Wonderful," she said, licking her lips. "I hope I don't become an alcoholic, because I'd hate to think of never enjoying one of these again after a shitty day."

"Really bad, huh?" Coughlin didn't mean it. He'd heard her complaints for years since becoming her agent and manager. It was an unofficial relationship at best. He'd been around Washington a long time, first as a congressional aide, later moving into public relations and lobbying. He headed a PR agency that handled mostly industrial association accounts, but had taken on a few local celebrities, first as their publicity agent, then moving into other areas of their professional lives, including money management.

Maureen finished her martini and looked across the small table at Joe. He was, as she sometimes put it to friends, right out of central casting, a ruddy-faced Irishman who wore expensive suits, was possessed of that mythical Irish gift of gab, and who could hold his liquor with the best of them. The only thing she didn't like about Joe was his lacquered fingernails. Her husband, from whom she'd been divorced for many years, had used clear polish and, aside from a myriad of other factors that had caused them to separate after only five months of marriage, his shiny nails had played their part.

"So, my friend, tell me about New York," Coughlin said.

She motioned for the waiter to bring her another, then turned to Joe and said, "I don't think they'll give it to me."

"Why do you say that?"

"Tits and ass, that's why."

"Huh?"

"A song from *Chorus Line*. Without a nice tush and a set of boobs, a girl doesn't stand a chance in show biz."

Joe stifled a laugh that was building. Finally, he said, "Frankly, Maureen, I wasn't aware you lacked those things. In fact . . ."

"Don't take me literally, damn it." The waiter delivered her refill. "Have you heard anything about the Entertainment types being involved in finding a new female network anchor?"

He shook his head.

"I heard that up in New York. Do you know what that means, Joe? It means that Charlie's Angels will be doing the news pretty soon." She cupped one ear and mimicked an announcer as she said, "Good evening, ladies and gentlemen, we bring you nightly *jiggle,* featuring that vision of loveliness, that bombshell, that adorable young thing who gives T-shirts a good name, Miss Mammary Gland herself. . . ."

"You're overreacting."

"In a pig's ass I am." She grabbed his arm and leaned close, her voice taking on an urgency. "Joe, there isn't one goddamn newswoman in this business who can hold a candle to me. I've been paying my dues for a long time. I want that anchor slot, damn it. If News were making the decision, I know it would be mine, even though they're a gang of second-rate managers who wouldn't know a breaking story from a topless bar. But if Entertainment is involved, God help me and God help journalism.''

Joe waved to the waiter. "Steak all right?" he asked.

"Chicken hash," she said. "And a salad."

"I'll see what I can find out about it," Joe said after the waiter had departed.

Maureen seemed not to have heard him. She said, "I talked to Renée Ballantyne and Carl Schwartz while I was up there. They can't find the balls to level with me. All they say is that 'It's being considered. There's a possibility that we'll bring in a new female anchor for network, but nothing definite.' Bastards!"

Coughlin nibbled on a baked stuffed clam as he said, "Let me see what I can find out."

"Oh, shit."

"Don't get testy with me, Mo." He forced a laugh. "Look, the reason I said we should get together tonight was that I think I've worked out a nice deal for you on the radio side."

"The talk show?"

He nodded. "Sunday afternoons, from one to five. A call-in thing, with guests. I think I can get them to go for twenty a year."

She sat back in her chair and chewed on the inside of her cheek.

"Did you hear me?"

"What? Oh, I'm sorry, Joe. She's a pretty young thing, isn't she?"

Coughlin followed Maureen's gaze across the dining room. A young girl was about to leave with her parents. She was about sixteen, long-legged, and appropriately awkward. Her hair was auburn, bordering on red. "I guess so," Coughlin said, "only I'm not into young girls."

"I wasn't referring to her potentials in bed, Joe, I was talking about . . . oh, what the hell. How are the clams?"

"Fine." He couldn't be sure, but he thought he detected the threat of tears in her eyes. "Sure you don't want anything first?"

"Positive."

"How's things with Congressman Maitland?"

She snapped her fingers. "Damn, I have to call him. I was supposed to have dinner with him tonight. Got any change?"

He gave her what coins were in his pocket and she left the table, returning just as their entrées were being served. "He's pissed," she said. "Can't blame him, I suppose. The hash looks good. Want some?"

"No."

As they lingered over coffee, Joe said, "Mo, I think you're getting unnecessarily upset over this network anchor thing. I know how you feel whenever they bring in the pretty boys to read what somebody else wrote, but that's reality, the bottom line. No matter what they taught you at The U. of Missouri, the news, at least TV news, is, to a certain extent show biz."

"I should have stayed with print."

"No, you shouldn't. You're making a classical buck in TV, you're on the tube nightly in one of the ten biggest markets in the country, and you've got enough awards to paper a ballroom. What did you have working print, Mo, ink all over your fingers and half the money?"

She sat back and sighed. "I know, I know, but there's something wrong with a business where, if you're a woman, being the best at what you do doesn't get you to the top unless your nose is cute and . . ."

He added with a chuckle, "By the way, your tits and ass are dynamite."

She grinned. A close friend had recently told her that she'd forgotten how to smile. She'd responded with a string of cynical statements about there not being much to smile about in the world, but had been reflecting on the comment ever since. Another remark about her hair being too short had also been dismissed, but months later she'd begun allowing it to grow to its present shoulder length.

Coughlin paid the bill and they left the restaurant. It had started to rain lightly, which gave the streets a clean, fresh look and smell. Maureen shivered, and Joe put his arm around her.

"Drop me home?" she asked.

"Sure."

They walked to where his Lincoln was parked. He put the key in the door, then turned and asked, "Home or Maitland's place?"

"Home."

Which was a Georgetown town house that had been refurbished in the late thirties after Eleanor Roosevelt had launched a campaign to clean up the deteriorating Georgetown section of the nation's capital. It was on a small, quiet brick street. Maureen owned the house, had bought it with money left her by her father. Friends had suggested that she invest the money in stocks and bonds and rent a place to live, but that went against her nature. Her family, Irish immigrants who'd settled in Kansas City, believed that no matter what a man did with his life, his first obligation was to own a piece of property. She loved her house, not because it had appreciated dramatically in value over the years but because it was her home, her temple of refuge against a hostile world.

The drinks had done to Joe Coughlin what they usually did, had turned him into an expansive, talkative professional Irishman. As he drove through the streets of Washington, down Twenty-first to New Hampshire, southwest to the Washington Circle, then across Pennsylvania to M Street, he waxed poetic about the city. She'd heard the Thomas Moore poem before from him, but always enjoyed his recitation of it:

"And what was Goose Creek once is Tiber now.
This famed metropolis, where fancy sees,
Squares in morasses, obelisks in trees;
Which second sighted seers e'en now adorn,
With shrines unbuilt and heroes yet unborn."

She applauded quietly.

"Only a real Irish broad appreciates things like that,

Mo," he said as he turned into her street. "Maybe that's why my Jewish wife and I haven't gotten along for thirty years."

"I think you got the better of the deal, Joe," she said. "Thanks for dinner and the lift. When will the radio thing be firmed up?"

"Just a matter of dollars. It's yours if you want it."

"Make whatever deal you can. Are they still bitching about my using an agent?"

"Of course. They consider it a betrayal, but as us Irishmen say, 'Take the shamrock from your hat and cast it on the sod. It will take root and flourish still, though under foot it's trod.'"

"Who said that?"

"I have no idea. Invite me in for a nightcap and I'll regale you for the rest of the evening."

"No, you won't. The last thing I want is regaling. Thanks again. I'll call you tomorrow."

"Good night."

Inside, she quickly undressed and slipped into a yellow terrycloth robe, picked up the phone to again call Jack Maitland, then replaced it in its cradle, poured herself a gin on ice, flicked on the television, and stared absently at the screen. Her mind wandered, first to her assignment in the morning to interview Speaker of the House Tip O'Neill about a pending tax reduction package before the House, then to the meetings she'd had in New York, and finally to the young girl she'd seen in the Jockey Club. She went to the bedroom and opened the bottom drawer of her dresser. She rummaged through old sweaters until she found a large brown envelope, which she opened; she spread its contents on the top of the dresser. There were a dozen photographs, most of them old, but two having been recently sent to her by her mother from Kansas City. One was of her mother standing in front of the small, solid house in which Maureen had grown up. The other was of her redheaded daughter, Julie, who looked not only like the girl in the restaurant, but like Maureen.

"Good night, baby," she said, shoving the pictures back into the envelope in such nervous haste that an observer might have thought someone was about to steal them. She returned the envelope to the drawer and covered it with sweaters. "Good night, baby," she repeated as she turned down the covers of her bed and slipped beneath them.

CHAPTER 6

The screening was held in a cramped, stuffy projection room just off the main network newsroom. Machlin had suggested to Carl Schwartz that they screen materials in a projection room serving the Entertainment and Talent divisions, a large, cheerfully decorated facility that allowed everyone a comfortable chair. Up in News, the chairs were of the folding metal variety. The screen was small, and there hadn't been much of an attempt to soundproof the room, which meant that the noisy click-clack of wire-service machines interfered with sound from speakers that flanked the screen in the front of the room. But his suggestion had been turned down. That was the trouble with News, he muttered to himself as he rode the elevator. Everyone so damned elitist and preferring to put up with discomfort than leave their precious domain.

After everyone arrived, including Carl Schwartz and Renée Ballantyne, Schwartz said, "These are the entries in the Shay Brickhouse competition. Ordinarily, we never screen these pieces outside News, but because of the situation with the new female anchor, we thought you'd be interested in seeing them."

He directed his final comment at Machlin, who nodded and said softly, "Thanks. I appreciate it."

"We'll see the Cindy Lewis Klan piece first. We were going to use the three-part series she did on the rally in Amarillo, but the follow-up interview she did with Monty Jamison is just too good to pass up."

"When did that air?" Machlin asked.

"It aired in Amarillo last week," Schwartz said. "We're going to run it as a series on the network beginning Wednesday. She did a hell of a job even getting him to sit down and say what he did. At any rate, let's take a look at it." He dimmed the lights and a videotape monitor came to life.

Ever since Cindy Lewis had covered the Ku Klux Klan rally, the phone hadn't stopped ringing. Some of the calls were congratulatory and they'd pleased her. It was the others that were upsetting, calls from teenagers and middle-aged people, not only in Amarillo and the rest of Texas, but in Florida and Alabama, Massachusetts and California. Some of them threatened her life and the lives of her family for having distorted the facts to paint a negative picture of "one-hundred-percent red-blooded Americans" who cared a lot more about their country than "you bleeding-heart liberal scum in the media, you Jew bastards and nigger lovers . . ."

It was the first time she'd been exposed to such vehemence over her reporting, and she suggested to Hal that they change their number to an unlisted one. He balked, as angry as he was about the calls. They'd had the same phone number for years. His friends and clients knew it by heart. When Cindy started in TV her boss had suggested that she change her number. Everyone else at the station who was in the public eye had done so. It made sense to her, but Hal had refused. Until the furor over the Klan piece there really hadn't been a problem, just a few stray crank calls. Now, with the calls increasing in number and nastiness, he agreed.

She picked up a telegram that had arrived a few days

ago and read it again. It was from Renée Ballantyne, producer of *This Night,* the nightly network news program on which Cindy's Klan reports had appeared. It said: "Nice job on Klan series. Congratulations. Any follow-up would be appreciated. Ballantyne."

She went to the kitchen, where Maria, the housekeeper, was busy preparing a large vat of chili. Hal had invited a dozen friends to the house for what he termed "an elegant chili party." In Amarillo, elegant meant wearing a shirt with a collar.

The counter was covered with ingredients to go into Hal's recipe—meat, garlic, chili pods, chopped onions, paprika, cumin powder, Tabasco, and red peppers.

"Please, Maria," Cindy said, "go a little easy on the peppers. The last time we had it I thought half the guests would die from internal combustion."

Maria laughed, said, "*Sí, Señora.*"

Cindy went to the bedroom and browsed through her closets. She would have preferred to stay home that night to greet her guests, but that was impossible. She had to be at the station by five to anchor the six o'clock news. Hal had asked her to take the night off and she'd promised to try, but she hadn't even bothered. Her coanchor had already arranged to have the early evening off, and it was an unwritten rule that one of the two would always appear, to give viewers a sense of continuity. At least she'd succeeded in freeing herself from the eleven o'clock newscast. Her coanchor would be back in time to cover that.

She chose a white blazer to wear over a teal-blue blouse, and white slacks. It really didn't matter what she wore from the waist down, because she never left the desk while delivering the news. The director didn't like a news team strolling about the set, even though that practice had become popular elsewhere. Each person had a spot and was expected to stay in it. The cameras would provide any sense of motion.

Hal arrived home at four. He'd taken off early to help

prepare for the party. "You couldn't get off, huh?" he said as he came through the door and kissed her cheek.

"No, I'm sorry."

"You should tell them to go to hell."

"I can't do that and you know it." She was suddenly gripped with a desire to leave. His increasing complaints about her job had recently filled her with a need to escape to the hectic calm of the studio.

She kissed him on the mouth, smiled, and said, "I'll tear right out of there the minute it's over. You told everybody seven, didn't you?"

"Six-thirty."

"Why? You knew I . . ."

"I thought you were taking off. I wish you had."

"I couldn't. They wouldn't let me."

"All right. Did you buy the liquor?"

She hit the side of her head with the heel of her hand. "No, damn it, I forgot. I'm sorry."

Hal almost said something, then smothered his words with a sigh. "It doesn't matter. They can deliver."

"Hal, please don't be mad. There's no need."

"Who's mad?"

"You are."

"No, I'm not."

"I have to go. See you soon."

"Sure. I'll be watching."

"At least I don't have to do the late news."

"I count my blessings." He grinned. "I'm sorry, too, Cindy. It's been one of those days. Knock 'em dead."

"I'll try."

Hal and his guests sat in the den and watched the end of Cindy's newscast. There was, of course, the usual round of compliments about how good she was and how fortunate Hal was to be married to her. He agreed wholeheartedly.

Cindy arrived home at seven-fifteen, hugged and kissed everyone, and accepted a bourbon on the rocks Hal held out for her. "You were sensational," he told her, punctuating his remark with a bear hug.

"Thanks," she said. "Whew, it's good to be off for the weekend."

They went outside to a large fieldstone patio where Hal had set up a bar. An outdoor speaker piped smooth, mellow string music from a tuner inside the house. The sun had set, and a cool breeze came up from the northwest. A darkening sky created a scrim against which emerging stars played.

"Still receiving crank calls?" Cindy was asked by one of the guests.

"Nope," she said. "We changed the number." She glanced over at Hal, who was busy making drinks.

"You know, Cindy," the guest said, "I can understand some people, especially here in Texas, getting a little uptight over your report on the Klan."

She stopped the motion of her glass toward her mouth, looked over, and asked, "Why?"

The short, balding man, who owned a string of fast-food outlets in town and was Hal's weekly golf companion, raised his eyebrows and smiled. "Well, it's not as though Texas is a Klan state, Cindy. The fact that an offshoot of it chose to hold a rally here that got out of hand doesn't reflect what the whole state is about."

"My report never claimed that it was. The rally happened to be held here in Amarillo and that's why it became a Texas story. It could have happened anywhere."

"I know, I know," the man said.

His wife, the only person at the party for whom Cindy didn't care, joined the discussion. "I think it's a shame the way media slants things," she said. "I mean, Cindy, with all due respect to you, you have to admit that it does."

"No, I don't have to admit anything," Cindy replied, sipping her bourbon. "I don't think anybody in TV, or in newspapers, for that matter, slants the news to suit a political purpose. What does happen is that the interesting side of an issue makes for better film, and that side gets more play. But that's due to the demands of the media. Actually, I . . ."

The man's wife smiled, turned, and walked toward the bar. Cindy was grateful for her rudeness. She didn't want to get into controversial issues. The night had been designed for light chatter and laughter and she wanted to keep it that way.

Still, thoughts of what had occurred at the rally were never far from her. She walked to the edge of the patio and looked out over carefully manicured grounds. A face from the rally, one twisted into a mask of hatred, suddenly popped into her consciousness. It belonged to a Klan member who'd removed his white mask and attempted to attack her while she was doing her commentary.

She'd arrived at the rally with a camera crew from the station, including the black sound man named Chip. It wasn't a large gathering of local Klan members, two dozen at best, but a large crowd of local citizens had gathered to witness the event.

Cindy instructed the cameraman to set up in front of a makeshift platform from which the leadership would speak. She was aware of interest in her and the crew. A few hooded Klansmen overtly made reference to them, one saying in a loud voice, "They even brought a nigger with them."

Cindy also knew that they would welcome any coverage they would receive, and she'd thought about that on the way to the rally. She was never able to come to grips with giving media exposure to unsavory, dangerous groups. In doing so were the media perpetuating their goals, or did the exposure illuminate for decent people just how destructive these groups were? She always chose the latter interpretation, not only because it made sense to her to expose evil, but, from a more practical point of view, it was her job.

"Do you want just straight coverage of the speeches, Cindy?" the cameraman asked.

She looked around the growing crowd that had begun to press closer to the platform. "No," she said over the noise, "get some of it, but try to pick up reactions, too."

A heckler shouted an obscenity at the Klansmen. The leader came to the edge of the platform, pointed his finger, and shouted, "It's slime like you that has sold this nation to the niggers and the Catholics and the Jews."

Someone to Cindy's right challenged the Klan leader to take off his mask and step down into the crowd. For a moment, Cindy thought the Klansman might do it, but he didn't have to. Sympathizers in the audience turned on the challenger and told him to shut up or leave.

"Looks like it might heat up," Chip said as he adjusted settings on his recorder and pressed earphones against his ears.

"Let's hope it doesn't," Cindy said. But she also knew that the more heated the confrontation, the better the report would be. That was another reality of her profession. Without controversy and confrontation, without floods and wars and murders and rapes, a journalist was left with nothing but positive, happy news that, despite public clamor for reporting the good in society, seldom built audiences for very long.

A group to the rear of the crowd began to chant, "Let's go, let's go, let's go . . ."

The Klan leader picked up a microphone, raised his hand to quiet the crowd, and said, "Ladies and gentlemen, we are Americans standin' on this platform this morning, and any of you out there who don't understand what bein' an American is ought to get your asses out of here right now."

Cindy looked over to make sure the camera was rolling. It was. She again looked up at the speaker, who said, "This country is goin' to hell, and goin' there damn fast. There isn't a decent value left, the sort of values that this country was built on. You may not know that because the knee-jerk bleeding-heart liberals and the media run by 'em won't tell you the truth." He looked down at Cindy, who returned his stare without flinching. Inside, however, she'd begun to tremble, and she pressed her clipboard closer to her body.

"We sold this nation to the drug pushers and pimps, the liberal do-gooders and foreign nations who sell their goods here and put our people out of work," the speaker said. His remarks were met with a smattering of cheers.

Cindy noticed a woman with a two-year-old child on her shoulders. The child had blond curls and big blue eyes, and waved a small American flag in the air while her mother cheered.

"Catch some of that," Cindy told the cameraman.

Cindy searched the faces of those who had gathered. She spotted a familiar one, Jeb Cooney, who ran a successful public relations agency in Amarillo. He had a number of industrial and commercial clients, although lately he'd moved more into the political arena. Cindy and Hal had known him a long time. Recently, Cindy had done a favorable story on one of his industrial clients and Cooney personally thanked her after it appeared on the air. What interested her most, however, about Cooney's presence at the rally was his long-standing relationship with Monty Jamison. Jamison was one of the richest men in the Texas panhandle. His influence was felt throughout the state and beyond its borders. He was known as a primary force behind a variety of leading Texas politicians, including those who'd transcended state politics and had reached loftier chambers in Washington.

There had been speculation on the part of assassination buffs that Jamison, along with other wealthy and powerful leaders in the Southwest, might have been behind the murder of John F. Kennedy. It had remained only speculation, however, and even the most dedicated followers of the continuing Kennedy saga held out little hope for making such a link. Jamison, despite being a rich, elderly, and eccentric recluse, remained a constant source of public interest, and the rumor had always been that he was a source of financial backing for the Klan. He'd admitted long ago that he'd once been a member, although he vehemently insisted that it was no longer the case.

"Where are you going?" Chip asked as Cindy started to walk away from the crew.

"Over here," she said. "If I have something, I'll wave."

She approached Cooney and greeted him. He smiled, held out his hand, and said, "Good to see you, Cindy. I knew somebody from the station would be here."

"Why are you here?" she asked.

"Just curious, that's all."

"Are you sure, Jeb?"

"Why do you ask that?" He frowned, his large round face becoming a mass of wrinkles.

"Oh, come on, Jeb, you know why I ask. Are you representing a curious citizen or Monty Jamison?"

The directness of her question took him aback. He glanced around, then said, "That's ridiculous, Cindy, and you know it. Good God, a nice gal like you getting so involved in the media that you end up suspecting everybody."

"Can I ask you some direct questions about Mr. Jamison on camera, Jeb?"

"Hell, no." He laughed.

"Is Mr. Jamison here?" she asked.

"Not that I know of."

"What's the chances of getting an interview with him, Jeb?"

"About as good as getting those guys up on the stage to donate money to the ACLU."

She laughed, said, "I really would like some time with Monty Jamison, and you're the only conduit to him I know. How about taking a shot at it for me?"

"I'll ask him."

They were interrupted by a sudden surge of noise from

the crowd. Cindy turned and saw a young bearded man
leap up on the stage and lunge at one of the Klansmen.
Police stationed at the four corners of the platform quickly
grabbed the attacker and pulled him to the ground. She
saw that the scuffle was being recorded by the crew, which
pleased her. She quickly turned to Cooney and said, "I'd
appreciate being able to ask Mr. Jamison about Klan activities in Texas, Jeb. Let me know."

He nodded absently and pushed his way through the
crowd toward the rear of the field. Cindy watched him,
then joined her crew.

The Klan leader screamed into the microphone, "That
young man there who just attacked a loyal American is
typical of the kind of scum this country has fallen victim
to. I'll be interested to see how the news media shows
what happened." He laughed. "They'll probably slant it
so that it looks like we all beat up on that poor little fella
who smokes pot and spits on his mommy and daddy and
who thinks bein' an American is a free ride."

Cindy and the crew returned to their original position in
front of the stage. The Klan leader concluded his remarks.
When he was finished, Cindy yelled up at him, "Could we
have a few words with you, sir?"

The hooded Klansman peered down at her, came forward, leaned over, and said, "Only if you promise not to
distort what I say to suit your own purposes."

"I won't slant anything," Cindy said, "but I won't
promise you anything in advance, either. I'd like to ask
you questions, and I'll do my best to see that your answers
are accurately presented."

The Klansman turned to one of his colleagues and said,
"Feisty little lady, ain't she?" Both men laughed as the
leader hopped down from the stage.

He was taller than she'd realized, and she felt a twinge
of primitive fear. She said to the crew, "Let's do an interview with this gentleman." They quickly set up and she
held a microphone out to him. "Sir, why did you call this
rally today?"

The Klansman hesitated, then said, "Because all over this country decent God-fearing Americans are fed up with what's been happening to them. What this country needs is for the decent men and women to stand up tall and to let the people know what they're thinking instead of turning over television and radio and newspapers and magazines to the pornographers and dope addicts and do-gooders who are selling us down the drain."

"But what is your message?" Cindy asked. "You talk about what's wrong, but you don't offer a solution."

"The solution is to get rid of everybody who isn't a one-hundred-percent American, who loves his country and who understands why it was great before the subversive element took over."

"Who is the subversive element?" Cindy asked. "Give me a name."

"Hell, lady, all you have to do is go down the roster in Congress, or turn on your television set every night."

"I'm on television every night," Cindy said, "and I consider myself every bit as good an American as you are."

"That's a matter of opinion. You're probably a nice enough person when you're at home, but maybe female liberation got to you, too." He laughed beneath his hood.

"Who's behind this rally?" Cindy asked, resisting the temptation to respond to his comment. "Who finances the activities of your organization in the state of Texas?"

"The members. We pay dues."

Cindy looked up on the stage at the remaining Klansmen. She said, "You don't seem to have many members. They must pay a lot of money to support your activities."

"That's your opinion, ma'am," he said.

"It isn't an opinion. Obviously, you're getting money from someplace other than just dues."

"You think what you want," he said, his voice reflecting a growing anger. "That's the problem with people like you. You've got your own opinions and you infect millions of people who watch you every night with those opinions instead of presenting the facts."

"Then tell me the facts," Cindy snapped. "Do you have financial backing other than membership dues? Do certain people support your activities but refuse to take public credit for it? Is Monty Jamison a contributor to the Texas Ku Klux Klan?"

The Klansman stood silent for a moment; then he said in measured tones, "If I were you, lady, I'd be careful throwing around the names of some good, decent Americans like that. You and your goddamn television station might find yourself in court bein' sued for libel."

He started to walk away but Cindy grabbed the sleeve of his white robe. He spun around and, for a moment, she thought he might physically attack her. She said in a loud shrill voice, "Why won't you answer my question about Monty Jamison? Why do you hide behind a mask if you are so proud of being an American? Why do you do nothing but attack by innuendo and slander?"

It happened so quickly that she did not have a chance to react. His left hand shot up from his hip and grabbed her throat. The assault lasted for only a second. He quickly withdrew his hand, pivoted his head from left to right, then jumped up on the stage, gathered his hooded compatriots, and herded them off the back of the platform to waiting vehicles.

Cindy was speechless. When she'd regained her composure she turned and looked at the cameraman. "I got it all, Cindy," he said.

"So did I," Chip said, removing his earphones.

"I don't believe it," she said.

"You'd better," Chip said. "We just got us a hell of a report."

She literally ran into the station and sought out her boss, Bob, who was manager of news operations. She told him what had occurred and he was as excited as she was. He suggested that they immediately get the tape to editing.

"Obviously, Cindy, you came up with a lot more than the network bargained for. I'll call Ballantyne in New York and tell her to keep the slot open. If it's as good as you say, you've really made a score."

She stayed at the station through the afternoon and did her newscast, which preceded the EBS network news. She watched with interest as the feed from Amarillo was smoothly worked into the network broadcast from New York. When her report on the Klan rally was over, the half-dozen people watching with her broke into applause. She smiled broadly and thanked the crew members who'd helped her get the story.

She was preparing to go home when Renée Ballantyne called from New York.

"I'm glad you enjoyed it," Cindy said.

"It was marvelous," Ballantyne said. "What we'd like is an interview with Monty Jamison."

Cindy laughed. "That's easier said than done. He doesn't give interviews to anyone."

"Well, because of your report, Cindy, there's great interest in developing more pieces on the Klan and similar organizations, especially about those people who seem to be behind their activities. Do what you can. We're all very impressed here with your story."

"I feel so good hearing that," Cindy said. "I'll pursue the Jamison interview."

She checked her watch. She'd missed dinner. She called home and Hal answered the phone.

"Did you see it?" she asked.

"Yes, I did. It was good." He sounded very cold.

"I'm packing up now. Did you save me anything to eat?"

"I don't know. Maybe Maria did."

"Hal, please don't be angry with me. I . . ."

"We can talk about it another time, Cindy. See you later." He hung up.

Her boss suggested that they all go out for dinner to celebrate the success of her story.

"I really shouldn't, Bob." she said. "I just talked to Hal and . . ."

"Ah, loosen up, Cindy. You had a big success tonight and that's cause for celebration. Just tell that old stick-in-the-mud that his wife's public is demanding her."

She didn't want to go, knew that it would only fuel the fires at home, but at the same time was not anxious to walk into a house filled with hostility and tension. Besides, she was hungry. She smiled at Bob and said, "Great, where to?"

"Let's go to Rice's. It's prime-ribs night."

"Sold," Cindy said.

She returned home at eleven. Hal was asleep. She undressed quietly and slipped beneath the sheets next to him. He stirred.

"I'm home, honey. I had dinner with some people from the station at Rice's."

He muttered something unintelligible.

"Good night," she said, kissing his cheek.

"Good night."

Hal came from the kitchen and announced that the chili was ready. Someone cheered, someone applauded, and everyone adjourned to a long table set up at one end of the patio. Crisp white tablecloths covered it, and there were place settings and chairs for fourteen people. After they were seated, Hal clapped his hands and said, "Be prepared, folks, for Hal Lewis's masterpiece, the hottest and best chili this side of . . ." He stopped, looked at Cindy, and said, "You didn't tell Maria to alter the recipe, did you?"

"Me?" Cindy replied with exaggerated shock. "You know I'd never do a thing like that."

"Oh, yes, you would," Hal said, laughing, as he headed for the house.

The faint ringing of a telephone was heard from the bedroom wing.

"At least I know it's not another nut," Cindy said. She

saw Hal move toward the bedroom and silently hoped it wasn't the special line to the station. She wanted no interruptions, not so much for herself as for him. She'd thought a lot about the problems between them and had recently decided that her career had perhaps gotten out of hand. She was not a feminist who held that a career was as important as a family. She basically believed in a woman's right to choose a role besides that of mother and wife, but her own needs were less strong than those of other women she knew who'd embraced the women's movement. She enjoyed being a wife and mother, drew deep and enriching substance from it. If her career truly threatened her life with Hal, there was little doubt in her mind what choice she would make.

"It's for you," Hal announced flatly as he came to the patio area. "The station."

She asked for his understanding with her eyes but received none. Maria came from the kitchen carrying two large wooden salad bowls. Cindy excused herself, went to the bedroom, and picked up the red phone. A young man from the station's assignment desk asked whether she was free to go out on an interview.

"No, I'm not," she said. "I'm sorry, but I have a houseful of guests." She hung up and returned to the patio. The phone rang again.

"Damn it," Hal said. He wiped his mouth and was about to leave the table when Cindy placed her hand on his arm and said, "Please, Hal, it's not such a big deal. I'm sure this will be the last interruption." She picked up the phone and said gruffly, "Who is it?"

"Hey, Cindy, take it easy, this is Bob."

"I'm sorry, Bob, but I have a dozen people sitting down for dinner and . . ."

"And they can stay there. Cindy, I just got a call from Jeb Cooney. The interview with Monty Jamison is on. Right now."

"Why? He's turned down every interview request we've ever made."

"He's evidently upset at the way the rally was covered. He's also mad as hell that his name was ever brought up during the interview you did with the freak in the white sheet. He wants to set the record straight about himself and the Klan."

"Does the network know?"

"Yes, I just called. They've offered anything, including funds, to put together a series on Jamison."

Cindy looked over her shoulder toward the patio. "I can't, Bob. Hal will blow his stack."

"Let him blow it later, Cindy. The crew is on its way over. You go out to Jamison's spread, do the interview, grab what background footage you can, and run it back here. You'll be back at the dinner table before anybody knows you're gone."

"No, I can't."

"The crew will be there in a few minutes, Cindy. Don't disappoint me or the network. This is big stuff. See you here when you're finished."

Despair and fear swept over her as she hung up. She was immobile. The idea of returning to the patio and announcing to Hal that she was leaving on an assignment was inconceivable. She was tempted to simply slip out the front door without saying anything to anybody.

She walked to the doorway and peered through it. Hal was telling a joke. She couldn't hear his words but she knew it was a funny story because of his gestures and his expression.

The front door chimes sounded. Hal looked toward the house. Cindy did not want him to answer the door. She quickly moved up the hallway and into the living room. Hal looked through the glass patio doors and squinted. She waved him away, indicating that she would get it.

"Ready?" the sound man asked her. He was a crusty older man who was never without a wet cigar between his teeth.

"Give me a minute," she said. She closed the door, turned, and was face to face with Hal.

"Who is it?" he asked.

"Horace, from the station. I have to go out and interview Monty Jamison. He's agreed to it and it's the only time we can make it work."

Hal's face was filled with anger and disbelief. After what seemed an eternity of silent staring, he said, "Don't do it, Cindy."

"I have to. I won't be long. Enjoy dinner and tell everybody I'll be back for dessert."

"Jesus, Cindy, this is too goddamn much."

"I don't like it any more than you do. I don't like it when you have to run out for some dinner meeting to nail down a client, either. I have my job, just like you do."

"That's right, but I know when to separate it from my private life." He was yelling.

"Not so loud."

"I don't give a damn who hears."

"Well, I do. Monty Jamison has agreed to an interview with me about the Klan, and the network wants it."

"I told you to lay off Jamison, Cindy. I carry some of his industrial coverage."

"I know that, Hal, and I'm not trying to make trouble for you in your business. But Monty Jamison is a national figure, someone the public has always speculated about. No one has been able to interview him until now. I have to do this. Can't you understand what an opportunity it is for me?"

He looked at the floor, then into her eyes. He said softly, "Cindy, this has got to stop. I mean it."

She withheld the words that had formed on her tongue, saying instead, "I can't keep them waiting. I'll be back as soon as I can." She extended her lips to him but he turned away. "Tell everybody that I'm sorry."

"Tell 'em yourself."

"All right." She walked briskly to the patio, announced that she was leaving and that she would return as soon as possible, grabbed her purse from a chair, and joined the crew in the station wagon.

"Where to?" the cameraman asked.

"The Jamison ranch," Cindy said as she started to write the questions she wanted to ask on her clipboard.

When the tape of Cindy's four-part interview with Monty Jamison ended, Carl Schwartz turned up the lights in the screening room and asked if anyone wanted to comment. There was unanimous praise for the interview. Cindy had done a superb job of getting Jamison to comment on many issues, including the Klan and, to everyone's surprise, on the rumors that had hounded him ever since the assassination of President Kennedy.

"She has a marvelous way about her," Carl Schwartz said.

"Yes, she does," Renée Ballantyne said, "but I'd rather screen all three entries before discussing them. Okay, we've seen the Lewis series. Let's look at the tapes Veronica Frazier did in San Francisco."

Schwartz lowered the lights and the first of three parts concerning a San Francisco drug scandal filled the screen. It involved high-ranking members of the police department, and word had it that the series would win Veronica Frazier and her station a local Emmy.

_____CHAPTER 7

"Congratulations, Ronnie," a friend said to Veronica
Frazier as she stood with a small group in the Mark
Hopkins Lower Bar. She'd just come from Peacock Court,
where the National Academy of Television Arts and Sci-
ences had held its annual Bay Area Emmy Awards dinner,
at which Veronica had picked up her own Emmy for the
drug series.

"Thanks," she said. She glanced at her mother, who
stood apart from the small crowd. Veronica was ambivalent about having her mother there. She was proud,
yet uncomfortable; and her discomfort made her ashamed.
Certainly, she could not have succumbed so completely to
the superficial worldliness of her colleagues that her
mother's lack of sophistication would matter. Yet, it did.

Mrs. Frazier wore a plain dress splashed with purple
and green flowers that Ronnie remembered from childhood. Beneath it jutted two short, gnarled legs covered by
dark opaque stockings. The only new item in her wardrobe
was a pair of black shoes with laces. She'd done her own
hair before leaving Detroit, and wore garish red nail polish
given her by a neighbor in the apartment building.

"You deserved it, Ronnie," said another well-wisher.
"It was a hell of a series."

Which it was. She'd gone undercover in Oakland at the start of the investigation, then had called upon unnamed contacts in San Francisco to develop the necessary evidence to support the charges. When the investigation was completed, she realized it had been the most exhilarating experience of her life. She missed feeling that her work was meaningful and had suffered a predictable letdown when the final segments were edited and narrated. She liked the action, and hated having to return to the sterility of the studio.

Stanton came through the lobby, his wife on his arm. "You must be very proud of your daughter," he said to Mrs. Frazier.

"Yes, I certainly am," she replied, still maintaining a distance from the others.

Veronica put her arm around her mother's shoulders and drew her into the circle.

"You live in Detroit?" Mrs. Stanton asked Veronica's mother.

"Yes."

"I've only been there once, to a convention with Craig." She turned to Veronica and said rather coldly, at least to Veronica's ear, "Congratulations. You must be very satisfied."

"Yes, I am," said Veronica, smiling. "It's the first thing I've ever won in my life."

"Yes." Mrs. Stanton placed her hand on her husband's arm and said, "We really must be going."

"I know," he replied. "It was a pleasure meeting you, Mrs. Frazier. We're all fans of your daughter. She's quite a young woman."

Veronica's mother nodded and looked away. Stanton said to Veronica, "Don't stay out too late celebrating. That nine o'clock meeting is important." The Stantons left the bar and were swallowed by the lobby crowd. Veronica knew he would not look back, not even for a fleeting glance. She understood. Wives had a way of noticing those things.

A friend, Lester Sims, joined them. Veronica had to stifle a giggle as he approached the group. Lester was an odd-looking man, very tall and thin. A wisp of red hair curled up from the top of a pale, freckled bald dome. He walked awkwardly, long legs flailing out in front of him, arms dangling and moving in no predictable pattern. He wore a dark-green velvet jacket, a white shirt open at the neck, paisley ascot, wrinkled gray trousers, and brown molded shoes. "The winner, the star," he said loudly as he wrapped his arms around her. People turned to look. It was one of those times when she wished he was a little less flamboyant.

Lester was a poet and author, although he tended to talk more about what he was going to write than actually produce it. There was little pressure on him to produce anything. His father owned a successful seafood restaurant on Fisherman's Wharf and Lester lived off a comfortable trust fund. Because he was homosexual, Veronica often found him a perfect escort, and would probably have been on his arm this night had her mother not been visiting. There was never any sexual pressure with Lester, no fumbling at evening's end.

"Do you think she knows?" Lester whispered into Ronnie's ear.

"Who?" she asked, thinking for a moment he meant her mother.

"Tarzan's old lady. Does she know you do her husband?"

"*Do* him?" She glanced at her mother, who seemed not to have heard. His snide reference to Craig Stanton angered her and she attempted to end the talk by narrowing her eyes.

"Did she say anything, Ronnie, Tarzan's legal Jane?"

"Excuse me." Veronica moved to her mother's side. She spotted another friend in the lobby and told her mother she'd like to introduce her to someone. Once away from the Lower Bar, she glanced back and saw that Lester was talking with another homosexual, a scenic designer named

George. Her sigh of relief was short-lived. Lester and George crossed the lobby, and Lester indicated he wished to speak to her alone. She reluctantly excused herself from her mother and joined them.

"Ronnie," Lester said conspiratorially, "George has come up with a dynamite supply of coke, haven't you, George?" George nodded. "Why don't we meet up at my place later and relax?"

"I'm sorry, Lester, I can't. I have my mother with me and . . . besides, I don't enjoy those things anymore, and you know it."

"She'd understand, Ronnie. I mean, after all, you're not her little girl anymore. Besides, she looks exhausted. The night is young for those young at heart, and it would be such a shame to cut short this celebratory evening filled with personal accolades from your peers for your achievements in your art form. Art form? Well, the electronic medium you serve with such devotion and skill."

She hated gay men when they slipped into such exaggerated female bitchiness. "Good night, Lester," she said.

"Don't be too quick to dismiss us, dear. Ordinarily, we wouldn't share anything this good, but for a legitimate star, one who's been recognized by her peers, we decided to make an exception."

Veronica had had enough. "Don't call me, I'll call you," she said, turning and rejoining her mother.

A half hour later Veronica and her mother sat in the living room of Veronica's rented house on Lombard Street. Veronica had kicked off her shoes and made herself a drink. "Well, Mama, what did you think of the dinner?" she asked.

"Real nice," her mother said, her eyes taking in her surroundings.

Next to her on a table was a vase of fresh roses. Veronica looked at them and smiled. "Aren't they beautiful, Mama? Did you smell them?"

Her mother shook her head.

"Why not?"

"I knew the minute I seen them that they weren't plastic like the ones at home. No need to prove it to myself."

Veronica smiled, although she was annoyed. She'd wanted to provide her mother with the kind of opulence she'd never experienced before, yet the old lady would not allow herself to savor it. Everything she tried to do to make her mother feel elegant seemed to backfire. Again, she was faced with ambivalent feelings. She'd been filled with happy anticipation at having her mother share her new life in San Francisco, if only for a few days. But here she was, and Veronica found herself awkward, embarrassed, and unable to relax. "Can I get you something?" she asked.

"No, no need for anything. I don't want to be a burden. I don't want to get in your way."

"Will you stop saying that?" Veronica said angrily. She reminded herself that there was nothing to be gained by expressing pique at her mother. She softened her voice and said, "You didn't eat much of the dinner, Mama. I watched."

"It was fine, just fine, only my stomach ain't what it used to be."

"Would you like something now? I can order food delivered, Chinese or a pizza."

"No, don't pay no attention to me. I ate enough."

Veronica refilled her drink and paced the room. "You never said whether you liked the house, Mama."

"It's fine, Ronnie, just fine. I never thought my little girl would make enough money to live in such a fancy place. But I guess I always knew you'd live good no matter what you had to do to get it."

Veronica stopped pacing and faced her mother. "Why did you have to say that?" she asked.

Mrs. Frazier didn't look up. She continued to sit in the chair, her feet up on a hassock as she said, "I am impressed, Ronnie, with all the nice things you have. I sure am proud of you winning an award, just like I was proud when you graduated from college. Nobody in our family ever did that before, and I tell my friends about how well you're doin'. But life ain't just having pretty things. Everybody's got to answer to God.''

''Mama, it's not like the way it was, not the way you think it is. I'm my own person now. I don't need other people to help me.'' She came to her mother's chair and fell to her knees, took her mother's hands, and said, ''I did what I had to do to make a better life for myself, and I've tried to share it with you. That's why I send you money every month, and that's why I wanted you here when something good was going to happen to me.''

Her mother turned her head slightly so that she was looking into her daughter's eyes. She turned away again and said, ''I've never been critical of you, honey, for what you've done. It ain't an easy life, Lord knows. But when it's all added up and you face your maker, the only thing that matters is the kind of person you've been, whether you've lived a good, moral life.''

''I know that, Mama, and I want you to be proud of me for the person I am, too, not just for what success I've achieved. More than anything in the world I want you to be proud of me as a daughter.''

Her mother coughed, and Veronica put her arm around her back. When the spasm had stopped, her mother said, ''You pay for all of this yourself?'' Before her daughter could answer, she added, ''They must pay you an awful lot of money to read the news every night.''

Veronica was tempted to continue the discussion, but instead she stood and went to the bathroom, where she looked at herself in the mirror. She returned to the living room, snapped on a large color television set that Craig Stanton had given her, and asked her mother if there was anything she wanted to see.

''Whatever is on,'' her mother said. ''I'm sleepy.''

''Would you mind if I went out for a while?''

''Of course not, Ronnie. Like I said, I don't want to be

a burden, to get in your way. You just go on and do whatever it is you want to do and don't worry about me."

"All right, Mama. You settle in here and watch some television. I promised someone I'd join them for a drink. I won't be long. I have a meeting in the morning but I'm free tomorrow afternoon and we can spend it together. I'll show you more of the city."

Her mother yawned and sat back in the chair. "I get so sleepy these days," she said. "Flying in an airplane would make anybody sleepy."

"That was yesterday, Mama," Veronica said. She smiled, kissed her on the forehead, and said, "I'll be back soon."

She put on her shoes, slipped a cape over her shoulders, left the house, got into her Porsche, and quickly drove to North Beach, where she stopped in front of a nightclub called Jammers.

A hand-printed sign in the window informed passersby that the Red Garland Trio was performing nightly, and that there was a four-dollar cover charge and six-dollar minimum at the tables, no minimum at the bar.

Inside, to her left, a dozen people stood at a long burnished bar that stretched from the entrance to an archway leading to the main music room. There were three musicians on the bandstand, Garland with his head hanging over the keyboard as he injected fragments of chords behind a bass player's solo, and a bearded drummer wiping wire brushes over large cymbals.

The bar patrons' loud chatter and laughter all but obscured the music. Why did they bother coming? Veronica asked herself as she moved along the bar's length to the end closest to the music room.

"Hello, Ronnie," one of the two bartenders said. "Been to a ball?"

She still wore her formal dress, a delicate salmon-colored strapless acetate-and-rayon velvet sheath that appeared to have been poured over her. She'd pulled her thick black hair into a severe chignon, and had attached a dusty-pink rose to it, which gave her an Oriental look.

"A dull awards dinner," she said. "It's nice to get back to real people."

The bartender laughed. "One thing this joint doesn't have is real people. What'll you have?"

"A kir, not too sweet. Is Bill around?"

"Yeah, he was a minute ago. He said he hoped you'd come by tonight."

A beefy red-faced man at the bar, who'd loosened his tie and appeared to be drunk, nodded at her and raised his glass. She turned away and looked down at her drink. She knew he thought she was a prostitute. It was not new to her, being mistaken for a professional. A woman alone in a bar often elicited propositions from drunken business-men, although it seemed that black women received the brunt of it, especially on the street.

"Well, look at Cinderella."

Veronica turned. Bill Teller, who owned Jammers, had come from the kitchen. He leaned close and kissed her on the cheek.

"Hi, Bill, how are you?"

"Waiting for midnight and for you to give me your slip-per. You look great. I heard you won. Congratulations."

"Thanks."

A waitress came up behind them and pointed at a couple at one of the tables who'd sat through a set of music, then had complained bitterly about the minimum charge.

"Don't worry," Bill said, "I'll talk to them."

Veronica watched him go to the dining room and re-called the first time they'd met. It was at a party, and he'd immediately made it known that he was attracted to her. He was six feet, two inches tall and had a weight lifter's body, although he didn't lift weights. Massive shoulders and arms threatened to break through his shirts, and his waist was the envy of many a woman. His face, large, square, and open, was framed by a mass of curly black hair that had begun to gray at the temples. Veronica often kidded him about his hair, accused him of having it teased into an Afro to assuage his guilt over the way his Caucasian ancestors had mistreated her people. As far as she knew, he carried no prejudice against anyone, which made kidding him easy and natural.

There was a quality of brother-and-sister in their relationship, although they had slept together from time to time. Even those sexual moments, however, were characterized by a sense of friends getting together to enjoy each other's company. While their sexual experiences had been physically satisfying, there was a certain absence of passion that was comfortable for both of them.

Bill had been divorced for twelve years from, as he put it, "a woman whose attitude was that if it wasn't important to her, it wasn't important." He often tried to dismiss his failed marriage as a temporary and transient mistake, but Veronica knew it had left him scarred. It was as though he was tethered to that temporary and transient mistake, and was afraid to let himself go again and repeat it.

You could get close to Bill Teller but never too close, a situation Veronica was at home with. She'd vowed after leaving Detroit for a new life in California that no one would ever gain access to what had been. She viewed California as the place where she'd been born again at twenty, a creature of the Bay, unencumbered by events of the first twenty years, a serious student, fresh and pure, neuter in color and attitude, and with a new world stretching out before her. The mistakes of those initial and now erased twenty years were, as Byron had said, "Gone, glimmering through the dream of things that were."

Of all the courses she'd taken at Berkeley, it was the literature courses that had most excited her. She'd devoured every book she'd been assigned, and had made the time to read dozens of others from the library—Balzac, Kafka, Shakespeare and Twain, Byron and Thurber. H. Allen Smith had made her laugh, and she'd cried reading Malamud. She avoided black authors. She'd read one of

Baldwin's books, but found that it dredged up too much of what she did not want to be.

Bill's detachment suited her, although there were times when it caused her to wonder whether in shedding her skin of twenty years she hadn't discarded the ability to love. Each time she reflected upon this she came to the same conclusion, however, that there was a price to be paid for everything. No such thing as a free lunch. It had been worth it, she inevitably concluded after bouts of introspection. Anything was better than what she'd had. If there had been the capacity to love while she was in Detroit, it would never have been allowed to surface anyway.

The drunk at the bar winked and said, "How ya doin', baby?"

She ignored him, although she could not deny her anger. She drank from her glass and sighed.

"Some of these clowns are not to be believed," Bill said as he rejoined her.

She laughed. "You seemed to resolve it easily."

"Yeah. I haven't seen you in a while. What's new besides winning an Emmy?"

"Not much. How was your vacation?"

"Good. I met a hundred Hungarian relations I never knew I had. I guess that's what happens when you're Hungarian and go to Hungary."

"You're the only Hungarian I've ever known," she said.

"Actually, I'm not Hungarian all the time, just when we run out of chicken and I have to steal one."

Her face said that she was about to burst out in either laughter or tears.

"What's the matter?" he asked.

"Nothing."

"Sorry, Ronnie, but your face says you're lying. I know you well enough to spot it."

"Well, my friend, your ESP needs servicing. I'd love another drink. I really shouldn't, because my mother is alone at my house and I have to get back, but I couldn't resist stopping off and winding down."

After her drink was served, Bill again asked if anything was bothering her. She repeated her denial until he casually inquired, "Who's this guy Roscoe?"

She felt as though he'd slipped a knife between her ribs. She turned away and tried to collect her thoughts. How could he even be aware of Roscoe Williams? She'd never mentioned him to anyone, had actually forgotten about him until his call that night when Craig Stanton was at the house. Roscoe had said on the phone that he was in town, but when she hadn't heard from him again she'd assumed he'd packed up and left.

"Who is he?" Bill repeated.

"Just an old friend," she said, still with her back to him. "We grew up together."

"That's very sweet. What'd he do, carry your books home after school?"

She turned and touched his arm, tried to tell him with her eyes that this was all too painful and that she wished he'd drop the subject. When it became obvious that he wouldn't, she said, "He's a character out of the old neighborhood, a loser who decided to look me up out here. He'd heard I'd made it and tried to put the touch on me for a few dollars. That's all there is to it."

"Did you?"

"Did I what?"

"Give him a few bucks."

"No. Bill, how do you know about him? Did I tell you?"

"No. Gus, the bartender, told me. He evidently stopped in here one night while I was away, got to talking with people, and mentioned you. Gus didn't think much about it until the conversation went further. This Williams character made some comments about how he 'knew you when,' nothing too specific, just implications that dripped with threat."

Her laughter was overtly forced. "Threat? That's silly."

Bill shrugged. "Maybe so, but that's the way he played to Gus. Gus didn't like the guy's style—flashy suit, rings on half his fingers, big gold smile, and too damn friendly."

She downed her drink and swung around on the stool. "I really have to get back. My mother will be worried."

"You're not going to tell me?"

"Jesus, Bill, stop making such a big deal out of it."

"Judging from the look on your face, you're the one who's making a big deal."

"Thanks for the drink. We'll catch up." She got down from the stool and was about to leave when he grabbed her arm. "Please," she said.

"You're afraid of him, aren't you, Ronnie?" He motioned to a bartender to fill her glass.

"I don't want another. I want to go."

"Not until you level with me."

"Leave me alone, Bill." Eyes that had been filled with sadness were now ablaze with anger. "Why do you care, anyway?"

"Because I like Veronica Frazier."

"I thought you stopped liking women twelve years ago."

He tightened his grip on her upper arm. "Don't come on professional female with me. I don't know where you came from or what your act was, but I do know you're good people. This cat Roscoe is bad. Good and bad don't mix, oil and water, an old Hungarian philosophy. Another one I picked up in my travels is that people who say they're friends take care of each other. Last I heard I was your friend."

She fought the urge to cry and thought she might succeed. Then, tears ran down her cheeks. She brought her hand to her face and squeezed her eyes shut.

Bill led her toward the back of the club, where his office was behind the kitchen. She'd been there before, had once made love with him on a battered green couch wedged in between gray file cabinets and a tall hutch. "Sit down," he said. He took a half-filled bottle of cognac from the hutch and poured some into two snifters.

"I don't want anything," she said from the couch.

"It's good for you."

She accepted the glass, sniffed its contents, then enjoyed the burning sensation as the amber liquid slid down her gullet to her belly.

"So, lady TV star, tell me about Roscoe Williams," Bill said as he joined her on the couch. Someone knocked on the office door before she could reply. "I'm busy," he shouted.

"They'll think we're doing something in here," she said.

"Let 'em think what they want. Look, Ronnie, the worst thing we can ever do to ourselves is to let problems build up inside. I'm not prying, I'm really not. Your life is your business, and if there's nothing to all this, terrific. I apologize for coming on like an old lady and that'll be the end of it. But if there is something bothering you, and Williams is the cause of it, lay it out for me. We'll talk it over and come up with a way to make it—and *him*—go away."

She started to say something, then washed the words down with cognac. Finally, she said, "There really isn't anything to tell. I'm surprised, that's all, that he came in here."

"So am I. Here he is, the quintessential dude, laying heavy tips on everybody and bragging about how he knew you a long time ago."

"That's true, he did."

"That'd be okay, except that the hints were clearly there, according to Gus, that he knew things people might not appreciate hearing about you."

"What could they possibly be?"

"That's the laugh you use on TV when you're supposed to laugh at something you don't think is funny. What could he know about you? You tell me."

"Nothing except how much my books weighed."

"Funny. Gus says . . ."

"Gus should mind his own business."

"And you should take lessons in appreciation for your fellow human beings. Gus is a good guy, likes you, and wouldn't give a flying fuck about Roscoe Williams if he didn't."

"I'm sorry."

"You should be."

There was another knock at the door. "Come in," Bill said. A waitress stuck her head in and said she was having trouble with a party of four who insisted on talking during the set. Bill told her he'd be out in a moment, said to Veronica, "People are a pain in the ass."

"I've noticed."

"Do you have a gun?"

"Of course not."

"I'm surprised. Everybody in the public eye ought to have one. You'd have no trouble getting a permit, you know, nuts after you because of stands you take on the tube, things like that. I have a permit. In this business it's as necessary as a cash register."

She nodded.

"Get a gun, Ronnie. I know someone down at head-quarters who'd grease the skids. They'll run a simple background check on you, check out references, no big deal."

"I don't want a gun. Guns frighten me."

"So does Roscoe Williams. Wave a gun at him and he'll run. Never fails with people like him."

"No, thanks, and you'd better get out there before Garland throws a left hook at the customer. He was a fighter before he became a pianist, you know."

"Yeah. Give me a kiss." He took her chin in his large hand and gently kissed her lips. She wanted to wrap her arms around him and spend the night secure in his embrace, and almost suggested she wait until the club closed so that they could spend the night together. But she remembered her mother.

Bill went to his desk, opened a drawer, took out a .22-caliber pistol, and handed it to her.

"I don't want that," she said, pushing the weapon away.

"Take it. It's not registered. Stick it in your purse and take it home. Tomorrow you can apply for a legal permit and give this back when you buy your own."

She took the gun. It seemed to weigh a ton. She lowered it to her lap, looked up at him, and said, "I appreciate the thought, Bill, but this isn't the answer."

"Suit yourself. I'd better get outside. Be back in a minute."

Veronica stood and placed the gun on his desk. She looked around the small cluttered room. Framed black-and-white photographs of jazz greats who'd appeared at Jammers filled what wall space there was. She looked at some of the photos and thought that if things had gone differently, her father's picture might have hung among them, his trumpet in his hands, a wide, infectious grin on his face. A punk kid who'd attempted to rob the Detroit liquor store in which her father worked part-time had canceled forever that possibility. The kid had panicked because her father refused to hand over money, and fired his cheap handgun. The bullet hit her father in the face. He lived for ten hours before life slipped away on an operating table in a metropolitan hospital that served the black ghetto in which they lived.

"You should be up there, Daddy," she said as tears again welled up. "People have no right to make another person's life unhappy." It was what her mother often said, abbreviating it to, "People have no right . . ."

She returned to the desk, picked up the .22, and weighed it in her hand. No, she decided, she'd had enough of violence. As she was about to leave the office, Teller returned. "Where are you going?" he asked.

"I have to get back to my mother, Bill. Thanks."

"For what?"

"For being a friend. I feel better now."

"Good."

They hugged and enjoyed a long, lingering kiss. "Let's get together soon," he said.

"Absolutely."

Her mother was asleep in front of the television when Veronica returned. "Mama," she said gently, touching her cheek. Her mother awoke easily, quietly, smiling. "I'm back," Veronica said.

"That's good," she said, touching the back of her daughter's hand.

"Come to bed."

Later, much later, long after her mother was asleep, Veronica sat up in the living room. The room was lighted by a single floor lamp. She looked around at the expensive furniture, beautifully framed prints, tall, gleaming brass candlesticks, an expensive and extensive stereo system built into the wall. She pulled her robe tight around her, took her purse from on top of the television set, and returned to her chair.

"People have no right . . ." she said to herself as she climbed into a bed in the guest room, closed her eyes, and wished, if only for a moment, that there was a way to go back in time, to redo a life, to start all over again.

CHAPTER 8

They broke for coffee following the screening of Veronica's series in EBS's New York headquarters, then settled back to watch Maureen O'Dwyer's entry in the Shay Brickhouse competition. It had to do with the sexual abuse of children, and from the moment Maureen's face filled the screen it was obvious that the series would be tense, jarring, and highly professional.

Maureen O'Dwyer walked through the newsroom of EBS's Washington O & O and glanced up at a large assignment board. A staffer carefully wiped clean stories that had been done and replaced them with new ones. Maureen's name was on the board; next to it was written in grease pencil, "Sexual Abuse (kids)." The names of the cameraman and sound man assigned to her also appeared on the board. A code was written—"HFR." It meant hold for release, which indicated that no one was counting on it for that evening's newscast.

The assignment editor, a young bearded man who'd recently been hired away from the *Washington Post,* called Maureen to his desk. "What time do you think you'll wrap up today's abuse taping?"

"Today? By one. Why?"

"Proxmire is holding a press conference at two. I thought you might like to cover it."

"No way, Ritchie. The only reason I'm back in the pot this week is to do the abuse piece. Remember, you're talking to an anchor, not your run-of-the-mill reporter." She wasn't certain he realized she was kidding, so she added a chuckle to make the point. "I really can't, Ritchie. Another time."

"Yeah. Maybe Jake can grab it."

She strolled into Tom Golding's office. He was the station's news director. He was on the phone with Carl Schwartz in New York, and the call was being amplified through a speaker on his desk.

Schwartz laughed. "Well, let's see, Tom, we're in the midst of a garbage strike, a ninety-two-year-old lady was raped last night, and I just bought a boat. What's new in the nation's capital?"

"Did the old lady put up a fight?"

"She gave him an hour to get out. What can I do for you?"

"What's this I hear about Machlin and the Entertainment people getting involved in choosing a new anchor?"

"It's true."

"What the hell does Machlin know about news?"

"Lots these days," Schwartz said. "It's been proclaimed from above that Entertainment must have its say in revamping us. Frankly, Tom, I'm all for it. Laverne and Shirley will make a hell of an anchor team, and having *Tattletales* as a sustaining feature should prove boffo in the ratings. Are you complaining?"

"Get serious, Carl, is Machlin really calling the shots?"

"He's in the game, if that means anything. How did you hear about it?"

"My source is sitting right across from me."

Schwartz said without hesitation, "Hello, Maureen, how's things?"

"Absurd, according to this conversation. How are you, Carl?"

"Tip-top."

Maureen liked Carl Schwartz, often said he represented a bastion of sanity in Network News. She knew, too, that he admired her work and openly expressed it to the brass in New York. Schwartz had a professional irreverence that she found refreshing in a business overflowing with sacred cows. She asked, "What's in it for me?"

"Play your cards right, Maureen, and you'll end up a contestant on the newest quiz show."

"Which is?" she asked.

"A spin-off from *Family Feud*. Couples compete and the winners get divorced. Look, Maureen, ignore the Machlin business. He's on a power trip and he's drunk with it. Everybody is letting him and his goddamn Entertainment Division think they're really involved in shaping the news, but it ain't quite that way. We're basically letting them go through the motions. When it all settles, the decision is coming out of here anyway."

"That's refreshing."

"What are you working on these days?" Schwartz asked.

"A piece on sexual abuse of children. It's going to be damn good."

"Everything you do is good," he said. "Send it up when you're done. It sounds like network."

"I will."

"By the way, did you see the piece we ran last night on Monty Jamison? What a hell of an interview the Lewis gal did with him."

"Yes, I saw it," Maureen said, "but, frankly, I wondered why anybody bothered. Sure, it was a good interview, but Monty Jamison is an anachronism."

"That's what I love about you, Maureen, always telling it like it is."

"Just an opinion, Carl," she said, "but who am I? Just another overworked and underpaid field reporter and local anchor."

She couldn't admit she'd been jealous of Cindy's interview with Jamison making the net after so little time had passed since her Klan report. She did have to admit to herself that it was good, solid reporting. Maureen knew that, had she been running Network News, she would have used it, too, despite what she'd been thinking during the report: *I don't like her type, all cuddly and blond and oh-so-sincere, with that trace of southwestern accent, the breathlessness and wide blue eyes.*

She headed up the hall toward the cafeteria. She was to meet her crew in front of the building in a half-hour, and a cup of coffee would pass the time.

The cafeteria was virtually empty. She sat in a corner and picked up a discarded copy of that day's *Washington Post*. She'd already read it over coffee at home, along with the *New York Times* that was delivered to the house. She couldn't begin her day without reading at least two newspapers. She'd also caught an interview on the *Today* show with Norman Mailer, and had watched a portion of *Good Morning America* in which the repair of dripping faucets had been analyzed.

"Mind?" the general manager of the local radio affiliate asked as he stood over her, a tray in his hands.

"Be my guest," Maureen said as she slid over to make room.

"Set for Sunday?" he asked.

"Rarin' to go," she said.

The final details of her Sunday afternoon radio call-in show had been ironed out and she was slated to start that weekend. She was looking forward to it. As a journalist on nightly newscasts, she was professionally restricted from injecting her own ideas and opinions into them. Any editorializing was left to management, and was clearly labeled as such.

The radio show, all four hours of it, would be a breath of fresh air, a chance to stretch out and to vent her own feelings about topics and issues. She'd been assigned a young woman fresh out of a local graduate school as her producer, and they'd discussed the guests for the first show. The format had been pretty much left up to Maureen, and she'd decided that she would present a different guest and topic each hour, unless, of course, a guest was of sufficient interest to warrant more time.

She enjoyed working with the younger woman, whose youthful zeal reminded her of her own early days in the field. But most of the producer's suggestions were too weighty for a Sunday afternoon listener-participation show. The young woman had pushed for guests in the areas of inflation, police brutality, and drug abuse. Maureen had bought the drug abuse idea but vetoed the others. She'd do the first hour without a guest; listeners could call in about anything on their minds. The second hour would feature a spokesperson from the Children's Diabetes Foundation discussing the problems of the youthful diabetic. Drugs would occupy hour number three. The fourth hour had remained up for grabs until that morning, when she'd received a call at home from an old friend, author Donald Bain, who told her he'd be in Washington that weekend promoting a new book.

The general manager told her that if Sunday turned out to be sunny and pleasant, she could expect a paucity of calls from listeners. "They'll be out there listening, Maureen," he said, "only it's hard to call from picnics and cars. Just be prepared to bullshit a lot."

"Me?" she said, eyes wide. "I wasn't born Irish for nothing."

She went outside, where her crew was waiting in a new company station wagon. Management had recently purchased a fleet of them, new models that had sliding sunroofs through which a cameraman could grab moving shots.

"Good morning," she said.

The sound man's name was Jimmy. He was young, black, and pleasant. The cameraman was a grizzly veteran of the station, a dedicated union man who insisted that every union regulation be observed and honored. Maureen had requested a different cameraman, but schedules hadn't allowed it.

"How are you, Harry?" she asked him as she climbed into the backseat and wedged herself between boxes of equipment.

"All right, Mo. What are we doing?"

"An interview in Rockville."

"Jesus, we'll run into lunch," he said.

"No problem, Harry. The people we're interviewing will give us all the time we need."

He pulled away from the curb and down a long, winding road leading to the main highway. Maureen settled back, dug into her briefcase, and pulled out materials pertaining to that day's interview. She'd found, through a nonprofit center established to treat victims of childhood sexual abuse, a woman who'd been a victim of it in her youth, and who was willing to publicly discuss it. There would be other interviews throughout the week, with counselors at the center, a child who'd recently been sexually assaulted by her father, law enforcement officers and judges, and a boy who'd sold himself on the street as a prostitute and participant in pornographic films. It would all eventually be edited together in a cohesive five-part report.

They drove northwest on Connecticut Avenue, caught the beltway to the Rockville Pike, and came to a stop in a Ramada Inn parking lot. The subject of the interview had stipulated that her face be kept in shadow and that her name not be used, and although Maureen had agreed to the conditions, she didn't like them. A certain impact was lost without the viewer having visual access to the speaker. There had been little choice but to agree, however. Finding someone willing to openly discuss such a deeply personal and intimate experience wasn't easy.

The room had been reserved in Maureen's name. She led the crew to it, opened the door, and went inside. "We'll do it over there," she said, pointing to two chairs and a table by the window. Heavy yellow drapes would provide a suitable backdrop and shield the camera from unwanted light.

"Where is she?" Jimmy asked as he began to take lighting equipment from cases.

"She should be here in a half-hour," Maureen said. "Don't forget, we have to shoot her in shadow."

"Oh, shit," Harry grumbled. "I hate that."

"Yeah, so do I, Harry, but that's the deal."

He continued to complain as he set up the camera. Maureen wanted to tell him to shut up, but didn't. She'd learned long ago that she could only be as effective as a crew allowed her to be. Getting along with crew members, no matter how abrasive or annoying their personalities, could make the difference between a mundane story and one that sparkled. There were cameramen who actively sought out interesting supporting shots, who would haul equipment up stairs and over bridges without being told. And, there were the "Harrys," who had to be prodded into every set-up, and who complained about each one. It was a lottery for reporters. The assignment desk assigned the crews, and although those who'd been around as long as Maureen could sometimes arrange to work with a particular person, it didn't happen very often.

"All set," Harry told her.

"I hope she shows," Maureen said. "I offered to pick her up, but she didn't want us near the house. She's a nice gal, married and with two kids. Her husband knows about what happened and what she's doing, but that's as far as she wants it to go."

"What happened to her?" Jimmy asked.

"Her father raped her. More of that goes on than we know."

There was a knock on the door and Maureen opened it. A slender, wide-eyed blonde lady stood in the hall. Next to her was a buxom woman of approximately the same age.

"Mrs. O'Dwyer?" the blond asked.

"Mrs. Johnstone?"

"Yes. This is my friend, Emily. I asked her to come with me to . . ." She smiled. "To hold my hand, I guess."

"Of course. Hello, Emily, come in."

The sight of the equipment seemed to overwhelm them. They stopped halfway into the room.

"Don't be concerned," Maureen said, "just a lot of necessary garbage to get the job done."

Mrs. Johnstone glanced at her friend, then said to Maureen in a voice barely above a whisper, "Could I speak with you in private?"

"Sure." They went to the bathroom and closed the door.

"Are you sure no one will know who I am?" she asked.

"Absolutely, unless somebody recognizes your voice. That never happens, though. I really wouldn't worry about it if I were you." *But I'm not you,* Maureen told herself, *and if I were, I'm not sure I'd go through with it.* She expressed none of those feelings to the woman because she didn't want to lose her. She touched her arm and asked, "May I call you Sue?"

"Yes. Not on the air, though. You said I didn't have to use my real name."

"Of course not. We'll use any name you choose."

"Marie?"

"Sounds fine. Any reason?"

She shook her head. "I guess I don't know anybody named Marie."

"Makes sense. Ready?"

"I'm so nervous."

"Don't be. We'll take it nice and slow. And you do know what a marvelous thing you're doing for others who've gone through what you've been through."

"That's what you told me when you called. I don't think I would have agreed except for that. My husband says it, too. He says that I'll be helping people."

"Absolutely. That's why we're doing this series, to help people."

"I feel better," she said, managing a smile.

They returned to the room. Jimmy was sitting on the bed reading a magazine, and Harry was perched on a shelf that contained the heating and air conditioning.

"All set?" Maureen asked.

Emily approached her friend and looked closely into her face. "You could use a little blush," she said.

"Her face won't be seen," Maureen said, sensing Harry's annoyance.

"But it's TV," said Emily. She took Sue Johnstone's arm and led her back to the bathroom. "We'll just be a minute," she said over her shoulder. "She should look her best for TV."

Maureen shrugged for Harry's benefit and took her seat.

"We're going into lunch, Mo."

"How about shooting through it and we'll eat after?"

"If you want to shoot through lunch, we just won't eat," he said. Maureen knew he'd be just as happy skipping lunch and putting in for overtime. She wanted to avoid overtime because the budget was tight, but there didn't seem to be much of a choice. If they delayed shooting, she might lose her subject. "All right," she said, "we'll skip lunch."

"Maybe we can grab a sandwich on the way back," Harry said, "to eat in the car."

She smiled to herself. That was the way Harry operated. He'd get his overtime and still not miss a meal.

Sue Johnstone and her friend returned. Sue's hair had been combed, her cheeks were alive with color, and fresh lipstick had created a larger mouth than the one she'd arrived with.

Maureen settled Sue in a chair. Jimmy attached a clip-on mike to her bright orange dress, and did the same to Maureen's blue blazer. He flicked on the lights, and the sudden glare startled Sue.

"Just relax," Maureen told her. "Actually, you're lucky. If you were going to be on camera, they'd really hit you in the face."

She received her cue from Harry, drew a breath, then asked, "Sue, could you tell me . . ."

"It's Marie," Sue said.

"Cut," Maureen said. "Sorry." She wrote in large black printing on the pad in her lap: "MARIE." "Let's go again." She received her cue. Jimmy slated the piece. "Marie, could you tell me what happened to you when you were a child?" There wasn't a need to establish the subject and topic. That would be done later, in the editing room and in on-camera comments she'd record in the studio.

"Well, when I was about eight years old, I guess, my father came into my room one night and . . . my mother was someplace else, I guess . . . and he came in my room and made me take off my clothes."

"All of them?"

"Yes."

"Then what did he do?"

"He . . . well, he took off his clothes and got into bed with me."

"What did you think about while this was happening? Do you remember what you thought and felt?"

Sue hesitated, and Maureen wished her face were on camera. It was filled with pain and anguish. Finally, she said, "He took his hand and did things with me. I was afraid of him and did what he wanted me to do. He took my hand and put it on his . . . penis."

Maureen knew certain lines and words would have to be cut in the final edit. She hoped the use of the word *penis* would be acceptable, considering the nature of the report and the circumstances of the interview.

"Did he try to have intercourse with you?"

Another pause. "Yes, he did."

"And you were only eight."

"Yes. It hurt a lot. It wasn't just that one time, either. Every time my mother went out he'd make me do it with him."

"How often?"

"I don't know, sometimes three or four times a week."

"How long did this go on?"

"Until he left. He left us about a year after he started doing it with me."

"You must have been very happy that he left."

"I guess I was, only I didn't want to say that to my mother and to my brothers and sisters."

"Did you ever tell your mother what your father had done?"

She shook her head.

"You'll have to answer, Marie, because we can't see you. I'll ask the question again . . . did you ever tell your mother what your father did to you?"

"No, I was afraid to."

"And you carried it with you silently for all these years?"

"Yes. I didn't know who to tell. I guess I was afraid all the time."

Maureen thought for a moment, then asked, "Who did you finally tell?"

"My husband."

"Why did you tell him?"

"Because . . . well, because we were having troubles between us."

"Sexual troubles?" She thought she might have gone too far, but then Sue said in almost a whisper, "Yes, we were having sex problems. I told him one night about my father."

"What was his response?"

"He was upset at first, said I should have told him about it before I married him. He was right, I guess, but I was afraid that if I told him he wouldn't love me."

"But that didn't happen, did it?" Maureen said. "He eventually convinced you to seek professional help, didn't he?"

Sue was about to cry. Maureen could have stopped the interview, but didn't. She wanted every possible inch of tape from which to edit the finished report. She also wanted tears from her subject. It would add to the poignancy of the piece.

"My husband is a very good man," Sue said, managing to hold back her tears. "He helped me, and now things are very good between us."

"How did he help you, Marie?"

"He took me to a clinic for people like me."

"Did they help you?"

"Yes, very much. There were other people like me and that made me feel better."

"Marie, do you think all your scars are gone now?"

"I don't know. Sometimes I wake up in the middle of the night and think about it. Sometimes I dream about it."

"I'm sure you do. What about the other people you met at the clinic? Were their experiences the same as yours?"

"Pretty much, only some were worse, I guess."

"I have to change tape," Harry announced loudly.

"Time for a breather," Maureen told her subject. Jimmy killed the lights and the two women sat in silence. It was going nicely. Although she'd run through her prepared list of questions, Maureen intended to stay with the interview as long as she could. Her questions about Sue's husband and their sexual problems hadn't been met with resistance. Perhaps she could explore that more fully. A counselor at the clinic had told her that adult sexual problems often resulted from the trauma of childhood molestation.

"All set," Harry said.

"Ready?" Maureen asked Sue.

"Do we really have to do more? I don't know what else I could tell you."

"Just a few more questions. I'd like to find out more about how you feel today, what problems you still face because of what happened to you."

"I guess there aren't any problems," she said. "I have a nice life now."

"You did mention problems with your husband. Could we talk more about that?"

Sue looked across the room at her friend, then said, "I don't think so. He might not like it."

"Just a few minutes more," Maureen said. She nodded at Harry, who started the camera rolling.

"Speed," Jimmy said when the videotape was rolling.

"Sue, perhaps you could remember for me some of the feelings and thoughts you experienced when your father climbed into bed with you."

"No, Sue's not the name to use. You said . . ."

"Shit! All right, again, Marie, would you tell me what went through your mind when your father was sexually abusing you?"

"It was so long ago. I guess I was just too scared to think about anything."

"Did you love your father?"

The pause was long and painful. "Yes. He was good to us until he left."

"You didn't hate him for what he did to you?"

"I wanted to kill him, but that was later."

"Later?"

"When I knew what had happened. I mean, I was too young to really know."

"But you eventually wanted to kill him."

"Yes."

"Can you say it today without fear or pain?"

"Say what?"

"That you wanted to kill your father."

"I . . . oh, yes, I wanted my father dead for what he did to me."

Maureen was pleased. She'd wanted the words from the woman herself rather than as a reply to a question. Her statement would cut nicely into the series. "I think that's it," she said.

"Good," Harry mumbled as he turned off the camera. Jimmy killed the lights and removed his earphones.

"Was I all right?" Sue asked as Jimmy came around behind her and removed her microphone.

"You were terrific."

93

"Those times you called me Sue won't be on TV, will they?"

"Of course not. I really appreciate your courage in coming here and being so candid. If more people did that, the problem might surface and something could be done about it."

"That's why I agreed. My husband said the same thing."

"Your husband is right." She looked at Sue's friend, Emily. "Thank you for coming with her."

"My pleasure. I watch you all the time and I think you're great."

"Thanks."

"Better than the others on TV."

"I really appreciate that. Well, careful driving."

"When will this be on TV?" Sue asked.

"I'm not sure. I'll give you a call and let you know."

"Will you? That would be nice."

"I promise. Good-bye."

Maureen and the crew stopped at a deli on the way back to the station. As they sat in front of it and ate sandwiches, Jimmy wanted to talk about the interview. She avoided the conversation except to nod or to mutter simple responses. For some reason—and she could not identify its origins— the interview with Sue Johnstone had been unsettling, had caused a free-floating anxiety to attack her. She'd been detached during her research; the reading she'd done represented only black marks on white paper, statistics, psychological jargon about those who sexually abused children, and a list of names of potential interview subjects. That was all Sue Johnstone had been, a name.

Now, the story had moved from conception into reality, and Sue Johnstone's reality was not pleasant.

She heard Jimmy's words, yet could not connect with them. Her mind wandered as she nibbled on an egg salad sandwich, went back in time, and, for a fraction of a second, she was *there* again, so young and frightened, his fist coming at her, hitting her face very hard. Her trance state ended at the moment of impact, hands clasped to her round belly, a scream of pain, then all black.

". . . I knew somebody once back home who had a thing for little kids," Jimmy said. "Not his own kids, but other kids in the neighborhood. Weird, really weird. He had a family, but he used to hang around the school and do the black raincoat bit." He laughed. "Weird guy, but not his own kids. You got kids, Mo?"

"What time is it?" she asked.

Jimmy checked his watch. "One-forty-five."

"Let's get back."

"I'm not finished yet," Harry said.

"As soon as you are," she said.

She answered phone calls in her office, riffled through mail, and played with possible openings for the sexual abuse series. The young women assigned to produce her Sunday radio show stopped in and asked about the vacant fourth hour. Maureen apologized for not telling her that she'd booked a guest. The producer appeared hurt at the slight. "It came up this morning," Maureen said. "I'll be glad to get this first show out of the way. Why don't you put together a guest list for the following week? Mix it up, that's all I ask."

Joe Coughlin called and invited her to dinner. She declined, said she was tired and felt grubby.

She went to Makeup at five, where her hair was combed out and rearranged and light makeup was applied. She dozed off while sitting in the chair.

At twenty minutes to six she entered the studio in which the early news was produced, settled behind the desk, and perused copy that had been written during the day by other staffers. The director gave her a fast rundown of visuals slated to be used on the newscast. The weatherman, a boyish fellow with a large smile, strolled onto the set and fussed with meteorological symbols on a huge colored map of the United States. The sportscaster, who'd been with the station for almost twenty years and who'd built a solid reputation with the D.C. area's sports fans, greeted her and took his position. Maureen noticed on the rundown sheet that an additional two minutes had been allotted to sports that evening. She mentioned it.

"The drug thing," the sportscaster said. "Got some good tape with a couple of locals who say, 'Maybe the rest of the guys in the league, but not us.'" He guffawed and went back to editing copy.

Maureen was to be solo anchor this night. Her partner was off on assignment and it had been decided not to replace him for the evening, which suited her fine. She preferred working alone, although she'd never expressed that to people at the station. Men could get away with such comments, but women who made them were viewed as pushy and uncooperative.

"One minute to air," the director said over the intercom. "Mo, we'll open on two. We go right to tape on the press conference after your one-line intro."

She looked up at the control room and nodded. There was a word in the first line of copy she didn't like; she came up with another and penciled it in just as the floor manager, his finger pointed at camera number two, counted down, "Five, four, three, two, one." The camera's red light came to life, and the floor manager pointed to her.

"Good evening, I'm Maureen O'Dwyer and this is what happened today."

The red light shifted from camera two to camera three, and the floor manager pointed to it. She turned and faced it. "A presidential news conference this afternoon turned into a shouting match between the President and a reporter. Joel Marshall was there and filed this report."

Videotape of the press conference rolled, and the reporter's voice came through the monitor. The director said over the intercom, "Back to you, Mo."

"Okay."

The videotape of the press conference ended and Maureen continued.

After two more tapes a commercial for a local tire dealer filled the monitor.

And so it went for the rest of the half-hour, smooth and professional, without a hitch. An HFR she'd done weeks ago about two teenagers bicycling from coast to coast to promote the Heart Fund ran after the sportscaster's extended report. The weather in the Washington, D.C., area would be pleasant and cool overnight, with a chance of showers the following evening.

"That's our report for this day," she said. "Jeff Poulson, who's away on assignment, will be back tomorrow. I'm Maureen O'Dwyer, have a nice evening." Production credits crawled up the screen as the camera pulled away from the desk and reduced her to a small background figure.

"Okay, nicely done, troops," the director announced. "Mo, you've got a long-distance phone call on six."

"I'll grab it in the office."

She went to her office and pushed a lighted button on her phone console. An operator asked whether she was Miss O'Dwyer.

"Yes, I am."

"I have a person-to-person call for you. Hold on, please."

Moments later the familiar voice of her mother came on the line. "Maureen?"

"Mama? Hi, how are you?"

"All right. How are you?"

"I'm fine. Is anything wrong?"

"I'm afraid there is."

"What?"

"It's Julie."

"What's happened? Is she sick?"

There was a damnable pause. Then her mother said, "They sent her home from school today?"

"Why did they do that?"

"They found things in her locker. Drugs."

97

"In Julie's locker? I don't believe it." There was no response. "Mama, are you there?"

"It's a terrible thing, a terrible thing."

Maureen lighted a cigarette. "What kind of drugs did they find?"

"Marijuana."

Relief replaced the initial panic she'd suffered. "Well, Mama, that's not good, but it isn't all that bad. Kids today are all into it. I'm not for it, but . . ."

"They found other things, Maureen, pills."

A portion of the panic returned. "What sort of pills?"

"I don't know." Her mother started to cry.

"Mama, crying won't help anything. What kind of pills did they find?" Her voice had risen and she was sorry for that, if only because when it had happened in the past it sometimes prompted her mother to hang up.

"I don't know, I don't know. They say that she had lots of them and that she was selling them."

"Selling them? Why would she . . . who's *they,* damn it?"

"The principal and the police."

"Oh, God. Are you sure?"

"I'm the one who's here, I should know. You should be here. I can't do anything with her. She treats me like I was a piece of dirt on the floor. She's fresh to me, and whenever I tell her to do something she gives me terrible looks. I tell her to do her homework and she lies about it. She's seeing this boy who I don't like. I just know he's the cause of all this. I didn't like him since the first time I saw him. I told her . . ."

"Is she there?" Maureen asked in a controlled voice.

"In her room. She won't come out."

"Go tell her I want to speak to her."

"I don't know what to do. She needs a mother."

"She has a mother, goddamn it, only her mother is someplace else at the moment. Get her on the phone."

"I'll try."

A minute later she returned and said that Julie refused to

leave her room. "She's playing that music, that music all
the time. You have to come out here right away."

"Mama, I can't. I'm so busy and I start a new radio
show this Sunday. Just get her on the phone."

"I don't know what's going to happen to her or to me.
A child should be with a mother."

Maureen sensed that someone was behind her. She
swiveled her chair and saw the producer of her radio
show. She carried a clipboard and looked as though she'd
collapse if she didn't speak with Maureen that moment.

"Just a minute," Maureen told her. Then, to her
mother, "Mama, I'm sure this will all pass. It's probably
overblown. Julie's going through a teenage phase, that's
all. The best thing to do is not push her, leave her alone.
Do you understand?"

"I don't understand why you can't even bother to come
and visit your daughter. She should be living with you."

Maureen felt the temper rising within her. She tried to
control it but it spurted out of her mouth. "And I'm not
about to pay for the rest of my life for one mistake. We
agreed, remember, Mama? Do you remember?"

"I'll never understand you, Maureen. It's not fair."

"Mama, I have to go." She was again aware of her
producer's presence. "I'll call tomorrow. See if you can
get Julie to agree to talk to me on the phone tomorrow.
Will you do that?"

"Yes, I'll try."

"Good, Mama, I love you. I have to run now."

There was a click as her mother hung up.

She turned and said to the producer, "Mothers."

"Here's a list I made of guests for the next show," the
producer said, handing her the clipboard.

Maureen glanced at it, knew it was all wrong, but decided not to discuss it at that moment. "Leave it with me,
hon. It looks good, but I want to think about it. Thanks."

"You don't want to discuss it now?"

"No, I can't. I have an appointment. Tomorrow."

The girl's face reflected her disappointment. Maureen

stood and put her hand on her shoulder. "I think you're going to work out fine," she said, forcing a smile. "Sorry, but I do have to run."

"All right."

"Have a good night."

A few minutes later she was in the parking lot and unlocking her car door. She drove toward the center of town, her mind on everything except the road. Eventually, she pulled up in front of Clyde's, the granddaddy of Washington saloons. Other bars and restaurants had opened on M Street and had tried to capture the same ambience, but they hadn't succeeded, at least according to the core of regulars who flocked there. Maureen tended to go to Clyde's when she was low in spirits and needed an artificial boost. This was one of those nights.

She walked through a milling crowd in the front and to a rear room. Her hunch was correct. Joe Coughlin was there with a couple of cronies and, as usual, was drunk and singing Irish songs. Coughlin had the most remarkable memory for song lyrics and poetry Maureen had ever seen. There was no comment or situation that didn't trigger an appropriate line from a song or poem, especially after he'd had a few "tranquilizers," as he called martinis. He spotted her as she came through the door, stopped the song, met her halfway across the room, and wrapped her in a bear hug. "My goodness, it is my favorite lady newscaster."

She kissed his cheek and followed him to a corner where his friends waited. Joe introduced them, hailed a waiter, and ordered her a martini. She started to protest, then gave it up. A martini was exactly what she wanted.

The first drink hit her hard. She accepted the offer of another from one of Joe's friends, and, after consuming it, knew that she was drunk. She hadn't eaten since the sandwich with the crew. A pulsating headache had developed at the base of her skull, and a wave of nausea came and went.

"All right," Joe announced in a booming voice, "time

for a little bit of Paddy Murphy." He started to sing with great flourish, his arms conducting an imaginary band, his normally red face rendered even redder by the liquor. He beamed with pride as others in the room directed their attention to him.

"*The night that Paddy Murphy died, I never will forget.*
The Irish got so goddamn drunk, that some ain't sober yet.
Of all the things they did that night that filled my heart with fear,
They took the ice from 'neath the corpse and poured it in the beer."

Everyone, including Maureen, joined in the chorus. Joe eventually went through every verse of the ballad. When he was through, his face and collar were soaked with perspiration.

"Time to move on," Coughlin announced. He put his arm around her and said, "The night is young, my dear. There are many more places to see and battles to win."

"Joe, I can't," she said, angry with herself for having trouble with the words. "I have to be up so goddamn early."

"Nonsense," he said. "I insist."

"No, I'm sorry, another time soon."

"Struck out again, Joe, huh?" one of his friends yelled.

She kissed him on the cheek, thanked him for the drinks, waved to his friends, and left the club. The cool night air hit her in the face like a wet rag. She looked up the street and saw a telephone booth, walked to it, inserted a dime, and dialed. After repeated rings, Congressman Jack Maitland answered.

"Jack?"

"Who's this? Is that you, Mo?"

"Yes. How are you?"

"Fine. I tried you but there was no answer."

"That's because I wasn't there," she said, giggling. "Jack, can I come over?"

"Now?"

"Yes."

"Jesus, Mo, I'd love that, but . . ."

"Please, I need you right now."

"I was about to go out. You've been busy and . . ."

"Damn it, Jack, I need somebody right now. I can't be alone."

"All right, Mo. Where are you?"

"I have my car. I'll be there in a little while."

She knocked and Maitland opened the door. He wore a blue velour robe and sandals. She felt his erection spring up and press against her belly.

"You smell like a brewery," he said.

"Just hold me, Jack, please hold me."

"In bed."

They walked silently into his bedroom, where a single lamp cast a warm, welcoming glow over a king-sized bed. She quietly undressed. Maitland slipped out of his robe, pulled down the covers, and sprawled on his back. When she was naked, she took unsteady steps toward him, stumbled, and fell into his outstretched arms. The feel of him against her sent a jolt through her body. Absently, mechanically, they fondled each other, hands tracing contours of their bodies and pausing at particularly provocative places, lips tasting the recesses of their mouths, subdued moans mingled with wet sounds, all leading up to the moment when he mounted her and, after a long series of sustained and steady thrusts, ejaculated. She hadn't quite reached her own orgasm and, before he went limp, he withdrew and massaged the exterior of her sexuality with his own until she tensed, her legs trembled, and she audibly announced her release.

They lay together, he on his back, her face nestled against his neck and one leg tossed over his body. She smelled of gin, which he didn't like, but he didn't say anything about it, did not suggest that she go to the bathroom and brush her teeth. He had mixed feelings at that moment. He was annoyed at her last-minute phone call and the drunken state she was in when she made it. Then again, there was the feeling of serenity in having her against him, absently running his fingers through her thick red hair, the sound of her steady breathing as she drifted into sleep, the feel of her. There had been other women since his divorce, but none that aroused as much pleasure and pride as Maureen O'Dwyer. He admired her success and standing in Washington, and in quiet, introspective moments admitted to himself that if he married again, it would be someone like her.

When she was fully asleep he gently slipped from bed and looked down at her. He smiled. She was very beautiful and childlike. He put on his robe and went to the den, where he spent an hour going over committee reports. When he returned to the bedroom she'd turned on her stomach and was snoring lightly. He sat beside her and placed his palm on her buttocks. She stirred under his touch.

"Just go to sleep," he said. "I'm here."

"That's nice," she said into the pillow.

CHAPTER 9

After viewing the three entries in the Brickhouse competition, Howard Monroe and Renée Ballantyne had lunch in a local health food restaurant.

"Well, what do you think?" he asked after finding table space against a wall.

"I have trouble responding to any of them, Howard. The idea of having Entertainment calling the shots in finding a new anchor is enough to handle at the moment."

He took a forkful of bean sprouts and slowly chewed. "I can take this stuff only so often," he commented.

"It's good for you, Howard," she said.

"Let's assume we can get over the business of having Drew and Machlin involved in the process, Renée. If we can do that, which of the three this morning would get your vote?"

She screwed up her face as she absently played with her food. She then looked up and said, "Maureen, I guess. She's certainly earned it. There's nobody in the business with better experience and more integrity."

"But would she boost ratings?" Monroe asked.

Renée shook her head as though to scold him. "Have you become enough of a media creature to choose journalists based on their ratings appeal?"

"Not deep down inside, Renée, but I have come to appreciate the reality of this business called broadcast journalism. Rachoff *means* business. If the ratings don't come up on News, the entire network suffers, and he'll be forced to bring in new people. That means . . ."

". . . that we won't have jobs," she said, completing his thought.

"Yup, that's the reality I'm talking about."

They lingered over herb tea and discussed the videotapes they'd just screened of Veronica Frazier, Cindy Lewis, and Maureen O'Dwyer. Monroe felt that Maureen's performance was the most professional, but also felt it was a little too slick. As far as he was concerned, Veronica Frazier's undercover approach had much more impact.

Renée agreed with his comments, although she was more impressed than he with Cindy Lewis's four-part interview with Monty Jamison. "That was a coup," she said. "Jamison has been on everyone's mind since the Kennedy assassination. There's some solid envy in the trade over that report."

They walked out onto the street. The sidewalk was filled with noontime diners and shoppers. Monroe stretched and rubbed the back of his neck. "I hate to go back," he said. "Until Entertainment stuck its nose in our business I used to enjoy coming to work. Now, I wake up in the morning and have to convince myself to put my feet on the floor."

Renée looked into his eyes and saw the fatigue. Touching his arm, she said, "Don't let it take too much out of you, Howard. It will all be resolved and we'll forget about it. Like my father used to say, 'A hundred years from now who'll remember?'"

Monroe smiled and nodded. "It's those hundred years that are tough," he said. "Let's go back to the circus."

Chapter 10

Herb Machlin sat at his typewriter and wrote another draft of a memo to go out under Renée Ballantyne's signature. He made a note to his secretary to personalize each of the memos, and that they were to go to Cindy Lewis in Amarillo, Veronica Frazier in San Francisco, and Maureen O'Dwyer in Washington.

The Shay Brickhouse Foundation has nominated you for one of its annual awards for excellence in broadcast journalism. I'll be in touch with you shortly with details. In the meantime, I suggest you make plans to be in New York the week of October 10 to attend the Brickhouse dinner and to engage in activities related to the awards that are of benefit to EBS. Congratulations on performing the quality of work that has brought attention not only to you, but to all of us at the network.

Sincerely,
Renée Ballantyne

He sat back and reread the memo. He was glad he wouldn't have to be the one to give it to Ballantyne. Her animosity toward him had become more overt, and ghost-writing a memo for someone who'd spent most of her professional life writing would probably send her into a rage. Jenkins Drew could give it to her.

He put the draft into an envelope and wrote Drew's name on it. He checked his watch; a few minutes after six. He walked down the hall to Drew's office and placed the envelope on his desk, returned to his office, picked up the phone, and dialed. A female voice answered.

"Jeneen?"

"Yes."

"Herb Machlin."

"Oh, yes, how are you?"

"Fine."

"Glad to hear it."

"I wondered if you had time this evening," he said.

"Some, but not much. When were you thinking of?"

"How about right now?"

"That would work, although we won't have much time."

"I'll be right over."

He arrived twenty minutes later. She opened the door and he walked into her lavish living room. The floor was covered in white shag carpeting, and interesting original paintings were illuminated with pin spots. He tossed his jacket on a chair. Jeneen came up behind him and wrapped her arms around his middle. "You've put on a few pounds since the last time I saw you," she whispered into his ear.

He wished she hadn't commented on his weight gain. After all, she was being paid to be with him, and what she thought of his physique was irrelevant. At least, that was what he preferred to think. In fact, he wished he hadn't put on extra pounds since last seeing her.

He turned. "You look terrific," he said, his hands going to the tie of her green silk robe. He opened it and slipped it over her shoulders. She was naked beneath it.

"One of those days, huh?" she said as she pressed against him and kissed his neck.

"Yeah, one of those days." He stepped out of her embrace and removed his clothing. She led him into a bedroom cast in a pale pink light. The bed was circular, and there were mirrored squares on the ceiling directly above it. He glanced at himself in a full-length mirror on a closet door. He hadn't put on too much weight, he told himself as he inhaled so that his stomach flattened out. The hue of the lighting was flattering, and he felt better.

She pulled down a silk spread and curled up on the bed. He stepped close, then glanced up into the ceiling mirrors. A growing bald spot was visible, and he ran his hand through his hair to spread what was left of it around.

"Come to baby, Herbie," she said, extending her arms.

He lay beside her and gave himself over to her soft white perfumed flesh. She played with him with her fingers until he'd become semihard, then got on her knees and took him in her mouth until he was fully erect. She glanced up at him and asked, "How do you want it, Herbie?"

He said, not returning her look, "Just come here and let me hold you for a while."

"I can't. I told you that I don't have a lot of time."

"Please, just a few minutes."

She lowered herself onto him and nuzzled her face in his neck. "Oooh, you feel so good," she said.

"So do you, Jeneen." He ran his fingers up and down her spinal column, then caressed the upper portion of her buttocks.

She slid off him, leaned her face over his, and said, smiling, "Do you know what I need, Herbie?"

"What?"

"I need that wonderful big cock in me. You're one of the few customers I have who truly satisfies me."

He knew that she was lying, was telling him what she probably told every john who paid for her services, yet the words were pleasant to hear, even if it meant suspending judgment.

She straddled him and lowered herself until the tip of his penis brushed against her vagina. He didn't want to complete the act yet. He wanted to stroke and love her, to have her treat him as though he were her only lover, but he knew that would never be the case. The sex was almost irrelevant. It was the warmth, the touching, the intimacy that prompted him to visit her on occasion and to pay her fee.

As she settled on him and uttered a satisfied moan at the feel of him inside, he said, "I'd like to spend a whole night with you, Jeneen."

She began a slow circular motion with her pelvis. "That would cost a lot, Herbie."

"I know, but I'd like to sometime."

"We'll see, we'll talk about that someday," she said, never breaking her rhythm.

He tried to hold back but decided there was nothing to be gained by it. He let himself go and enjoyed his ejaculation.

She walked him to the door after he'd dressed. "I loved it, Herbie," she said. "I feel satisfied for the first time all day. Don't be a stranger so long again."

"Yeah, I'll be back soon. Have a nice night, Jeneen."

Before hailing a cab he went into a phone booth and dialed home.

"Where are you?" Marcie asked.

"I told you I might get hung up late tonight on this project with Drew. I'm heading for the train now."

"You could have called and told me definitely."

"Well, I didn't, so get off my back. I've had one hell of a bad day."

"So have I, Herbie. The dishwasher broke and I can't get anybody to come until next Wednesday."

"I'll call them. Maybe I can get them to move faster."

"Do you want me to meet you at the station?" she asked.

"No, I'll take a cab."

"Stop at the deli on the way home and pick up some milk. We're out of milk."

He sighed, said he would, found a cab, and told the driver to take him to Grand Central Station. His train was delayed a half-hour, and by the time he arrived home Marcie was sufficiently angry not to talk to him.

"Hell of a thing," he snapped as he went into the den and turned on the television set. "A man works all day and this is what he comes home to?"

"A woman works all day and this is what comes home to her? I'm going to the movies. Make yourself something to eat."

He went to the kitchen, paused in front of the refrigerator, and touched his belly. "Time to go on a diet," he said as he returned to the den, settled in his chair, and tuned to the beginning of an old movie on EBS. And remembered he forgot the milk.

_____Chapter 11

Veronica Frazier settled in seat 5A, by a window in the DC-10. It was the Redeye special, and would get her to New York at 6:15 the next morning.

She'd upgraded her ticket from coach to first class at her own expense. EBS had placed a ban on all first-class business travel except for selected executives. For Veronica, coach class was all right under normal circumstances, but to sit wedged in between people on a long overnight flight was intolerable.

One of the flight attendants was a black woman, much darker than Veronica and with features less fine. She was businesslike in the cabin, quick and sure in her actions, a professional, thought Veronica, well trained and proud.

Veronica's seatmate was a man in his forties. He was dressed casually, like someone in the film or record business, although she knew dress was too often misleading. He was pockmarked and not openly pleasant. Soon after takeoff he told the stewardess that he didn't wish to be awakened for food. "It's never worth it," he muttered.

"Yes, sir," she said, glancing at Veronica and smiling.

There was no movie. A deli platter was served. Veronica didn't complain about the food, even to herself. It was always a wonder to her that food was served at all in a silver tube flying at six hundred miles an hour over thirty thousand feet in the sky. She tended to view many things that way, with wonder.

She looked at her sleeping seat companion. There was cruelty to his mouth. He hadn't introduced himself. Not that she cared. She probably wouldn't have enjoyed a conversation with him anyway. She often judged people by whether she'd like to be cornered by them at a party for more than fifteen minutes. When she told Craig Stanton of her criterion, he'd said that he always judged people by whether he'd like to be stuck next to them on a long flight. Either way, the man next to her would not qualify.

They hit choppy air over Utah and the seat belt sign lighted up. The captain, who'd had little to say, came on the PA system and advised passengers to keep their belts fastened. "Veteran travelers always do anyway," he added. Which Veronica already knew.

The aircraft's movement woke the man next to her. He growled, tried to go back to sleep, then sat up and rubbed his eyes. "Where are we?" he asked.

His voice took her by surprise. She said, "Over Utah. There's rough air."

"I noticed." He yawned and stretched, scratched his belly beneath a purple velour shirt. After a few minutes of silence he rummaged through a leather carry-on bag, found what he was looking for, and turned to Veronica. "Want a joint?"

"No . . . I don't use it." She did not add, ". . . anymore."

He went to a vacant lavatory, then returned ten minutes later, slumped in his seat, and closed his eyes.

Veronica suddenly felt fatigued. She twisted in her seat, tucked her stockinged feet up under her, and put her head on a small pillow. She thought of the recent past, of her Emmy and her mother's stay in San Francisco, of Bill Teller and the gun that she'd hidden in the recesses of a clothes closet, of Craig Stanton, and of Roscoe Williams.

Her thoughts weren't clear; they came and went as in a dream, fragments floating in and out of reach.

The only thought she could focus on was the reason for her trip to New York. Initially, receiving Renée Ballantyne's memo had excited her. She couldn't wait to show it to Craig. When she did, his reaction was disappointing. He dismissed it and suggested she do the same. That conversation had taken place in his office.

That night they'd had dinner at L'Orangerie, on O'Farrell, where Stanton was a regular. They sat on a love seat. She was still in an expansive mood because of the memo. She pushed against him and ran her fingertips over the top of his thigh. There were only occasional times in their relationship when she felt loving toward him. Love? Never that, but warm, at peace, and able to take from him emotional nourishment. This was one of those times, and she was disappointed with his unwillingness to reciprocate.

"What's wrong?" she asked.

"Nothing. Do you want an appetizer?"

"The salmon sounds good."

Stanton waved to Andre, the captain, and ordered for both of them. The wine was a California Charles Krug, 1964, the salad termed a "money salad," because, as the story went, someone had once said it was so good that it must be made of money; it had artichoke, mushrooms, celery, and watercress.

"I wish you'd tell me what's bothering you," Veronica said.

"And I wish you'd stop asking me," he said in a low, angry voice.

"Is it the memo?"

"What memo? Oh, that. Of course not."

"Aren't you happy for me?"

He laughed. "Yeah, I suppose so. The Brickhouse Awards are a sham, just something to hang on the wall. If you want to get off on that kind of thing, be my guest."

She couldn't fathom his response. He'd been her mentor, had been instrumental in bringing her to a point in her career where winning awards was possible. Didn't he experience pride in seeing a "pupil" succeed? She knew she'd feel that way.

"Are you coming to New York for the dinner?" she asked him.

"No, why should I?"

"I just thought management from stations up for an award would be invited to . . ."

"Look, Ronnie, this award bullshit is just that. Why don't you demonstrate some class and turn it down, refuse to show up like Brando did at the Academy Awards?"

Refuse to show up? The walls of the station were lined with awards garnered by staff members. Radio and television stations displayed them like badges of success, sponsors were wooed with them, print media flooded with releases praising the accomplishments of station newsmen and -women.

"Why?" she asked. "I thought the station would want to be represented."

"Nobody said you won anything. You've been nominated, that's all. They'll fly you into New York, feed you some bad meals, make you feel important, and send you back to reality."

She didn't want to offend him, but she couldn't help laughing. "This is reality?"

"It looked pretty good to you before."

She stopped laughing and touched his arm. "Don't be mad, Craig. I didn't mean anything. You know how important it was for me to succeed. I appreciate everything that's happened to me since coming out here and meeting you. I hope you know that."

"Why should I know that, because you go down on me every once in a while?"

She turned away from him and stared straight ahead. There was a table of six people directly in front of her. One of the men, younger than the other two males, was loud and continually tried to impress the others. Veronica had always been fascinated by groups of people who obviously had a business link. The younger man's wife sat quietly, wearing a thinly disguised expression of pain. To succeed seemed always to demand posturing and bravado, establishing turf and importance. Veronica hated it, yet was good at it. Her father had once said that the beauty of working as a jazz musician was that your horn did all the talking. It either talked good or it wasn't allowed to talk again. "I go play, the man pays me, and that's that," he'd said. "Don't have to lick nobody's boots, just talk through my horn."

"What do you want?" Stanton asked, referring to the menu.

She'd drifted away from the table, now was snapped back to it. "I don't know, I haven't looked."

He checked his watch. "This can't be a late one for me. Make up your mind."

"Veal."

"Which one?"

"Any one, it doesn't matter."

"What's your problem?"

"You."

"Why?"

"I hate you."

"Good." He motioned for Andre and placed their order, then asked her, "Do you want a soufflé? It has to be ordered now."

"No."

"One raspberry soufflé," he told Andre.

"Let's clear the air," he said to her, sitting back and sipping his wine.

"Fine. Why are you upset about my being nominated for the Brickhouse Award?"

"I'm not. It's just that I've been around this business a lot longer than you."

"I'd never argue that, Craig. I respect it and learn from you."

115

"This is all a network game run by a bunch of airheads in the Entertainment Division, that's all. They've been making noise about finding a female anchor for the seven o'clock news, and this year's Brickhouse shit is evidently tied into it."

She was silent as she allowed his words to sink in. Was he suggesting that she was a candidate for such an anchor spot? It couldn't be, but what else could she take from it? The realization that he might be suggesting it caused her even further confusion over his response to the invitation to New York. If there was even a remote possibility of it, wouldn't he be proud, want her to succeed? She couldn't raise these questions because she was afraid of shutting him off. She wanted to hear more.

She said, "But that has nothing to do with me. The drug series picked up an Emmy and now it might pick up another award, that's all."

He said nothing.

It wasn't easy but she added, "If you'd rather have me not go to New York, I won't." She hoped he wouldn't take her up on it.

He cocked his head and looked at her. "Really?"

"I don't understand it, but I won't go. If I do go, would you like to come with me? We could make it a little vacation, get away. I'm sure there's business you could do there and we could spend time together. I've never seen New York. Maybe that's why the telegram excited me so. I don't care about any stupid award." It wasn't true, but she was compelled to make the claim. "But I would enjoy seeing the city."

Their entrées were served and they ate in silence. The young man at the other table had evidently had too much to drink and was now even louder.

"What a pain in the ass," Craig said.

"I know."

"Well, are you going?" he asked.

"To New York?"

"Yes."

"You tell me."

"You might as well go. Forget me. I can't get away."

"You're sure?"

"Yeah, I'm sure. Let's get out of here." He paid and they went to his car, which was parked directly in front. He drove her to Lombard Street, parked on Powell, and walked her to the house. She turned on a single lamp in the living room and asked if he wanted a drink. He looked at his watch. "I have time. Scotch will be fine."

They sat on the couch and she leaned against him. "I'm glad we resolved this thing about New York," she said. "I guess I'm excited because it's all so new to me. You'll have to forgive me, Craig. I'm not a grizzled veteran yet."

"Get close to that gang in New York and you soon will be."

"Are they *that* bad?"

"Worse than that." He placed his glass on the coffee table, turned, and put a hand on her shoulder. "Look, Ronnie, I . . ."

Was he about to cry?

"What is it?" she asked.

He turned away and rubbed his eyes. "Nothing, just dead-ass tired."

She ran her fingers through her hair and realized that she felt sorry for him for the first time in their relationship. She didn't like the feeling, but found herself responding by stroking him, licking his wounds, whatever they were. He reacted, squirmed to accommodate an erection, took her in his arms, and kissed her with an urgency and force that usually wasn't present. They moved quickly to the bedroom, where, without even a modicum of foreplay, he entered her and reached his climax. He quickly withdrew, turned on his back with an arm beneath his head, and stared at the ceiling, on which the light of a small lamp formed a half-moon. She knew he was angry, but was afraid to mention it for fear of evoking even greater anger. Finally, she got up and slipped into a robe.

"Where are you going?" he asked, not moving.

"The kitchen. I'll make some coffee, if that's all right." She hadn't meant it to sound snotty, but it did.

He picked up on it. "Don't come off nasty with me, Ronnie. Just because you're becoming a star doesn't mean you forget where you came from."

She froze in the middle of the room, her hands holding the robe's cord in midair. "What do you mean by that?" she asked.

He sat up against the headboard. "Give me a cigarette."

She hesitated, then took an open pack from her dresser and tossed it to him. "Why did you say what you did?" she asked.

"No reason, except that I've seen it too many times before. Local girl makes good with generous help from friends, rises to the top, and forgets the names of her friends when they come backstage."

She shook her head and threw up her hands. "And you think that's happening to me? That's absurd. Because of some dumb award that you even say is nothing, a waste of time? You're crazy, Craig."

Two things happened then. It hit her that he knew more than he'd told her about the circumstances surrounding the Shay Brickhouse Award and the network flying her to New York. A star? Was that possible?

Then he came off the bed and struck her across the side of the head with the back of his hand. The blow sent her reeling against a wall. She grabbed drapes to keep from falling and they came down on her in a heap. She pulled them from her face and watched as he quickly dressed and walked to the bedroom door.

"Why?" she asked.

"Because I don't like to be used."

The pilot of her flight to New York announced that they'd passed through the choppy air and that the seat belt sign was turned off, adding, "I won't be back on with you until we get closer to New York. Have a pleasant sleep."

Her seat companion was snoring. Veronica sat up straight, put on the complimentary earphones, and dialed in a channel on which jazz was featured. It was after one song had finished and another had begun that she understood what had transpired between her and Craig Stanton the night he hit her. He was jealous, was afraid to expose her to something bigger and better because that would increase the potential of losing her. It took another full tune before she amended the realization. He wasn't afraid of losing her. He was afraid of losing control over her. Once she reached that conclusion, she felt immeasurably better.

_____CHAPTER 12

A party for Maureen O'Dwyer was held at Clyde's. Joe
Coughlin had invited an assortment of friends, mostly his
but including a sprinkling of her TV buddies.

"A toast," Joe said as he raised his glass.

"To what?" someone asked.

Coughlin looked at the questioner as though he'd broken
wind. "To Maureen, of course," he said, smiling to temper his obvious annoyance. "To the best goddamn female
journalist in the business."

"Just *female?*" she asked.

"Isn't that enough?" a friend of Joe's said as he put his
arm around her and kissed her cheek.

"To the best goddamn journalist in the world, male *or*
female," Coughlin said.

"I'll drink to that," said Maureen, aware that her words
were coming out in hesitant bunches. When Maureen was
upset, she drank, and she'd been upset since she called
Jack Maitland's apartment early in the morning two days
ago and heard a woman answer the phone.

A few friends gathered around her and offered congratulations on her Brickhouse Award.

"I didn't win anything yet," she said. "Besides, it's no
big deal. I won a Brickhouse six years ago."

"Toe in the sand," a male friend said. "Modesty doesn't become you."

Maureen laughed. She considered Joe's idea for a going-away party absurd. She was always flying up to New York and this was just another trip. Besides, she meant what she'd said about the insignificance of the Brickhouse Award. She had a den overflowing with awards from almost every foundation in the country. Giving out awards was what kept some of those groups in business, just as the framed eight-by-ten glossies with politicians that adorned her wall were nothing more than an ongoing PR effort.

Once, while in New York, she'd watched a short dark man in a plaid suit pose with celebrities in a posh hotel while a photographer snapped their pictures together. Later, she met the photographer and asked who the other man was and why he was having his photo taken with celebrities. The photographer told her that the man owned an Italian restaurant on Cape Cod in which photographs with the rich and famous hung on every wall. Once a year he came to New York, hired the photographer, and went celebrity hunting. The man's wife, as well as employees of the restaurant, wrote flowery greetings on the finished pictures and forged the celebrity signatures.

Yet, there were always irrefutable twinges of excitement at being recognized, and she sometimes wondered whether she'd been born a victim of a disease that only went into remission with daily doses of adoration, not personal but certainly professional. A man she'd been seeing once had told her, "There's no room for a man in your life, Mo, because you're married to a goddamn typewriter and TV camera." She always denied it, but when alone and reflective she had to acknowledge that there was an element of truth to what he'd said.

"Think you'll win?" Joe asked her after another round of drinks had been served.

"No, and what difference does it make?"

"You're right, it doesn't matter. By the way, the ratings on the radio show are spectacular."

She grabbed his arm and her face came to light. "How do you know? They don't come out for another week."

"The Coughlin Mafia. Believe me, the ratings are solid."

"That's good to hear. I'm really comfortable with the call-in format now, Joe, into a groove on the phone. I hated that initial awkwardness, but maybe it was that nit of a producer I was saddled with."

"She's gone."

"Right. I had to fire her. Hated to do it. She's a nice kid and all, but so damn young. Young people don't *know* anything, no matter how bright they are. Did you know that, Joe? Young people don't *know* anything."

He laughed. "They're not supposed to know anything, Mo. They're supposed to *do*. Knowing comes later."

She downed half her drink and looked at her watch. "I'd better get my tail out of here."

"It's early."

"Not for me. I have to pack, take care of some things before tomorrow. I'm taking the first shuttle."

"Why? I thought you weren't due there until late tomorrow afternoon."

"I thought I'd see some people early in the day, spend some time with Schwartz. We're having lunch."

"I heard some scuttlebutt about Schwartz today," Coughlin said.

Maureen's eyebrows went up.

"Somebody was telling me, and I can't think of who it was, that Schwartz . . ." He stopped because her attention suddenly shifted to the front door of Clyde's. Standing in it was Congressman Jack Maitland. He quickly crossed the room, kissed Maureen on the cheek, and shook Joe's hand. He said to her, "I didn't think I'd get here, but here I am. We ended up conferencing the wetlands bill and I was afraid for a while we'd be there all night. Thank God some of the others had commitments. I wouldn't have missed this for . . ."

"I was just leaving," Maureen said.

"My timing is even better than I thought," said Maitland. "Another few minutes and I would have missed you."

"You did," she said as she picked up a white shawl from a chair and took a step toward the door. She stopped, turned, and said to Joe Coughlin, "Thanks for the party, Joe. I'll talk to you from New York."

Maitland was obviously dismayed and looked to Joe for sympathy and understanding. When he received neither, he followed Maureen across the large room and out to the street. "What's bugging you?" he asked.

She walked away from him, stopped next to a mailbox, placed both hands on it, and drew a deep breath. He came up behind and put his arm over her shoulder.

"Please, Jack," she said.

"Mo, tell me what's the matter. I'm sorry I'm late, but you know as well as anybody how hard it is to plan anything when you're in Congress."

She turned and looked up at him with her green eyes. He felt her tremble beneath the weight of his arm. She said, "I've just been under a lot of pressure, that's all."

Maitland shook his head. "No, there's more than that, Maureen, and you know it. Is it because of what happened the other night?"

"Of course not." She said it with conviction, too much conviction.

"I apologized for that, Maureen. Why can't you drop it?"

"Maybe because I don't want to. You know, Jack, despite my shell of toughness and professional detachment, I'm capable of being very hurt. You hurt me."

"I didn't mean to. That girl was someone from before we met."

"And still very much a part of your life."

"Why not?" he asked. "I'm divorced. There have been other women since we split, including you. I've told you that you mean more to me than the others." He tried to lighten the tone by saying, "I could almost believe that I'm falling in love with you."

She stepped back and laughed, and said, "Jesus, Congressman, when are you going to stop couching your statements like a politician and say something honest and true to me? Do you love me?"

"Yes, I think I do."

She slapped her hand against the side of her head. "There you go again."

"No, I'm not being a politician. I'm being honest. We haven't known each other that long, Mo, and I can only tell you what feelings are developing. Frankly, you scare me at times."

"Scare you? How?"

"That very shell you talk about. You want me to open up and to love you, but you keep that shell around you."

"I've been hurt too many times before, Congressman. If I'm self-protective, you'll have to understand that."

"And what about me? Because I'm a man I'm not supposed to admit hurt? I've been hurt, too, and if I feel a need to go a little slower with us, you'll have to be as understanding as you expect me to be."

She thought about what he'd said; then she stepped into his arms and they embraced. A couple passing by observed them and made a comment.

"I have to get home and pack," Maureen said. She spotted a cruising cab and energetically waved it to the curb.

"My car is right around the corner," Maitland said.

"Please, I really need to be alone tonight, Jack. Is that okay?"

"It will have to be, won't it? You sure I can't buy you a drink, or make you one at home while you pack?"

She shook her head. "Positive. Are you going home now?"

"Yes."

"I'll call you a little later." She kissed him, climbed into the cab, and gave the driver her address.

The moment she was inside her house she poured herself a stiff drink, turned on the television, and sat in a black vinyl reclining chair. There was nothing on TV that interested her except a repeat of an old documentary on animal behavior. She sat through it, nursing her drink until the final credits; then made herself another and watched part of a variety special featuring a popular rock group. She hated the music, turned off the set and put on an album of big band jazz. She was unsteady from the drinks and knew that if she gave in to the feeling she would fall asleep and not accomplish anything. She pulled two suitcases from a closet, opened them on the bed, and transferred clothing to them from drawers and closets. She couldn't make up her mind what dresses to take to New York, particularly which one to wear to the Brickhouse dinner, and wished she'd planned her wardrobe a little sooner. Eventually, she made her choices and carefully folded them on top of other items in the bags.

The phone rang just as the record came to an end. "Damn it," she muttered. The last thing she wanted was a telephone conversation.

"Maureen O'Dwyer?" an operator asked.

"Yes."

"I have a collect call for you from Mrs. O'Dwyer in Kansas City. Will you accept the charges?"

She almost said no, but told the operator, "Yes, I will."

"Maureen?"

"Yes, Mama. Why are you calling at this hour? Is something wrong?"

Her mother started to cry.

"Mama, stop crying and tell me what's the matter."

It took her mother a few seconds to pull herself together. When she did, she said in a voice that Maureen could bearly hear, "Julie is gone."

"What do you mean she's gone? Where did she go?"

"I don't know. That's what's so terrible. She didn't come home from school and wasn't here for dinner. I didn't want to call the police because I thought she was just being spiteful. We had a big argument at breakfast and she was nasty to me. But she still isn't here. I looked in her room and some of her clothes are gone. So is a suitcase she kept in her closet."

"Hold on," Maureen said as she dropped the phone on the bed and got a cigarette. When she picked up the receiver again, she said, "She's probably staying at a friend's house."

"I think she ran away."

"Why would she run away, Mama? Where would she go?"

They discussed the situation for a few more minutes, and Maureen came to the conclusion that her mother was probably right, that Julie had left, at least for the night.

"Should I call the police, Maureen?"

"I suppose you should, but maybe that's just being premature. She's going through that rebellious teenager phase, that's all. Chances are she's staying with a friend to get even with you for the argument and she'll be back in the morning looking for breakfast."

"I just know I won't sleep all night," her mother said. She started to cry again.

"Mama, crying won't help anybody. Have you called her friends to ask about her?"

"No, I was embarrassed."

"Embarrassed about what? I'm sure her friends' parents have all gone through this kind of thing with their own kids. Why don't you make some calls and just ask if she's there."

"I suppose I could do that. I'm so worried. She shouldn't have done this to me."

"Of course she shouldn't have, Mama," Maureen said, unable to disguise the annoyance in her voice. "Look, make those calls and then get back to me."

"All right, and if she comes in, I'll have her call you right away."

"Fine. I won't be here tomorrow or for the rest of the week. I'm going to New York."

"You don't care, do you?"

Maureen waited for her mother's tears to subside, then said, "I'll be here all night in case she comes home. I'll call you tomorrow during the day and let you know where I can be reached."

"Maybe I should call the police."

"No, Mama, she hasn't been gone that long. Let's give it the night and we can decide tomorrow what to do. Now, try to go to sleep and forget about it. I'll talk to you tomorrow."

After they'd concluded their conversation, Maureen went into the bathroom, where she stripped off her clothing and climbed naked between the sheets. She was filled with confusion, as though all the nerve ends had been activated at once and were in conflict. The booze hadn't helped. She turned on a clock radio next to her bed and listened to a talk show. Eventually, she fell asleep, but awoke an hour later and looked at the clock. She turned off the radio and tossed and turned until finally drifting off an hour and a half before the alarm went off at five-thirty. She turned it off and stared at the ceiling. "Please, God, let her be safe," she said aloud.

A few hours later she was on the early shuttle flight to New York City.

_____CHAPTER 13

The young man from EBS's Public Relations Department who'd met Cindy Lewis at Kennedy Airport led her into the lobby of the Inter-Continental New York, formerly the Barclay, on Forty-eighth Street, just off Park Avenue. She stopped to admire a huge copper bird cage in the middle of the lobby that housed a variety of exotic birds. Shades on the cage, which were drawn at night to provide dark and quiet for the cage's inhabitants, were rolled up. Cindy knelt on a green circular leather banquette surrounding the cage and made a funny face at one of the birds, which, she was sure, was a half-moon parrot. The young man realized he'd lost her and retraced his steps.

"Isn't this wonderful?" she said, bubbling with excitement. "Imagine having a bird cage right in the center of a hotel lobby." She looked up at a domed glass ceiling above the cage and slowly shook her head. "How elegant," she said as she followed the young PR man to an elevator, where a bellhop waited with her luggage.

Once upstairs in her room on the fourteenth floor, after the bellhop had been tipped and had left, she pirouetted. The bed, which had a bamboo headboard, was queen-size. Cindy picked up one of two fluffy peach-colored terrycloth robes from the bed and held it in front of her. "They think of everything," she exclaimed. "Imagine, providing robes."

She went to a glass-topped desk where a crystal vase containing two pink roses stood next to an iced bucket of Nicolas Feuillatte Brut champagne. A handwritten note from the assistant manager of the hotel welcomed her to New York.

"It's lovely," she said to her escort. "I don't think I've ever been in such a beautiful room."

The young man smiled. "Well, I'm glad you're happy, Miss Lewis. I have to run now. Make yourself at home. We'll be in touch with you soon."

"Thank you, thank you so much," she said, walking him to the door.

She bolted the door behind him, then went to the window and looked out over Manhattan. There was no denying her nervousness; she didn't even bother to try. She put her hands on ventilation ducts that ran the length of the window, and allowed her body to shudder with excitement and anticipation. She couldn't believe it, being in New York City. She and Hal had traveled, but never very far from home. Once, they'd taken a trip to California with the children, and had also visited Arizona and Utah. Cindy had family in Seattle and St. Louis, and they'd flown there on occasion. Hal's business conventions also provided trips for them, although his few business trips to New York hadn't coincided with her schedule. She was never able to accompany him.

She stepped into the large bathroom and perused the items that were provided for her as a guest: a bar of Nino Cerruti soap in a black case, a vial of Rich 'n Lather shampoo, a shower cap, and a small sewing kit.

"VIP treatment," she said. "How wonderful."

She wasn't sure what to do first. It was four in the afternoon. She was tired, yet she could not conceive of wasting a moment by napping. She also felt grimy, and decided to take a shower. First, however, she must call Hal in Amarillo and let him know that she had arrived safely. She sat on the edge of the bed and read the card of instructions for placing calls. She finally figured it out, got up, took off her clothes, and went into the bathroom, where she stood under a hot shower for ten minutes. Clean and refreshed, she slipped into one of the robes and placed her call.

"Hello," one of the kids said.

"Hi, it's Mommy. How are you?"

"Great. How are you? Did you get there okay?"

Cindy laughed. "I guess so. I wouldn't be calling if I hadn't." She judged from his muttered response that she'd offended him, so she added, "I'm just fine, honey. I'm in the hotel and it's beautiful. They're treating me like a real important person, champagne in the room and a nice note from the manager. Is Daddy there?"

"Nope. He called and said he wouldn't be home as early as he thought. He figures he'll get here around six."

She looked at her watch and estimated the time in Amarillo at three-thirty. Hal had planned to be home by noon, but something must have come up at the office. She talked for a few more minutes with her son and told him that she would try to reach his father later. "I miss you already," she said. "I love you."

"Love you, too, Mom. Well, have a good time there. And good luck, I hope you win the award."

"Thanks, honey. I'll call every day."

She leaned back against the headboard after hanging up and considered calling Hal at the office. She decided not to. Chances were he'd gone to lunch with a client, or maybe decided to play golf that afternoon. She'd try him later, when she was reasonably certain he'd be home.

She felt tired again and closed her eyes, but reminded herself not to fall asleep. She didn't know what she'd do that night, but thought someone from the network might contact her and suggest some activity.

She then thought of Hal and of the circumstances surrounding her departure. They weren't especially pleasant, although there hadn't been open hostility. She'd desperately wanted him to come with her, had even suggested they consider it a second honeymoon. But he refused, claiming the press of business, which, although she didn't buy it, was not made an issue by her. She knew Hal was unhappy with her trip. He hadn't said as much, but reading between the lines with Hal was never difficult. He'd indicated great pride in her Brickhouse Award nomination, had called friends and told them about it, and had even suggested a party to celebrate. She'd nixed that idea, partially because she would have been embarrassed, but mostly because of the unstated tension surrounding the arrival of the memo from Renée Ballantyne.

Just before leaving she'd made one final stab at getting Hal to accompany her. She suggested that he arrive later in the week, certainly in time for the dinner itself, and that they stay over the following weekend and see some theater, enjoy interesting restaurants, and turn it into a relaxing vacation. He balked, although he did say he would consider it if things eased up during the week. She knew he wouldn't, but there was a certain comfort in hanging on to the possibility.

She turned on the television but didn't watch it, instead returned to the bed and read through a letter that had followed the memo. It didn't tell her much about what to expect in New York, although it did spell out her hotel accommodations, gave her phone numbers at EBS, and told her that shortly after she arrived she would be contacted by a network representative.

She dozed but awoke when the five o'clock EBS newscast came on. She watched it with great interest. There was a different feel to the way the news was presented, she thought, more polished and professional, certainly more big city, and she suffered a twinge of insecurity at being there at all. *It's all so silly,* she thought, *this housewife from Amarillo, Texas, being in New York with all the big shots.* But she also was gleeful at the thought of that same housewife from Amarillo, Texas, winning a coveted award in journalism, beating out all the hardened and experienced professionals. That thought caused her to giggle, and she wrapped her arms around herself and squeezed.

Maureen O'Dwyer had a piece on the second half-hour of the newscast, an interview with a high-level official of the IRS about new tax rules. Cindy was familiar with Maureen's work from having seen her frequently on network newscasts, but seeing her in New York added another dimension to the experience. She couldn't explain why, it simply did. She was also aware that Maureen was up for the same Brickhouse Award. The Brickhouse Foundation had sent her material about the awards, including a listing of those nominated. Some of the names were familiar, some were not, and she was anxious to meet as many of the nominees as possible. If nothing else, the trip to New York would provide an enriching experience that would remain with her for the rest of her life. She tended to view the world that way, as a place where enriching experiences came along from time to time and were to be gobbled up and cherished. Hal was not quite so romantic about life, although he always responded favorably to her sometimes childlike, always bubbling reactions. He'd once told a friend, "It's like being married to a teenager." When she'd been told of this comment she was initially hurt, but then realized that he'd meant it as a compliment.

She unpacked her things and hung them in the closet. She wasn't sure whether to remove everything from the suitcases; but then she decided to do just that. There was no sense living out of a suitcase for an entire week. Having things put away would give her a sense of home, which she'd already begun to miss.

She'd just completed the task when the phone rang. She quickly went to it.

"Cindy Lewis?"

"Yes." She was disappointed. She'd thought it might be Hal.

"This is Herb Machlin from EBS. Welcome to New York."

"Why, thank you very much," she said.

"Is everything satisfactory?"

"Oh, yes, it certainly is. The room is lovely and there's champagne and . . . yes, everything is just fine." She realized she was gushing and didn't want to come off like the teenager her husband loved. She deliberately slowed her speech and lowered her voice.

Machlin said, "Well, glad you made it safely. Have you any plans for this evening?"

"No, I don't think so. I thought maybe somebody from EBS had planned something, but I haven't heard anything." It was now that she tried to place his name, but came up blank. She resisted asking who he was, his position at EBS, whether he was involved with news. It would have been inappropriate, she felt.

He saved her any anguish by saying, "I'm with the Entertainment Division at EBS. I don't know if you're aware of it, but we're very much involved this year in the Brickhouse dinner and other aspects of the News Division. I'm very familiar with your work. In fact, I was the one who passed through Amarillo, watched you, came back, and suggested that we keep an eye on you."

She couldn't believe what she was hearing. Was that how it had happened, that simply? She said, "That's wonderful. I didn't realize that people were coming through town and looking at you that way. I don't know what to say except thank you very much for liking what you saw."

"Oh, I sure did. You're good, Cindy. I think you've got one hell of a future with EBS."

"Thank you. I . . ."

"We're a little disorganized today. We'd originally planned some sort of reception for everyone tonight, but there wasn't time to make that work. I thought you might be loose for dinner and I'd love you to be my guest."

"That would be wonderful. I don't have any plans and . . ." She felt as though a vise had been closed on her chest. Here she was accepting a dinner invitation from a strange man simply on the basis of his claiming to be professionally involved with her and having been instrumental in bringing her to New York. Who was Herb Machlin? she wondered. Not only that, was it right for her to go to dinner alone with any man while in New York? She realized that she wasn't very sophisticated, at least the way that term had been redefined these days, but she'd always been comfortable with her codes and with the rules of her marriage to Hal. She hated the confusion she was feeling and wished Machlin hadn't called. She also was aware that she had fallen silent, which must have been awkward for him. She quickly said, "I suppose dinner would be all right. Will anyone else be joining us?"

"Maybe. It depends. I'll see who I can round up, but if I can't, that's all right. I want to get a chance to know everyone involved in the Brickhouse Awards and I might as well start with you. Any preferences in restaurants? Like Mexican food, Greek, Chinese?"

"I like them all, but I eat an awful lot of Mexican food in Texas."

"Of course you do." He laughed. "How about steak? I know a great steak house."

"Whatever you say. What time would you like to meet me?"

He paused, and she knew he was looking at his watch. He said, "A coupla hours. I'll come by and pick you up. What's your room number?"

"I don't know, I'll go see."

"It's on your phone."

"Of course, how silly. It's fourteen-forty-four."

"Two hours. Nice talking to you."

"Thank you. Good-bye."

CHAPTER 14

Herb Machlin hung up the phone on Cindy Lewis and went to the window in his office. It had started to rain, and a brisk wind splattered raindrops against the glass. He wished it weren't raining. He hated moving around the city in wet weather.

Chris came into the office and told him his wife had called while he was in a meeting with Jenkins Drew.

"What did she want?" Herb asked without turning.

"She said to call her when you came back."

"Thanks."

Chris left the office and he returned to his desk, picked up the phone, and dialed home. Marcie answered breathlessly. "What did I take you from?" he asked.

"I was in the basement. Did you pick up the gift for Mom and Dad?"

"Damn it, I forgot. Jesus, I'm really sorry."

The gift was for her parents' anniversary the next evening. He'd ordered it from Crouch & Fitzgerald on Madison Avenue, a handsome matched set of luggage with their initials.

"Why not?" she snapped angrily. "It wasn't such a big deal, Herbie, all you had to do was . . . ."

"Goddamn it, Marcie, I ordered it, didn't I? The party

135

isn't until tomorrow night and I can pick it up in the morning.''

"And what if you forget it then?" The anger turned to tears.

"What the hell are you crying for?"

"You don't give a damn about them, do you? I break my neck for your parents when they have an anniversary, but you don't give a shit about mine.''

He almost hung up, then thought better of it, said in as calm a voice as he could muster, "Marcie, I went out of my way to order the gift. It's ready, and I'll pick it up tomorrow. I promise you. I'll bring it home with me and we'll go to your parents' fucking anniversary and bring the fucking gift to them.''

There was a long pause. "You are such a bastard."

"I have to go."

"What time will you be home?"

"I told you I was going to be tied up tonight with this Brickhouse project. I'll probably be late.''

"What are you doing?"

"Having dinner with out-of-town visitors. I should be doing the same thing tomorrow night, except it's your parents' anniversary party.''

"*Fucking* anniversary party, Herbie.''

"That's right, I forgot, your parents' fucking anniversary party. I'll see you later." He hung up.

Chris buzzed him on the intercom, told him that Renée Ballantyne wanted to speak to him. He punched a lighted button on the phone and said, "Hello, Renée, how are you?"

"Just fine, Herb.''

He always resented her icy tone and was convinced she reserved it for him. He said, "I talked to Cindy Lewis a few minutes ago. The others will be straggling in, but we'll round them all up as soon as we can.''

She said nothing.

"What can I do for you, Renée?"

"I wonder if you could stop up here within the next

half-hour. Howard and I have some questions we'd like answered."

The imperious tone coming through the phone rankled him. He didn't demonstrate his annoyance, however, simply asked, "What questions?"

"Why not come up and talk about it?"

He looked at his watch. "All right, I'll head up there in a few minutes. I can't stay long, though; I have a dinner engagement."

"It won't take long, Herb. By the way, since Entertainment is running this show, I assume all the plans for the week are under control."

He wanted to fire back at her that the plans were under a lot better control than if the News Division had been handling it, but he didn't want to precipitate a fight. Besides, he wasn't quite sure just how under control things were. He'd turned the nitty-gritty over to Sandy London. He said, "We're meeting with everyone at ten in the morning. I assume you'll be there."

"If I'm invited."

"I'll be up shortly."

He took an electric razor from his desk and went to the men's room, where he shaved, washed his face, and sprayed on Aramis. He carefully combed his hair, stepped back, and viewed himself from varying angles. Satisfied, he returned the razor to his desk, checked with Sandy London, who assured him that things were under control, told Chris to go home, and headed for Ballantyne's office. He was greeted as he came through her door by Carl Schwartz. Renée wasn't there. Machlin asked Schwartz if he knew what the meeting was about. Schwartz shrugged. "Who knows what any meeting is about around here, Herb? I'll be back in a minute." He left the office.

Renée came through the door, nodded at him, then sat behind her desk, half-glasses shoved up into her hairline. She picked up the phone, cradled it between her ear and shoulder, and lighted a cigarette. She nodded toward one of two vinyl chairs, and Herb sat in it, reaching down and hoisting a black sock that had drooped.

Renée listened silently to what the person on the other end of the phone was saying. Then she said, "And I'm telling you that people are fed up to their necks with stories on the ERA. In fact, Jack, they're fed up with feminism in general. Having a caucus in Des Moines might be big news for Des Moines, but we don't want it for the net." She again listened before adding, "I wouldn't care if Nancy Reagan were the speaker and was about to announce she'd decided to become an acid-head freaked-out love child. I don't want the story. Look, Jack, I have to go. Thanks for suggesting it and don't hesitate on the next one." She hung up, shook her head, and removed her glasses.

"Nancy Reagan?" Herb asked, laughing.

She nodded. "I just realized that if Nancy Reagan were about to make such an announcement we would take a network feed, but it's just another fem-lib convention. Thanks for coming up. Let me get Howard."

"Hello, Howard," Herb said when Monroe arrived.

"Hello, Herb." Monroe took the other chair and asked whether Renée had had a chance to fill Machlin in. Herb shook his head. Monroe looked at her before saying, "All right, I might as well lay it out nice and neat, Herb. The fact is that . . ."

"Let me close the door," Renée said.

Machlin was feeling increasingly uncomfortable. Obviously, what was about to be discussed was important and, in all likelihood, unpleasant. More than that, the seven o'clock network news broadcast would begin in forty minutes, which meant that everyone involved was working at peak capacity. Even though he hadn't arranged for this meeting so close to air time, he felt a strange responsibility for interfering in their busy lives. He crossed his legs, making sure that his drooping sock was in place, and said with a forced smile, "Well, what's this all about?"

Renée leaned forward on her elbows and said, "There's been a leak."

"About what?" Herb asked.

"About the three candidates for the Brickhouse Award also being considered as new anchor."

Machlin puffed out his cheeks and ran his fingers over his nose. "So what?" he asked, looking up and taking in both of them.

"So what?" Monroe asked. "It's bad enough, Herb, that Mr. Rachoff has seen fit to totally ignore time-honored principles of keeping journalism separate from game shows and sitcoms. That's a bitter enough pill to swallow, but the Brickhouse Awards carry a lot of prestige in the industry. The people who run the foundation take it damn seriously. You know we contribute to the foundation every year to foster higher levels of reporting. We fund a portion of their scholarship program. We send guest lecturers to courses offered by the foundation. In short, Herb, we have a very nice, solid, and professional relationship with the Brickhouse people."

Machlin still did not understand the apparent upset over the leak. In fact, he realized, he didn't even know what the leak involved. He asked.

"Zeneida Simmons called me an hour ago," said Renée, "and said she'd been called by a columnist. The story she got was that EBS had brought in the three candidates for the Brickhouse Award in order to hype the search for a new female anchor. I won't bother going into everything Zeneida said, but what it boils down to is, she's goddamn mad to think that the foundation would be used as though the circus were coming to town."

Machlin laughed. "In the first place, Renée, I have no idea where the columnist would have gotten that information. In the second place, I don't understand why it's such a big deal. Sure, we're going to use the fact that the three of them are in New York to our advantage. This isn't some college journalism exercise, although based on the ratings it looks like it has been for too long." He realized he'd stepped out of line and quickly added, "At least, according to Mr. Rachoff. We're trying to turn this network around, and it begins with News. There's nothing sacred about an anchor. You know as well as I do that every successful anchor is nothing more than a pretty face and a good voice, and I don't reserve that for the female side. It's all show biz, and the sooner *we* all understand that, the faster we can get this job done to Rachoff's satisfaction."

He sat back in his chair and waited for their reactions.

Ballantyne and Monroe looked at each other as though they'd just been spoken to in a foreign tongue. Monroe broke the silence by saying, "The Brickhouse Foundation has never allowed commercial intrusion into its function, and is not about to start now. You may gain publicity, but you're going to destroy in the process a very important relationship."

Machlin shrugged. "I'm sorry if that's what's going to happen, but I think there is a much bigger stake than wounding the Brickhouse Foundation's pride."

Renée slapped her hand on the desk and came out of her chair a few inches. "No, Herb, you're wrong. Howard and I have gone along with this charade long enough. We really don't have a choice. If the president of this network wants to bring into News the jiggle mentality of Entertainment, he's entitled to do that, and all of us here are pragmatic enough to go along with it, even though we see down the road something negative and destructive where the network's integrity is concerned. But those of us in News have a community of professionals to deal with, and I'll be damned if you're going to strip me of my dignity in the process of trying to pick up a rating point or two. I've spent my professional life in journalism and I'm proud of that life. I've paid my dues. I've crawled on my belly through a jungle, stood my ground in a riot when I thought my life was about to end, and worked my ass off to function as a professional in a field I have great respect for. Alot of anchors have earned that seat. But an anchor does not represent a network's entire news operation. Behind that pretty face and good voice is a team of dedicated people who like to hold their heads high when they walk out of this building at night.''

"Did you leak it?" Monroe asked.

Machlin put his hands to his chest and adopted a shocked expression. "Me? Of course not. It must have come out of PR.''

"It doesn't matter where it came from," Renée said. "The only point I want to make, and I have to make it fast because we're coming up on seven, is that it's one thing to play a role in revamping News, but it's another to go over the line, Herb, and to render a lot of hard work irrelevant."

Machlin wanted out of the room. He said, "Sorry, but I don't buy the purist approach, not in this business. Your Miss Simmons can take her attitude of being dedicated to independent journalism and disdaining anything that's tainted by commercials and shove it. The fact is, she, like all of us, takes the check every week, which makes us all whores when you think about it." He laughed, but when neither of them responded, he turned serious and said, "Look, I know this whole thing is hard for you to accept. It would be very nice if it weren't necessary for the divisions to cross lines. It never would have happened if News had been profitable, but the bottom line is that it hasn't been, and no matter what lofty ideals of journalism you learn in a classroom at the University of Missouri, this network has stockholders who want to see a return on their investment. The news isn't on the tube every night to inform the public. The news is on every night for the same reason that every other program is, and that's to provide a vehicle for commercials, which, as you well know, pay your salaries and mine. I know neither of you like me very much because of this, but I didn't ask for the assignment. I was given it from the very top. I'm trying to do the best job I know how, and if that steps on toes, that's the way it has to be.''

Monroe stood and came around the back of his chair. He leaned on it and slowly shook his head. "I find this truly offensive, Herb. I can't imagine there being such a gap in understanding between us."

Machlin stood and smoothed out wrinkles in his vest. He smiled. "Maybe there isn't such a gap, Howard. I started out in news, and I really respect what you people do. All I've been assigned to do is to see that the money starts rolling in to support your division, so that you won't have to worry about it anymore." He suddenly enjoyed the logic of his thinking and added, "Think about it, Howard, why should professional newsmen and -women have to worry about money in the first place? It's a waste of time. I'm not tampering with the news. I'm not telling anybody what news should go on every night or what news should be ignored. That's your business. What I am doing is applying my knowledge of entertainment programming to making news at this network attractive to viewers and, therefore, profitable. That's the mandate I've been given from above."

Renée looked at Monroe and burst out laughing. It took Monroe a few moments to understand what she was laughing at. When he did, he, too, laughed.

"What's funny?" Machlin asked.

"'From above'?"

Herb now knew they were laughing at him. Renée's phone rang and she picked it up, said, "I'm coming," hung up and muttered, "I have to go." She walked between the men and left the office.

"You understand what I mean, don't you?" Machlin asked Monroe.

Monroe looked directly into Machlin's eyes and said, "I certainly do, Herb. Thanks for coming up." He, too, left the office.

Machlin stayed for a few minutes and tried to analyze what had just occurred. He gave it up and entered the newsroom. Teletype machines clattered in the background. A bank of television monitors were filled with a myriad of pictures, some taken off the air, others showing material that was being fed to the network. Dozens of men and women focused in on the last-minute details of the telecast, their faces and bodies tense, reflecting the increasing pressure of every passing minute. Machlin was grasped in a fist of inertia. He was envious and resentful, just as he'd felt in the recent past when he was confronted with a large group of young people who seemed to have discovered a purpose in their lives, at least for the moment, and who had a long stretch of life ahead of them. There was always that feeling of urgency with young people, the same sort of urgency that permeated the newsroom.

"It's all bullshit anyway," Machlin told himself as he moved toward a door leading to the hall. A pert young woman wearing a tight purple shirt walked past him. She was braless and the outlines of her rigid nipples were clearly defined through the thin fabric. Herb stopped and admired her as she walked up the hall, then returned to his office, stopped in the men's room and checked his hair, and left the building, an umbrella under his arm.

_____Chapter 15

". . . and so I said to myself when I was sitting in that motel room in Amarillo, this is the sort of person who can really turn things around. People are fed up with slick, sophisticated newsmen and -women. They're looking for something real in their lives, looking for what Reagan promised them, a return to basics, a sense of dignity for the common man. Cindy, you might be that person, and if all my years of being right in this business count for anything, I'd bet heavy money on you."

Herb Machlin dabbed at his mouth with a napkin and sat back. He looked across the table at Cindy and tried to read her reaction. It wasn't easy. They'd killed a bottle of corvo red and her eyes testified to its effect.

"I can't believe this," she said. "I'm just a housewife from Amarillo who happens to work in a television station. My friends work in offices and factories. Why would I be considered so favorably above all the other people who've spent their lives in broadcasting?"

Herb smiled and leaned forward. "You can never figure this business, Cindy. The most unlikely shows succeed, and those that have all the earmarks of success fall flat on their face. There's no formula for success in television. You have to go with your gut, and if you don't, you find yourself out on the street damn fast. By the way, I don't like hearing you say you're just a housewife. In the first place, you shouldn't denigrate the role of a wife and mother. In the second place, you're a hell of a lot more than that. You have a style on the air that's extremely appealing. Maybe a lot of people wouldn't recognize it, but I did." He shrugged and came up with a self-effacing grin. "But maybe that's why I've been handed the job of deciding who the new female anchor will be for EBS."

She hadn't bargained for any of this. Here she was less than a day in New York, having dinner with an obviously very important executive at the network who was telling her, Cindy Lewis of Amarillo, Texas, that she might be offered the job of coanchor on the evening network news.

"More wine?" Machlin asked. The bottle was empty.

"Oh, my goodness, no. I don't usually drink that much wine in a month. It's such a pretty place and . . ."

"Did you enjoy the food?"

"Oh, I certainly did. It was wonderful, the best Italian food I ever had in my life. I'm glad we didn't go to the steak place. We don't have many Italian restaurants in Amarillo. There's a very nice pizza place that has table-cloths and candles and serves other things, but people there aren't very fond of Italian food."

"Glad you enjoyed it, Cindy. Let me ask you something, and I'd appreciate a very honest answer. I know you're married and have a family back in Texas. What will happen if you're offered the anchor job? It's something to consider very carefully. I don't know your husband or anything about him, but it's possible he wouldn't look too favorably upon a move to New York, especially with you becoming an important national figure. Some men have trouble dealing with that."

Cindy's eyes opened wide. "I can certainly understand how they would," she said.

"Well, maybe that's part of your charm. There's a move in this country back to great respect for the Middle-

American woman. I suppose it happens with every movement, the pendulum swings too far, then comes back in
the other direction. The feminist movement has brought
about some good change, but it's gone too far. The whole
trick to television programming is to anticipate trends far
in advance, and my gut says that the country is ready to
swing back to a more traditional model, which is one of
the reasons I'm convinced you're right for this spot. They
don't want the liberated woman, the big-city gal who's hip
and with-it. They want somebody like themselves, a solid
citizen who's proud to be a mother and wife. Another
tough question, Cindy. How is your marriage? Is it solid?
Any chance of it splitting up in the near future?''

She didn't know how to respond. Her initial reaction
was to tell him about the problems she and Hal had been
having, but she felt that would be terribly indiscreet. She
then wondered whether the state of her marriage really had
any bearing on the anchor position. It seemed that everybody in television had been divorced at least once. Why
would he care? She decided her question was more meaningful and asked it.

"Well, I think it will be important for you to be happily
married," he said. "I don't mean it has to be that way
forever, but it would help in getting you off the ground
here in New York." He leaned across the table and shifted
his eyes from left to right to make sure no one was eaves-
dropping, then said, "Nobody cares what you do in your
private life in this business, Cindy. I don't know much
about your personal life, and it doesn't matter to me if you
and your husband have a little something on the side now
and then. In fact, it can be positive, can keep a marriage
fresh, keep the individuals happy. The important thing is
that it not become public. Every contract we have with
talent has a morality clause in it, which lets us get out of
the contract if that person does something to offend public
decency. Just as long as you and your husband don't drag
your affairs out into the open is what counts.''

She slowly shook her head and looked at him as though

he'd uttered an obscenity. "Hal and I don't have affairs. We love each other."

He leaned back and said, "Yeah, of course. Ready to go?"

"I think so. This was very lovely and I thank you."

"My pleasure."

They paused at the elevator in her hotel lobby. He said, "There's a couple of other things I want to go over with you. Come on, I'll buy you a nightcap."

They took a table in the lobby. He ordered cognac. She wanted only club soda. "It's so pretty here," she said when their drinks had been served. She smiled as she noticed that the shades on the bird cage had been lowered for the night.

"Very European," Machlin said, "having drinks in a hotel lobby. That's what I like about this place. Ever been to Europe?"

"No," Cindy said, shaking her head.

"You'll get there if this anchor thing works out. You'll get to go lots of places."

"I like to travel. Hal and I go away sometimes."

"Tell me more about Hal. He seems like quite a guy."

"I wouldn't know where to begin," Cindy said.

She then spent ten minutes extolling Hal's virtues. When she was through, Machlin downed the remaining cognac in his snifter and said, "Cindy, there's something I have to know."

"What is it?"

"I have to know that if I offer you the new anchor spot, you'll accept it."

She opened her eyes wide and licked her lips. "I don't know. Obviously, it would be something that I'd have to talk over with Hal and the children. I could never make a decision like that without consulting them. It would mean picking up our lives and moving to New York, which would be hard on everybody."

Machlin scowled. "Sure, talk it over, but understand the difficult position I'm in. Choosing the new anchor has tremendous ramifications for EBS. If I were to put my neck on the line and give the spot to you, I'd look like a damn fool if you turned it down. You'd better talk it over with your family fast and let me know."

She started to say something but he cut her off with a wave of his hand. "Keep one thing in mind, Cindy. In this business you can't rely on what other people think. It has to be what you want, and you owe that to yourself as a human being. Either you grab the brass ring or it goes right by you and never comes back."

"I'm so tired. The trip, the dinner, all the wine, and now having to face this sort of decision is just too much for this Texas girl. Would you mind if we called it a night? I'd like to go upstairs and think about what you just said."

"Sure, I understand."

They looked at each other, and it suddenly occurred to Cindy that he was searching for the slightest hint of an invitation to accompany her to her room. She stood quickly, extended her hand and thanked him.

He looked disappointed, but only for a moment. He smiled, paid the bill, and walked her to the elevators.

"Well, good night, Mr. Machlin," she said, again shaking his hand.

"Good night, Cindy. Welcome to New York. And give it some serious thought."

She went to her room and placed a call home. Hal answered and enthusiastically asked how her day and evening had gone.

"Just fine, honey. I've met some interesting people. The city is so big and I just know I'll get lost, but I'm glad I'm here. The only thing is . . ."

"What's the matter?"

"I miss you so, Hal. Did you get your schedule squared away so that you could come here for the dinner?"

"I've been trying, Cindy, but I just don't know if I can make it work. If I can't, I want you to know that I'm with you every minute anyway and am rooting for you. So are the kids."

She managed to keep from crying but the catch in her throat was audible. "Hal, please come. I need you."

She heard him sigh. "I'll do my best, Cindy. I promise you that. Tell me what you did today."

"Just a minute." She placed the phone on the bed and went to the bathroom, took a Kleenex from a wall dispenser, and wiped her eyes, blew her nose. She came back to the phone as quickly as possible and said in a considerably brighter voice, "Well, let's see. I got here late. It took so long to get from the airport. A young man from the network met me and he was very nice. I took a shower and then a little nap and . . ."

"What did you do tonight? Did you have dinner with the people there?"

"Yes, with a whole bunch of them. Hal, there's something I have to talk to you about."

"What is it?"

"I think I might be offered a job here in New York."

He laughed. "What kind of a job?"

"As an anchorperson on the network news."

"Why? You didn't tell me anything about that before you left."

"I didn't know anything about it, honey. This all came out of the blue. It seems that the network is looking for a woman to coanchor the news and they're considering me. There's this big executive named Mr. Machlin who was in Amarillo. I guess he was traveling all over the country looking at different women on television. Anyway, he liked what he saw and feels that I'm the right one for the job."

Hal said nothing.

"Hal, are you listening?"

"Yes, I am. Who is this guy Machlin? Why would he be the one to make that decision?"

"He's very big in the network and was given the assignment of finding somebody. Oh, Hal, I know what you're thinking, but it isn't like that. He's a very nice man. But that isn't important. What is important is what happens if they offer it to me."

His tone that had been so pleasant earlier now turned to stone. He said, "It doesn't matter, Cindy, make any decision you want."

"Hal, that isn't fair. I would never do anything without discussing it with you and coming to a decision that made us both happy. You know that."

"It doesn't sound that way. I mean, how the hell could I say anything against a chance for the liberated woman to succeed in the glamorous world of television?"

Now she was angry. She understood his feelings, knew what emotions underlay his responses, but she resented them. She said, "I want you to come to New York, Hal. I want to sit down and talk to you about this before it goes any further. Please, I'm asking you to do this for me. We've had problems in our life but they've been minor ones, ones we always seemed to be able to solve together. This could be a big one and I don't want it to be. I love you, love the children, and wouldn't do anything to destroy that, but I think I'm at least entitled to be heard out."

Again, he said nothing.

"Hal, will you come?"

"I'll see. I'll talk to you tomorrow."

Neither said anything for a few moments. Finally, he said, "Cindy, take care of yourself. I love you."

"I love you, too. Good night."

"Good night. The kids send their love."

CHAPTER 16

Because Veronica had chosen to take the overnight flight from San Francisco, no one from EBS was on hand to meet her at Kennedy Airport when she arrived at a few minutes before six. She took a cab into Manhattan and checked into the hotel, unpacked, showered, and looked at the time. It was eight-thirty, and she was due at a meeting at ten. She was desperate for sleep, but knew that if she lay down she might not wake up.

She dressed for the meeting and went to the lobby restaurant, where she had breakfast. At nine-thirty she went to a public phone and called an old friend from San Francisco, Cale Jaleak. Jaleak had produced the occasional field reports Veronica had been allowed to do outside the studio, and he was one of the few people at the San Francisco station she truly liked and trusted. Short, pudgy, and prematurely bald, Jaleak had a keen sense of observation, a quick wit, and, most important to Veronica, a sincerity that was always visible. He'd produced the drug series that was responsible for her Brickhouse nomination and the trip to New York, and if she won, he, too, would receive an award. He'd left San Francisco only a month ago to take a more lucrative job with EBS in New York, and his departure had saddened Veronica. She was anxious to see him again. He'd sent her a note after arriving in New York with his home phone number on it. She dialed, he answered, and after some warm initial banter he suggested they get together for a drink later in the day. "I have to work tonight on a report we're doing on Long Island," he said. "But I could catch up with you about four."

"That sounds good. Where?"

He named an Irish bar on the East Side.

Veronica arrived promptly at ten A.M. at EBS's New York headquarters. She was directed to the floor on which News was located and, after waiting a few minutes in a reception area, was ushered into a small conference room where Cindy Lewis and Maureen O'Dwyer sat with representatives of the News Division, and with Herb Machlin from Entertainment.

"Welcome to New York, Miss Frazier," Renée Ballantyne said as she came around an oak table and extended her hand. She introduced Veronica to the others in the room.

"It's a pleasure to meet you, Miss O'Dwyer," Veronica said, meaning it. She'd admired Maureen's work ever since becoming interested in television journalism, considered her the most professional of all women reporting on network news.

"I've always wanted to see San Francisco," Cindy Lewis said when she was introduced to Veronica.

"You must come visit sometime," Veronica said pleasantly, not adding that she had absolutely no interest in ever visiting Amarillo, Texas.

Machlin spent the next half-hour briefing the three Brickhouse candidates on the week's activities. Veronica casually observed Cindy and Maureen during the briefing. Cindy's attention was total and unwavering. She seemed to hang on every word. Maureen, on the other hand, didn't even attempt to mask her boredom. Veronica also observed in the veteran reporter scorn for Machlin and for some of the things he said. She had the same impression of Renée Ballantyne, who seemed on the verge of getting up and walking out at any moment.

Machlin was apparently unaware of any of these reactions because he rolled along happily and in an expansive manner, gesturing freely, a broad grin punctuating many of his statements that he considered humorous. When he was through, Renée told the other women that they were free for the rest of the day and evening, but were expected to attend a luncheon the following day. Then she quickly excused herself.

As people drifted from the room, Howard Monroe, who'd come in halfway through Machlin's briefing, took Veronica aside. "I know you were expecting the rest of the day and evening off," he said, "but plans have changed a little where you're concerned."

"What changes?" Veronica asked.

He sensed her apprehension and laughed. "Nothing serious, just a favor we'd like to ask of you while you're in New York. Ms. Ballantyne and I wondered whether you were free for dinner tonight. There's something we'd like to discuss with you."

"I suppose so," Veronica said.

Monroe didn't give her a chance to ask any questions, said, "Good. Why don't you stop by up here sometime before seven? Once the network newscast is over we can go out and break bread together."

"All right," Veronica said. She disliked expressions like "break bread" or "welcome aboard," but had learned to accept them as part of the business world. She assured Monroe she'd be there and went straight back to the hotel, where she slept until it was time to meet Cale Jaleak.

Jaleak was waiting at the bar when she arrived. He got up and warmly shook her hand, then gave her a hug. Among many things she appreciated about him was the fact that he did not automatically assume the right to physical contact with everyone with whom he worked. People in television, at least from Veronica's experience, were big touchers, huggers, and kissers. She didn't like it, considered it a breach of personal privacy.

"What'll you have?" he asked.

"What are you drinking?"

"Irish coffee. Want one?"

She shook her head. "The coffee sounds good, but not the Irish."

"I have just the thing for you, Ronnie, just enough alcohol to remind you you're in a bar instead of a coffee shop."

He summoned the bartender and ordered her a glass of iced coffee with a Bailey's Irish Cream on the side. He suggested she pour the Bailey's into the coffee.

She tasted the Irish Cream first, smacked her lips, and dumped the rest of it into the coffee. "When did you come up with this drink?" she asked.

He laughed. "After a thousand nights in the Buena Vista drinking Irish coffee I decided I was an addict, not to the whiskey but to the coffee. I tried this combination one night and thought it was terrific." He raised his glass and said, "Here's to seeing you again."

After she'd tasted the concoction she asked, "If you like it so much, why are you still drinking Irish coffee?"

He grimaced and shrugged. "Not enough kick, I guess. So, tell me what's been going on since I left."

She filled him in on a number of things. When she mentioned Craig Stanton she discerned a tightening in his face and body. Jaleak hadn't approved of her relationship with Stanton, although he'd never stated it. The only time the subject had come up was when she'd complained to Cale that she was not allowed to go out on assignment as often as she'd like. It was during that conversation that he told her the word had come down from Stanton to keep her in the studio, and to limit her outside activities. That news had angered her and she'd expressed it to Cale, who'd passed it off by saying in as casual a voice as he could muster, "That's the problem owing the company store, Ronnie." She hadn't immediately understood, but soon realized he was referring to her mortgaged life with Craig Stanton.

She confronted Stanton about what Cale had told her, but didn't identify the source of her information.

His response was, "You're pure anchor, Ronnie. Stay that way and forget the crusading journalist role. Anchoring is where the power and money is. Don't question me, just do what I tell you. I haven't steered you wrong yet."

She never brought it up again.

She asked Cale about his new job and he enthusiastically explained it. Because of the investigative reports he'd produced in San Francisco he'd been given a job with a network special unit operating out of Chicago, with a branch in New York. The Chicago-based group traveled the country almost constantly.

"It sounds marvelous," she told him.

He nodded and smiled. "Yeah, it is. Nobody seems to mess with us. It's like a special strike force in the military, I suppose, although never having been in the military waters down that analogy. There seems to be a lot of independence in the stories we do and the way we do them. It's nice being out from under the corporate thumb."

"I envy you," she said.

"It would be a good spot for you, Ronnie. In fact, I'd like to introduce you to another producer who's active with the unit. I think you'd get along. Who knows, maybe something could come out of it."

"I'd appreciate it."

"His name is Gregory Oates."

"I see his credits from time to time."

"He's black."

"I'm surprised you noticed," she said, laughing.

"I always notice blacks, just like I notice Japanese. Noticing isn't the problem, it's what you feel."

"Of course. I was only kidding."

"I know. Black never seemed to be a hang-up with you any more than being Jewish is for me."

His comment brought forth a louder laugh from her. "There is a difference, you know, Cale."

"I know, I know."

They sat together for an hour, then left because he had to catch up with his crew for a trip out to Long Island. "At this hour it'll take us forever," he said. "New York is a hell of a place . . ."

". . . to visit but . . ."

"But I'd hate to die here." They both laughed. "I mean that. I miss San Francisco, miss California. If the job weren't so good, I'd head back in a second."

They parted outside and she watched him walk up the street and disappear around a corner. She was glad they'd had the time together. It had lifted her spirits and set a positive tone for the night. What he'd told her about the special investigative unit had piqued her interest, and she intended to follow up on the lead with Oates if the opportunity presented itself.

She arrived at EBS promptly at seven. One of Monroe's secretaries took her into his office, where he sat with Carl Schwartz and Renée Ballantyne. The seven o'clock network news had just started and the four of them watched with intense interest. Schwartz and Ballantyne made occasional notes but said nothing. Finally, at seven-thirty, Schwartz excused himself and left the office.

"Any special preferences in food?" Monroe asked.

"No," Veronica said, hoping they wouldn't choose anything Mexican or Greek. They went to Peng Teng, a Chinese restaurant a few blocks from the building.

Monroe ordered for them, taking into account Veronica's comment that she liked anything sweet-and-sour. She'd been nervous about the dinner, but realized as they were served drinks and Renée offered a toast to her successful career in San Francisco that she felt unusually relaxed considering the circumstances. She tried to put her finger on the reason and finally did, at least to her satisfaction. There was a quiet professionalism in the two people, particularly in their relationship. Craig Stanton had claimed all along that Renée Ballantyne had achieved her rapid rise through management ranks because of a long-term intimacy with Monroe. Veronica had no way to judge the validity of that claim, although as she sat with them it suddenly dawned on her that Stanton, because of his relationship with her, naturally viewed everyone else in the same light.

Monroe was a handsome man, she decided, patrician in bearing. His features were fine, his clothes fit naturally and correctly. His hair was thinning and there was the beginning of jowls, but even considering those telltale signs, she judged that he was probably older than he appeared. She assumed he came from money and had attended the right schools, and as he talked of his background her assumptions were proved correct.

Her response to Renée Ballantyne was positive, too. Her face was, of course, familiar from when she'd been an active field reporter on the network, and the image that had been presented electronically was an honest one. Like Monroe, she seemed very much in control of herself, which resulted in the ability to be always at ease. She wore a light-gray tweed suit over a pale-peach silk blouse that formed its own tie at the collar. The tie was fixed to the front of her blouse by a gold set of initials fashioned into a pin. Straw-colored hair was drawn back into a tight chignon at her nape. Long, tapered fingers were without polish or jewelry. Her skin was surprisingly tan considering her hair color. She wore only a hint of rouge and a modicum of lipstick. What was most striking to Veronica, however, were her green eyes, at once compassionate, yet perpetually probing, and defined by the beginnings of crow's-feet at the corners.

They talked mostly about the business of broadcasting, the conversation spiced from time to time with anecdotes from their individual careers. Veronica wondered whether she was being scrutinized by the two of them because of what Stanton had told her of the search for a new network anchorwoman. She chose to think not, because it took the pressure off. But she wasn't entirely successful in dismissing that notion. She also wondered what role her black skin would play in such a decision. She often told herself that she would never allow anyone to use her as a black symbol regardless of what opportunity it might open up. She had once had a friend who'd become the first black airline stewardess in America. The airline had conducted a long and diligent search until just the right person was found, not too dark, not too light, intelligent and educated, decent family, good background, and proud but never arrogant. Veronica felt that what her friend went through was distasteful, and could never imagine herself allowing her race to be used that way. Still, that attitude was not without hypocrisy, and she knew it. She'd been perfectly willing to allow herself to be used as a woman, and creating dividing lines was simply a matter of expediency and rationalization. Cale Jaleak had told her that one night in a moment of candor and she hadn't forgotten.

When dinner was over and they'd been served tea, Monroe smiled and said, "It's an old line, Veronica, but I suppose you're wondering why we're gathered here tonight."

Veronica returned the smile and nodded. "Yes, I was wondering when we'd get to that."

Monroe leaned forward and said, "Some of our people have gotten deeply involved in what could be a major investigative report. It has to do with drug dealing in local public schools here in Manhattan, something you're familiar with because of your work in San Francisco. It's shaping up into one hell of a story, and the people responsible for it have done a remarkable job. But they've reached a point where they need help, and we thought you might be the one to provide it while you're with us this week."

Veronica was unsure how to react. She hadn't planned

on working while in New York, and wondered whether others had been pressed into service this way. It really didn't matter, she decided, because she was not in a position to decline. She said, "Of course, I'll be happy to help if I can. What do you want me to do?"

Renée answered. "Go undercover for a day and act as a supplier to someone we've identified as a major source of illegal drugs on school playgrounds. We've tried to come up with somebody from the staff but we're afraid of blowing it by having one of our people recognized. When we knew you were coming to New York, we thought we had the perfect solution. Do we?"

Veronica felt natural defenses coming into play. She knew that being black was an important ingredient in the assignment. That was obvious, even though it wasn't stated. More than that, she had a natural reluctance to ever again set foot into the sordid, shabby milieu of the drug culture. She'd escaped that atmosphere long ago when she left Detroit and had resolved never to return again, to the city or to the situation.

"You don't seem particularly enthusiastic about this, Veronica," Renée said.

"I have mixed emotions about it, that's true. Why have you chosen me out of others who are here in New York this week?"

Monroe and Ballantyne glanced at each other before Monroe said, "The primary dealers are black. Our reporter on the story and producer are also black. They, of course, will fill you in on the details if you decide to help us. The important thing is that not only would you be a tremendous help to them and to the network, but in exposing this thing you might be saving some lives." He narrowed his eyes and looked for her reaction. She held his gaze for a moment, then shifted to Renée.

"You don't have to, you know," Renée said. "We'll find somebody else if necessary. It might delay us a little. That's not a catastrophe. It does make sense for us to ask you to do it, however, because of your experience as a reporter and your involvement with a similar story not long ago. Believe me, if you decide not to do it, it's okay.''

"I'd like to help very much," Veronica said, "but I . . ."

Monroe handed the waiter a credit card and said to Veronica, "Think about it. We will have to know by tomorrow morning. You can sleep on it and ask all the questions you want in the morning before making up your mind."

"I will," Veronica said.

"Will what?" Monroe asked. "Do it?"

"Sleep on it, and probably ask questions in the morning.''

"Fair enough," Monroe said. "By the way, Craig Stanton tells me you're quite a jazz lover."

Veronica would have preferred Stanton's name hadn't come up. She knew that Stanton and Monroe were old friends, and the thought of being discussed by them upset her. She also knew there wasn't much she could do about it. She told Monroe that her father had been a jazz musician and that she had followed the music ever since childhood. "I'm afraid there isn't much jazz left in San Francisco, however, except for a place called Jammers that a friend of mine owns. We used to have some great jazz spots, the Matador, the Jazz Workshop, good places that featured top names. But they're all gone now. Most of them have gone the way of topless and bottomless.''

"That's a shame," Monroe said. "There seems to be a legitimate resurgence of jazz in New York. Clubs are opening everywhere."

They walked outside and Monroe looked for a cab. He spotted one, waved it down, turned, and said, "I hope you have time to catch some good music while you're here, Veronica."

Renée hesitated for a moment, as though she was pondering her next words. Then she said, "How about tonight?"

"Not me," Monroe said as he opened the door of the

cab. "I promised Betty I'd be home at a reasonable hour once this week, and the way things are shaping up this might be the only night. Can I drop you two someplace?"

Renée questioned Veronica with a raise of her eyebrows. Veronica smiled and said, "I'd love to hear some good jazz." It was true that the thought of hearing music appealed to her, but more than that she welcomed the opportunity to spend more time with Renée.

Renée chose a jazz club on Third Avenue called Fat Tuesday's, where George Shearing and Brian Torff were appearing. They entered the downstairs club and were ushered to a tiny table to the left of the bandstand. They were just in time; Renée ordered a cognac, Veronica a kir as a male voice announced over the PA system that the Shearing Duo was about to begin the first set. He also reminded the audience, which was sizable, that there was to be no talking during the performance. Veronica made a mental note to suggest to Bill Teller at Jammers that he do a similar announcement prior to a set.

They sat in silence as Shearing and Torff wove intricate melodic and harmonic lines around standards and original tunes.

When the set was over and Torff led the blind Shearing from the bandstand, Veronica turned and said to Renée, "It was wonderful."

Renée nodded enthusiastically. "I've been a Shearing fan from way back when. I remember when he came from England and formed his quintet."

"I don't go back that far, but . . ." She cast a quick glance to see whether the remark was out of place, but obviously it wasn't.

Renée caught her concern, smiled, and said, "Not *that* far back."

Veronica told her a little of her father's brief career as a jazz musician, and when she detailed the circumstances of his murder, Renée winced. She said, "My father died a violent death, too. He worked on the docks in Houston and was killed when a crane snapped and its cargo landed on him.''

"How terrible."

"Yes, it was, but no worse than your story. I suppose life is a crapshoot after all. So many things contribute to what happens to us, timing, luck, circumstances.''

Veronica asked her how she got started in broadcasting.

"After my father died, my mother and I moved to Cleveland. I did most of my growing up there and put myself through Ohio State University. I majored in political science and had no intention of ever becoming a journalist. But I started writing in my senior year for the school paper, enjoyed it, and decided to try my hand at magazine articles. After a lot of rejections I sold one. After I graduated I was offered a job on a small radio station as a disc jockey, of all things.'' She laughed. "The owner of the station decided he ought to have a female voice on one of the shifts and gave it to me. It was fun. You did everything there, including running the board, ripping-and-reading news off the wire services, giving sports and the local weather, even doing interviews. Things just mushroomed from there, and timing did prove itself. Soon after I'd switched to television I got caught on camera in a hurricane and managed to keep my head. After that, everything just fell into place.''

"Just like that?'' Veronica said, shaking her head. "I'm sure there was a lot more to it.''

The waitress brought their check. Renée asked Veronica, "Like to stay for another set?''

Veronica pondered, then said, "Yes, I'd love to.''

"There's no cover if you stay for the second show,'' said the waitress.

"Fine,'' Renée said. "Just bring us another round.''

They said little while listening to recorded jazz between the sets. Renée turned and said, "Tell me about you, Veronica. I know you haven't been in this business very long, and I read the press release that accompanied your nomination for a Brickhouse Award, but what about you personally? What got you started?"

For the first time Veronica felt uncomfortable. As she'd listened to Renée's recounting of her beginnings in broadcasting she'd felt tremendous envy. Obviously, the woman with her had achieved great success in the field through hard work and sacrifice.

"You don't have to talk about it if you don't want to," Renée said.

"Oh, no, it isn't that," said Veronica. "It's just that it's been such a short career that I don't even think about it."

"Do you think it will be a long one?"

"What do you mean?" Her immediate reaction was that Renée was questioning her ability to forge a long and sustained career as a TV journalist.

"What I mean is, in order to succeed, really succeed in this business, you have to give up an awful lot of other things, things that most people cherish and are not willing to give up."

"A personal life?"

"Yes, of course. Sure, there is always a way to develop a private life of sorts around the demands of the profession, but it isn't easy, and usually that private life, because it takes such definite second place, is cursory at best."

Veronica sensed that Renée was talking about herself. She wanted to pursue it but wasn't sure she should. She decided to, and asked, "Have you ever been married, Renée?"

Renée looked at the table and said, "No, I haven't."

There was an awkward silence, which Renée broke by turning and saying, "I never really had time to marry. I started working very hard out of necessity, to pay back the money my mother had scraped together for me to go to college, and to help support my younger brother and sister. I felt good about that, considered myself a very grown-up and responsible young woman. When my father died, I became the man of the house. My mother worked hard at menial jobs but wasn't very good at taking care of everyday aspects of her life. I took over a man's role, in a sense, and the only thing that ever bothered me about it was worrying whether I was becoming too masculine. I don't mean sexually, of course, but my friends all seemed to play out a more classic feminine role, and I envied them.'' She again looked down at the table and reflected on what to say next. ''What happens,'' she said, ''is that you become so involved in a career, especially when it seems to be moving forward, that you tend to put off your personal life just another week, another month, another year, until you've exhausted your potential as a professional. I didn't dare let men get too close to me because they represented a threat to what I was achieving, just as men who are firmly committed to their careers can view women as a threat. They admire a career woman, but at the same time, natural needs come into play. They want that woman they admire to also have breakfast on the table in the morning and to make sure they have clean underwear and socks.'' She looked up at Veronica and said, ''It becomes a vicious circle, and at some point you have to decide whether you're going all the way or are willing to stop where you are. I decided to go all the way.''

Veronica was flattered that Renée was talking so openly and freely with her, but at the same time was uncomfortable with the candor. She felt a need to reciprocate, to display an openness, be a friend willing to share confidences. She said, in a feeble attempt to achieve this, ''I'm not sure what I want from life. All the clichés are appealing, a wonderful loving husband, two kids, lots of money, a big shaggy dog, and a house in the country, but I'm not sure that's what I'm all about. I've had to work very hard to put my past life behind me and to create something new, and it would take a tremendous amount to cause me to give up that effort.''

''Was the life you gave up that difficult?'' Renée asked.

Veronica nodded. ''I was brought up in the ghetto. My

mother still washes floors for rich whites in Detroit suburbs. There aren't many people who escape the ghetto, and I'm proud that I did."

"How did you do it?" Renée asked. "I'm always filled with admiration for people who could overcome adverse circumstances and go against the odds. I worked hard for what I have, but the odds were much more in my favor. I'm white, and although my family didn't have any money we certainly weren't reduced to ghetto living. How did you do it?"

"I . . . I think I just wanted it bad enough, that's all," Veronica said. "I . . ."

"I understand Craig Stanton has been very influential in your career," Renée said.

Veronica froze. Had Renée been gaining her confidence, laying enough of her own personal life on the table in order to seduce Veronica into an admission of something damaging to her chances at the anchor job?

"Craig is very high on you," Renée said.

"He's been good to me," Veronica said. She glanced around the room. "I wonder when they'll start the next set."

"Soon, I think. Would you like to leave?"

"No."

Renée sensed that mentioning Stanton had caused a stiffening in the young woman next to her. She dropped the subject and chatted amiably about the coming week in New York for the three award candidates. Then the announcer said over the PA, "Ladies and gentleman, a warm welcome for George Shearing and Brian Torff. May we remind you that the artists would sincerely appreciate your silence during their performance."

It wasn't until Veronica was back in the hotel, had changed into a nightgown, brushed her teeth, and climbed into bed, that she realized what had occurred at Fat Tuesday's. Renée Ballantyne had told her just enough to entice her to reveal personal things about herself. It was an old and effective interview technique, one she remembered being taught in a class at UCLA. She smiled as she pulled the covers up to her neck. It had been a fascinating evening. She'd learned something without having to lose too much. More important, a need that had been growing in her for a very long time, to succeed at something without having to mortgage herself, no longer seemed a distant dream. She could make it work as long as she focused her attention on what that need was, and did not allow herself to slip back into what had been so easy for her in the past. She was at a plateau, a launching pad, and where she flew from it was up to her.

She thought about it for a long time, and wondered whether she would ever get to sleep. But eventually fatigue, mixed with exhilaration, won out. She closed her eyes and remembered nothing else until morning.

Morgan Rachoff, president of the Empire Broadcasting System, placed a bookmark in the book he was reading, turned off the light, and walked toward the master bedroom of the triplex he and his wife, Helen, shared in Manhattan. The phone rang as he was halfway across the large carpeted living room. He picked up an extension and was greeted with the voice of Howard Monroe.

"How are you, Howard?" Rachoff asked.

"All right, I suppose, Mr. Rachoff, and I am sorry to call you at home this time of night."

"I assume it's important," Rachoff said.

"I think it is. It has to do with turning the revamping of News over to Entertainment."

"What's the problem?"

"It isn't working. More than that, I think we're heading for real trouble."

"Explain it to me, Howard. If we are, I certainly want to know about it."

Monroe spent ten minutes outlining his objections to what was occurring, stressing the long-term harm that could come to EBS's reputation within the industry. He talked of how every network's news operation was instrumental in establishing its public image, and touched upon the circus atmosphere that seemed to be developing around the search for a new female anchor.

Rachoff said nothing. When Monroe was finished, Rachoff said, "I appreciate this being raised with me, Howard. I've had indications that things might not be going as smoothly as I had hoped. Are you suggesting that the project be called off?"

"Not necessarily, although I would urge you to consider pulling Entertainment out of the project."

Rachoff said, "I might agree with you, Howard, from the standpoint of long-term ramifications. However, the reason this project was initiated, and especially the reason why Jenkins Drew and his people were brought into it, was to take charge of an immediate crisis. It's never easy balancing future considerations with present needs, but it seemed evident to me that we had reached a point where it had to be done."

"Mr. Rachoff, all I'm asking is that you reconsider how we're approaching it. If I didn't feel that it was within News's capability to turn things around, I wouldn't be making this call. But I have some ideas that I'd like you to consider, and so does Renée Ballantyne. All I ask while you consider them is to keep in mind that the immediate success we might have with this new approach could be rendered less than worthless down the road."

Rachoff sighed. "Do you want to come in and see me in the morning?"

"I'd appreciate that."

"All right. Come in at nine."

"I'll be there. Again, I'm sorry to have disturbed you at home. Please give my best to Mrs. Rachoff."

"I will."

Rachoff hung up, jammed his hands into his red silk robe, and went to the bedroom. He took off the robe and sat on the edge of the bed. His wife asked, "Who was that?"

"Howard Monroe. He wants to discuss the project we're involved in to boost news ratings."

"At this hour?"

"It's probably built up in him and this was the hour he chose to let it out."

"What do you think you'll do?" Helen Rachoff asked as her husband lay down beside her and turned off a small lamp at the side of the bed.

"Get some sleep, I suppose. It's funny, Helen, how you sometimes lose touch when you sit on top of such a diverse operation. I suppose it's inevitable. I think Monroe is right, but I may see things differently in the morning. I've gone along with him before, and ended up with the lowest-rated news division in the business. Well, we'll explore this tomorrow. Thanks for listening."

"Thanks for sharing it with me. I always appreciate that, you know."

Renée Ballantyne sat with her back against the headboard. She was naked; her breasts hung over covers she'd pulled up to her waist. Half-glasses were perched on her nose as she read through a copy of a memo Howard Monroe had handed her earlier that day.

The man in bed with her, who was also naked, pulled himself up next to her and asked, "What are you reading?"

She glanced at him and said, "An interoffice memo."

The man, who'd been her lover for more than a year, was vice-president of News at a rival network. He said, "Is it about the anchor fiasco?"

Renée nodded and continued reading. She realized she probably shouldn't have dragged the memo out of her briefcase while he was there. As close as they were personally, she was always aware that they were competitors, and had to remind herself not to be too open with him where her job was involved.

"What's new with that project?" he asked. His name was Jeb Stuart. Fifty, divorced twice, and the father of three daughters, he was held in high regard in broadcasting circles. He was also extremely handsome, which had caused Renée to respond the first time she met him.

She answered, "Things are getting straightened out."

He smiled and ran his fingers around the contour of her breast. "The only thing that will straighten that mess out is to take it out of the hands of the clowns in Entertainment."

"I know that," Renée said testily. She knew she shouldn't be annoyed. After all, she had told him about what was occurring within EBS and he obviously was interested and wanted to be helpful. Still, she was not anxious for him to cross over what she felt were clearly defined lines in their relationship. She tossed the memo to the floor, turned, and brushed her lips across his.

"You're avoiding the issue, my dear," he said.

"Funny, but I thought the issue might be to make love."

He laughed. "That, too, but first things first."

"I'd consider that a twisted sense of priority, Jeb." She said it playfully but meant it.

"I don't think so. You bring me halfway into this circus you've been so damned upset about, and then shut me out. I'm interested, and so would you be if the situation were reversed. What happens at EBS has an impact on all of us. If one of the four major networks gets away with putting News in the hands of Entertainment programmers, we're all in trouble. It gives the whole industry a black eye."

"Well, Jeb, maybe that's not going to happen."

He raised his eyebrows. "Have things changed since the last time we talked?"

"Everything changes. That's what's wonderful about life."

They looked at each other for a few seconds, and knew they were thinking the same thing. The attraction was mutually strong. They liked each other's looks, respected each other's successes in television. Sometimes, in more reflective moments, Renée admitted to herself that Jeb Stuart was someone to whom she could probably relate for the rest of her life. The thought of marrying him was, during those moments, appealing. He'd broached the subject a few times, but it had never gone beyond idle dinner-table conversation. Whenever the idea threatened to slip into the realm of possibility, she managed to shut it off and shift into other areas.

He said, "If you people in News were to get the project back, who would you go with?"

"Of the candidates?"

"Yes."

She said, "I'd be hard-pressed to choose one, Jeb. I suppose Veronica Frazier makes the most sense. She's black, beautiful, and the word from San Francisco is that the minute she came on the air, ratings soared. The gal from Texas is too parochial for me. Somehow, making a big deal out of a housewife from Amarillo being rocketed to stardom is a yawn."

"What about your old buddy, Maureen O'Dwyer?"

"I love Maureen. We've been through a lot together. I respect her talent and drive, but if ratings determine it, I'm not confident that the public is ready for anybody that good."

"The cynical Ms. Ballantyne," he said.

"I don't want to talk about it anymore. I hate bringing the office home with me."

"You did a pretty good job of it," he said, pointing to a bulging briefcase next to the discarded memo on the floor.

"I lost my head. I'm entitled to that once in a while."

He pulled the covers from her and nuzzled his face between her breasts. His hand slid over her belly and to the warm place between her thighs. The feel of his fingers exploring her sent a shudder through her body. She looked down and watched his penis slowly enlarge until it was almost fully erect. She reached for him, took him in her hand, and, after a few seconds of gentle stroking, brought him to complete hardness. They embraced, and the sensation of his engorged member sliding between her legs intensified the tremors within her. He slowly moved his pelvis back and forth, the wet firm contact with the core of her sexuality bringing her closer to that plateau from which total sexual satisfaction could be reached.

He kissed the length of her, her toes, thighs, and belly, took each breast into his mouth, and twirled his tongue over turgid nipples. When they were both ready, he lay on his back and she straddled him, slowly lowered herself. The sensation of being filled with him caused her to jerk and to utter a tight, passionate whine. She leaned forward on her hands and brushed his chest with her breasts.

"You're magnificent," he said hoarsely.

"Shhhhhhh," she said, smiling. She started a slow, gyrating movement, and she knew he was holding back for her sake. Although she appreciated it, she was ready for him to come. They rocked back and forth, the tension increasing until he grasped her breasts, closed his eyes, and convulsed in orgasm. She was only seconds behind.

When it was over she got off him and lay on her back while he slowly kissed her face and ears. He knew she'd had an orgasm, but also knew from a year of sexual exploration with her that there was still to come a different, more potent release. He poised his lips above her pubic patch, then lowered himself, and within a few minutes she writhed on the bed, her legs twitching uncontrollably, her moans reflecting the intense pleasure radiating from her sexual center to every part of her body.

_____CHAPTER 18

"She's still not back?" Maureen asked from her room at the Inter-Continental New York.

"No, she isn't. I'm worried to death," her mother said from Kansas City.

"Have you called everywhere you can think of?" Maureen lighted a cigarette.

"Of course I have. I don't know what else to do but call the police."

"No, Mama, not yet. There's no sense in sending up false alarms. Did you check hospitals?"

"Yes."

"No auto accidents, no drownings?"

Her mother broke into tears.

"I'm just being realistic, Mama. Please stop crying. It doesn't help anything."

Her mother calmed down and again urged that the police be called. Maureen stood firm, although she knew her mother was right. She just didn't want to act prematurely and cause unfavorable publicity. Kids often ran away, she reasoned, and returned after they'd made their point. But she was also worried, and tried not to transmit it to her mother. She said, "I have some sources I can call upon in Kansas City. Let's give it the rest of the day. I'll get on it right away and call you this evening. Okay?"

"It will have to be, won't it? You sit in New York while I sit here and suffer through this. What kind of a daughter have I raised? What kind of a daughter is she raising?"

Maureen's anger was tempered by guilt. She stubbed out her cigarette, told her mother that she would call as soon as she learned something, and hung up.

She perched on the edge of a windowsill and did what she often did when confronted with conflicting pressures, tried to compartmentalize them in the interest of resolving at least one. In this case she knew she could do nothing about Julie's disappearance. There was no person she could call, unless she alerted a friend at the EBS television affiliate in Kansas City. She was reluctant to do that for the same reason she didn't want to contact the police.

She focused in on information she'd received at lunch from Carl Schwartz. It had been a pleasant meeting; she always enjoyed his company, found his candor and irreverence refreshing. It wasn't until late into lunch that he brought up the question of a new anchor for the network news. He told her everything that had been going on, including the infighting between the Entertainment and News divisions. When he'd finished, she'd asked directly whether she was a viable candidate for the job.

"Absolutely, Mo," he replied. "The problem is that the bananas in Entertainment probably don't see you as pulling in instant bucks as fast as some of the others."

"Who are the others?"

"Well, I really shouldn't tell you, but, hell, we've been friends a long time. My understanding is that it's been narrowed down to three people."

"You're still not telling me anything, Carl. I'm one of them?"

"Yup. The other two are Cindy Lewis from Amarillo and Veronica Frazier from San Francisco."

She bit her lower lip and grunted. "Cindy Lewis from Amarillo? That's like bringing in Betty Boop."

Schwartz shook his head and said chidingly, "Don't let the claws come out, Mo; it isn't flattering."

She glanced at adjoining tables, then leaned close to him and said, "*You* think she's network caliber?"

"It doesn't matter what I think. I'm not making the decision. The point is that Machlin and Drew think she has a quality they can exploit. Frankly, I tend to agree with you, although she is adorable."

"*Adorable!* What bullshit to start judging network journalists on whether they're adorable or not." She sat back and ran her fingers through her red hair. "God, the lyrics were right, weren't they?"

"What lyrics?"

" 'Tits and ass.' I can't believe this network has been reduced to tits and ass where news is concerned."

"Mo, calm down. I know you're angry, but don't take it out on me. I'm just a hardworking cog in this wonderful, pulsating world of big-time show business." He grinned and put his hands on top of hers. "And I didn't say that Cindy Lewis was going to get the slot. I'm just telling you what the atmosphere is around here. I don't know for certain, but I get a sense that Monroe and Ballantyne might be finally pulling their collective balls together to stand up against what's been going on. It's kind of late in the game but it could help. If the decision swings back into News, I'd say you've got the inside track."

She mulled it over, then said, "Veronica Frazier, the black broad. I really haven't seen much of her work, but I understand she's pretty good."

"Yes, she is, has a nice style, very smooth and reserved. The fact that she's black helps, too."

Her laugh was bitter. "Where does that leave me, this fair-skinned, middle-aged broad who's done nothing but learn her craft and do a goddamn good job of practicing it?"

She saw in his face that he was annoyed at her, so she

175

quickly softened her tone and said, "I'm sorry, Carl, but I've been fighting this business for a long time."

"So have I, Mo, and I'll tell you something right now as a friend and a fan. The attitude that you've just expressed and have expressed for as long as I've known you is probably the thing that will keep you from ever reaching that star you're always going after. It's funny how the only negative comments ever made about you have to do with your attitude, your hardness. Nobody ever debates whether you're a top-notch reporter. You write rings around almost everybody in the business and have a delivery that can be believed. But that anger, that hostility, comes through and it's a damn shame."

She didn't know whether to yell at him or to ask advice on how to modify her image. She did neither, just sat there and drew her lips tight.

"Maureen, let me ask you something. Are you still tight with Renée?"

His question snapped her out of the funk she'd slipped into. She said, "Renée and I have known each other a long time, Carl. We worked together on stories when she was out in the field. We've always been good friends. I respect her, although I thought she sold out when she went into management."

"Thanks," he said.

"I didn't mean it the way it sounded, Carl. I don't know, I guess I was disappointed in her, but that doesn't taint my feelings about her. I like her and I think she likes me."

"Uh, huh."

"What does that mean? Are you trying to tell me something?"

He shook his head and lighted his pipe. "No, it's just that I get a sense of . . . I wouldn't call it rancor, but I'm not sure she's as big a fan of yours as you might hope she is."

"I'm sorry to hear that. Are you telling me it has a bearing on this anchor business?"

"Maybe. If Monroe and Ballantyne manage to shift emphasis back into the News Division, it could give Renée added weight in making the decision. I just want to be sure there isn't a complication there, something from the past, something that might get in the way."

"Nothing that I know of, Carl, but thanks for mentioning it. I'll think more about it."

They returned to EBS. He went to his office, she poked her head in a few doors to say hello to old friends. She then went to Renée's office.

"Maureen," Renée said enthusiastically, getting up from behind her desk and embracing her. "How are you?"

Maureen stepped back, sat on the edge of the desk, and lighted a cigarette. "I'm terrific. At least, I was a few minutes ago. I had lunch with Carl Schwartz."

"Yes, he told me that you were having lunch together. I'm sorry we didn't get a chance to talk the other day. You look terrific, as usual. How's things in the nation's capital?"

There was a hint of sarcasm in the question. Maureen picked it up, laughed, and said, "As insane and plastic as ever. Thank God we don't have to have reverence any longer for our elected officials, or for schoolteachers, doctors, and lawyers, too. When I was a kid I was convinced that my teachers didn't go to the bathroom the same way everybody else did. I always figured that they had some special way of eliminating waste."

Ballantyne laughed. "Do you still feel that way?"

"Sometimes. Anyway, here I am in exciting New York, nominated for a prestigious Brickhouse Award and thoroughly bored. Feel like talking for a few minutes?"

Renée looked at her watch and grimaced. "Sure, but it can't be long. I have a very important meeting with Monroe in twenty minutes."

"About the new anchor slot?" Maureen lighted another cigarette and took one of the chairs across from the desk.

"Yes, as a matter of fact. My goodness, how the grapevine grows in this business."

"It always has, always will. Want to level with me?"

"Sure. You want to know what your chances are?"

"I sure do."

"Fifty-fifty."

"What do I have to do to improve the odds?"

"There's nothing you can do. As long as the decision rests with Entertainment, I'd say your chances are fifty-fifty at best. If something happens today that I hope will happen, your stock goes up. So, all you can do is enjoy the town, get your nails and hair done for the big dinner, and keep in touch."

Maureen wasn't sure whether to press further, then decided to. She asked whether Renée was behind her for the anchor slot, and was disappointed in the nonresponse. The fact that she sat and said nothing said a great deal to Maureen. She quickly asked, "Why not?"

Renée threw her hands up into the air. "I didn't say I wasn't, Maureen. There you go again, being a hard-nosed reporter picking up on a cue from a subject. I'd be happy to see you coanchoring the nightly news and you know it. Do I have reservations? Yes, I do. Want to hear them?"

"Yes."

"Okay." The buzzer on her intercom sounded. She picked up the phone, winced, hung it up, and stood. "Maureen, I'm sorry, but I have to run this minute. I think things are moving even faster than I anticipated. Look, let's talk some more. How about tonight? What are you doing?"

"Nothing. Oh, I have some things I could do, but I'd much rather spend the time with you if you're available."

Renée went to the door and paused, looking thoughtful. She said, "Let's go to Antolotti's. I'll make a reservation and meet you there at seven-thirty."

Maureen stood. "Fine. I'll be there."

She'd returned to her hotel room, put on a robe, and sat on the bed. It looked good to her. Her instincts, which she had learned to trust over the years, told her that her chances were a lot better than fifty-fifty. If she was right, all the work and pain would finally pay off.

She deliberately shifted gears in her thinking and contemplated the situation with her daughter. She had to do something, but didn't know what. Her mother was likely to take action on her own if Maureen didn't give her some positive word that evening. She drew a blank, went to the window, where she closed the drapes tight against the afternoon sun, and returned to bed, this time getting beneath the covers. "Just an hour," she told herself as she nuzzled her head into the pillow. "Just an hour."

CHAPTER 19

They met in the executive dining room of the Empire Broadcasting System. A waiter in a stiff white jacket served coffee to Morgan Rachoff, Renée Ballantyne, Howard Monroe, Carl Schwartz, and Dick Hanratty, vice-president of corporate public relations for EBS.

Rachoff, who'd just taken a haircut, conferred quietly with Hanratty. Monroe, Ballantyne, and Schwartz sat across the table from them and waited for the meeting to begin. Finally, Rachoff sat back, checked his watch, and said, "We'll have to make this quick."

Monroe, who sat between his two colleagues from News, opened a file folder and said, "I think this decision, Mr. Rachoff, is one of the most important ones ever made at this network. As you know, news is no longer a step-child of broadcasting. It doesn't just provide public service anymore; it's capable of generating huge potential revenues, as evidenced by the success of our competitors. I think we're in a position to turn the corner here at EBS and put together a viable and profitable news operation, but . . ."

Rachoff, who'd sat stoically, again checked his watch, and said, "I know all this, Howard. You went over it with me on the phone, and the memo you delivered to me this morning makes the point very eloquently. Of course, you failed to mention that our news operation has lost money for years while others have been profitable. If that hadn't been the case, it wouldn't have been necessary to turn over certain aspects of news programming to Entertainment."

"I know that," Monroe said, "but we're ready to turn that around. The problem is that if we make a crucial mistake now and turn our News Division into an extension of the Entertainment Division, we'll not only destroy what upward morale everyone in the division is experiencing, but we run the risk of losing our credibility for years to come."

"Yes, Howard, I know that," Rachoff said rather testily. "I didn't ask you to meet with me to hear the arguments all over again. I've taken this question to other members of the executive team and the consensus seems to be that the decisions to turn over a reshaping of News to Entertainment might be a mistake. Therefore, I'm rescinding that order and handing the project back to you."

Ballantyne, Monroe, and Schwartz looked at one another in surprise. They hadn't expected it to be that easy. They also shared the realization that now that they had been given the ball, there was a sudden tremendous pressure to score points with it.

"Well, does that settle it?" Rachoff asked. "Is there anything further to discuss?"

Monroe was tempted to point out that the lateness of the decision placed a serious burden on the job of selecting a new anchor. He wanted to suggest that the project be shelved to give them more time to regroup, but thought better of it. They'd scored a major victory in wresting the decision away from Entertainment, and to qualify their demands would undoubtedly upset Rachoff. Instead, he stood and said, "Thank you, Mr. Rachoff. We'd better get moving right away to make this thing work."

Rachoff didn't respond immediately, but as the three representatives from the News Division were heading toward the door, he said, "I'm going out on a limb with this. I'm holding to the timetable and won't tolerate failure. Is that understood?''

"Yes, sir, it is," Monroe said.

Hanratty, who'd been making notes on a small pad, said, "Under ordinary circumstances I'd suggest we postpone choosing a new anchor to give us time to mount the right kind of publicity campaign, but it's too late for that. The leaks to the press about the Brickhouse Award and the three candidates being up for the anchor spot forces our hand."

"My sentiments exactly," said Monroe.

"Can we meet in ten minutes?" Hanratty asked.

"Sure," Monroe said. "My office?"

"Fine."

After they'd left the room Hanratty turned to Rachoff and said, "I have doubts about this."

"I know you do, Jim, and so do I, and I wish there had been some clearer thinking down the line. Frankly, we can't afford another losing season out of News, and turning it over to Entertainment still makes sense to me. The problem is that they make sense, too," he said, indicating those who'd just left.

Hanratty closed his pad and prepared to leave. He turned and said, "Actually, this might have been the best way to go all along. The concept of introducing a new anchor around the Brickhouse Awards was a hell of a good idea out of Drew. We've got the benefit of that input, and now we can get pure again and celebrate the sanctity of journalism." His smile brought no response from Rachoff, so he left the dining room and went directly to Howard Monroe's office.

He closed the door behind him and said, "Well, Howard, you pulled off quite a coup."

Monroe, who was sitting in his chair and had his feet up on the desk, managed a weak grin. He rubbed his eyes and twisted his head on his neck to relieve a tension headache.

"I'm glad it worked out this way, Howard," Hanratty

said as he took out a cigarette and lighted it. "I never was for Drew and Machlin sticking their noses into News.

Monroe knew Hanratty was lying, that he'd been instrumental in Rachoff's decision to bring Entertainment into the project, but he didn't say it, simply nodded. He swiveled in his chair and gazed out the window, then said absently, "Who's going to tell Drew and Machlin?"

"Rachoff said he'd call them. He probably already has."

Monroe turned back to face the desk and shook his head.

"What's the matter, Howard?" Hanratty asked.

"A coup? I'm not sure anything was won. Frankly, as much as I was against the decision to let Drew run things, there was a certain comfort in it. I've been fighting ratings here for a goddamn long time, and it would have been nice to see Drew fall on his ass, too."

Hanratty didn't respond, although he was dismayed at Monroe's attitude. Everybody, including himself, had an important stake in the future profitability of News, and now that Rachoff had reversed his decision, with Hanratty's enthusiastic blessing, he was more anxious than ever for it to work. He asked, "What are you concerned about, Howard? All the groundwork has been laid for a hell of a good campaign to launch a new anchor. I don't see anything coming of it but good, but maybe I'm missing something. Am I?"

Monroe shook his head, reached into a desk drawer, and took out a bottle of Tums. He popped one in to his mouth, chewed it, then said, "The News Division has been floundering under a lack of corporate leadership for as long as I've been here, Jim. The other networks have forged ahead, hired top talent, created interesting shows outside the usual newscasts, and have made heroes out of themselves. They did it because they had strong, enthusiastic leadership from on top. That hasn't been the case here, and what bothers the hell out of me is that after a lot of bumbling I'm supposed to work miracles again. Shit, that's no way to run a railroad.''

''I know, I know,'' Hanratty said as he lighted another cigarette, ''but the reality is that you got what you wanted about deciding the new anchor. All you have to do is make the right choice.''

Monroe laughed. It was not a happy laugh, was tinged with bitterness. He said, ''As far as I'm concerned, the right decision is to send the three of them back where they came from and go outside to hire somebody with credentials.''

Hanratty's eyebrows went up and he forced saliva through his teeth. ''That approach was scrapped early in the game, Howard. Frankly, I thought it was a pretty good idea to conduct a talent search within the O-and-O's.''

''Maybe you did but I didn't,'' Monroe said. ''That was Drew's brainchild. Christ, it was like one of those silly Hollywood talent searches where a thousand teenagers vie for fame and fortune, with the winner receiving two round-trip tickets to Hollywood for a screen test and lunch at the Brown Derby. I hate to come off a purist, Jim, because I'm not one, but it was a bullshit idea from the beginning. That's the problem. I may have gotten the project back in my lap, but I'm stuck with choosing one of those teenagers.''

Hanratty laughed. ''Maureen O'Dwyer a teenager?''

''Metaphorically speaking. Look, Jim, I'm all over the shock of getting this thing back from Rachoff. What I have to do now is make it work.''

Hanratty opened the pad on which he'd been making notes during the meeting, perused them, then said, ''I think we're in good shape. We have the three of them on *Lively Five* tomorrow night. We figured we might as well go with the leaks and lay it on the line with the public. I'm having releases hand-delivered all over town tomorrow. We've got some solid print interviews lined up and there'll be a lot of hoopla around the Brickhouse dinner. I just got final approval on the promotional budget. It's big, Howard. We'll be advertising in every paper and magazine in town. I've got people working on bus posters and direct mail. We're going to go with Drew's original idea of coming up with a contest for viewers . . ."

Monroe slapped his hand on the desk and said, "See, that's what I mean. We put somebody on national television to deliver news about war and famine and the viewers have the chance to send in a goddamned postcard for a chance to win a fucking toaster."

"A trip for two to Paris, a new car, and lifetime supply of . . . Tums."

Monroe rubbed his hand over his chin and sat back. "That's show biz, huh?"

"Yup."

Monroe stood, stretched, and went to the door. He said, "Thanks, Jim, I feel better." It was true; it had come over him that he'd been taking it all too seriously, which was something his shrink had told him years ago. There had also been a certain comfort in sharing his frustration with a man with whom he'd worked for many years, and who was in the same corporate boat that was filled with holes but managing to stay afloat.

Hanratty stood and extended his hand. They shook. Hanratty said, "this might turn out to be fun after all, Howard. All we have to do is run with it and make it work. By the way, who's getting it?"

"Getting what?" Monroe asked.

"The anchor job."

Monroe shrugged. "I really have no idea. I stopped thinking about it because up until this morning Jenkins Drew was making that decision. It's a damn good question."

"If you had to choose now, Howard, who would it be?"

Monroe furrowed his brow and licked his lips. "I suppose I lean toward Veronica Frazier from San Francisco, but . . ."

"Because she's black?"

"That helps, although there's more to it than that. No,

Jim, I really don't know. I suppose we'll have to make that decision after the Brickhouse dinner.''

"Can I give you a word of advice?'' Hanratty asked.

"Of course.''

"Now that the journalistic image is again intact, don't get too wrapped up in it. Remember, Howard, this *is* show biz.''

There were many expressions used by Cindy Lewis's children that bothered her, including "hanging out," but she realized that was exactly what she was doing that afternoon, hanging out in the EBS News Division. The telephone conversation with Hal had stayed with her, and she'd awoken that morning anxious and angry. She'd originally planned to go shopping for gifts to bring back to Amarillo, but her state of mind didn't lend itself to that activity, and so she decided to lose herself in the business that had brought her to New York.

She still felt out of place being with journalists who'd made it there, but as she watched them work she felt less insecure. It occurred to her that they were, after all, nothing more than men and women who did the same job she did, only they did it in a different city and in a larger context. The question of big-fish-in-little-pond crossed her mind and she realized she probably would always be more comfortable with a smaller challenge. Still, the thought of becoming a network personality sent rapid flashes of excitement through her body. As a young girl she'd shared the dream of becoming a famous movie actress, but it had faded quickly, as it does with most people. The difference was that most people never had an opportunity later in life to fulfill that childhood fantasy, as it appeared she might. Were she alone in the world, were there no Hal or children, no beautiful secure house in Amarillo, there wouldn't be a decision to make. She'd grab the brass ring Machlin had mentioned and hold on for dear life.

But that wasn't reality. There was a Hal and children and a house, and they meant more than anything in the world to her.

She was deep in these thoughts when a resonant male voice said from behind her, "Cindy Lewis?"

She turned and looked at Paul Satterfield, a familiar face on EBS news for years. Satterfield was a jack-of-all-trades who was as likely to turn up covering an insurrection in South America as he was reporting on a new medical breakthrough at the Mayo Clinic. Cindy had always responded favorably to him on television, not only to his professional bearing and deep voice but to his looks. But the tube didn't do him justice. He was remarkably handsome—a beautifully etched and tanned face, sparkling blue eyes, a perfect splash of gray at the temples, and an obviously trim and fit body beneath an impeccably tailored gray suit.

"Yes, I'm Cindy Lewis, and you're Paul Satterfield." She extended her hand and he took it. "I really like you very much on television," she said.

"Good to hear it, but I understand we might be seeing a lot more of you."

"Really?" Her eyes opened wide to indicate surprise, but she was aware that he was referring to the possibility of her becoming an anchor.

"Sure, that's the word around here. I saw the series you did on the Klan and on Jamison. It was good."

She didn't want to come off as a giggly, awestruck female, but wasn't entirely successful. She said, "I'm so happy you liked it. I'm . . . well, having someone like you appreciate my work means so much."

He smiled, displaying a perfectly matched set of teeth.

He narrowed his eyes and said, "Are you enjoying New York?"

"Oh, yes, very much. I've never been here before, and it's such an exciting city, so full of vitality and energy. I just love my hotel room and everybody seems so beautifully dressed and . . ."

"Don't let it fool you. It's a jungle like everyplace else, except it's bigger. Anyway, glad you're having a good time. Anything you'd planned on seeing but missed?"

She laughed. "A thousand things, a million things. I suppose people could spend their whole lives here and never see everything, not like Amarillo, where I live. It doesn't take long to see everything in Amarillo."

A leggy young female staffer came up to Satterfield and told him they were ready in editing for him to do a voice track. He thanked her, said he would be there in a minute, then said to Cindy, "I've been looking forward to meeting you very much. What are you doing for dinner?"

"Dinner ? Well, I . . ."

Again, the warm, perfect smile. "I just thought you might enjoy talking shop a little and seeing some of New York's better places. Have dinner with me. We'll go to Twenty-one."

"Twenty-one? I've heard so much about that."

"Well, it's an interesting place and one you should see while you're here. If things work out for you, you'll probably end up with your own table there, so let me be the first to introduce you."

She was faced with the same problem she'd had accepting the dinner invitation from Herb Machlin, but the dilemma seemed not nearly as treacherous. She said, "I'd love that. When?"

"I'll meet you here at seven-thirty." He turned and walked away, his stride screaming confidence.

Cindy checked her watch. It was three-thirty. Suddenly, she was filled with enthusiasm for shopping. She left the building, hailed a cab, and told the driver to take her to

Greenwich Village. She wasn't sure what she would find there, but it was on her list of places to visit and she thought she might as well shop there. As it turned out, she found perfect gifts for everyone in the family, and even bought herself a dress that under ordinary circumstances she would not have been caught dead in. It was a revealing Indian sun dress that she knew she'd dare wear only around the house, but that represented to her the sort of purchase one should make while in New York. She meandered along West Sixth Street, taking in the sights and sounds of the Village, appalled at the groups of people smoking pot but excited by it at the same time. It occurred to her as she stood on a corner and contemplated which way to turn that the exhilaration she felt at the moment had nothing to do with being in New York. Rather, it had to do with being alone, without the encumbrances of family and home, being respected for her professional qualifications just as Hal was when he received awards for selling the most insurance.

She turned and looked at her reflection in a store window that featured drug paraphernalia. "A head shop," she said to herself. "How awful." Then she noticed in the same window the reflection of a man openly admiring her. She quickly walked away, found a cab, and climbed in. She looked out the window and saw that the man continued to stare at her. "Creep," she said.

"What?" the driver asked.

"Nothing. The Inter-Continental Hotel, at Park and Forty-eighth."

As he pulled away from the curb she cast one final glance back, and, as much as she hated to admit it, was pleased that the man continued to look in her direction.

Maybe I've missed something, she thought. She didn't believe it, but the thought stayed with her for the rest of the afternoon.

_____**C**HAPTER **21**

Renée was late for her dinner at Antolotti's. She was greeted warmly at the door and led through the crowded front dining room to where Maureen sat in the smaller room at the rear of the restaurant.

"Sorry," Renée said breathlessly, "but I made the mistake of asking somebody a question as I was leaving. The only way to get out of there when the show is over is to wear blinders and walk a straight line."

Maureen laughed and finished the martini she'd ordered. "Hurry up, I'm one ahead."

After they'd both been served drinks, Maureen asked, "Well, did things work out the way you hoped they would?"

Renée drew a deep breath and nodded. "The ball is back in our court again. Finally, sanity prevails."

Maureen deliberately didn't show how relieved she was to hear the news, but inside she trembled with anticipation. If News was now to make the final decision, her chances had taken a quantum leap forward. Surely, she reasoned, none of the hierarchy in News would consider the other candidates over her. She was a pro, had spent years honing her skills as a writer and reporter. She also knew that the recognition factor was important to viewers.

She'd been reporting on television for years, and seldom went a day without bumping into someone who recognized her and who stopped to talk or to get her autograph.

"Let's order, I'm starved," Renée said as she picked up a menu.

Food was the last thing on Maureen's mind. She wanted to hear more about the decision that was to be made about the new network anchor, but didn't want to appear too anxious. She, too, picked up her menu and chose a dish. After they'd ordered, Renée lighted a cigarette and said, "Do you want it?"

Maureen knew exactly what she was referring to but asked, "Do I want what?"

"The anchor spot."

Maureen sat back and shook her head, then let out a burst of laughter. She again leaned forward and said, "I've never wanted anything so much in my life, Renée. Do I have it?"

"No, but I think you can."

"Is there a hitch?"

Renée screwed up her face in thought, then said, "The only hitch might be you, Mo. I'm not sure you should take it, even if it's offered."

Maureen's puzzled expression was genuine. Surely Renée, who went back almost to the beginning of Maureen's career, realized how much she wanted the anchor spot. It represented to everyone in the business the crowning achievement, maybe not in pure journalistic terms but certainly as a measure of having reached the top. She wondered whether this was a ploy on Renée's part, a more comfortable way of not giving her the job. Before she had more time to ponder it, however, Renée added, "I wouldn't take it if I were you."

Maureen's eyes opened wide as she asked, "Why not?"

"Well, Mo, you reach a point where security means something. You know this business. Anchors come and go depending upon the whims of management and the ratings numbers game. Blond macho anchors are in this week, next week it's sensitive homosexuals, the rating period after that sends everybody scurrying for Cronkite types with gray at the temples."

Maureen shrugged. "I know all that, Renée. That's the business and I accept it."

"It's worse for women. We're still, and probably always will be, window dressing on the set. Did you ever count the number of times the male half of a mixed anchor team gets to sign off?"

Maureen laughed and motioned for a waiter to bring another drink. She said, "I sure did, and I made a stink about it in Washington. Along with everything else, the AD keeps a running tab on it for us so that we come out even at the end of the month."

Renée shook her head and smiled. "Feminism gone awry."

"No, feminism at work. Look, Renée, what are you getting at? You know I want this slot, have been aiming for it since the first day I stepped into a studio. If you're simply protecting my best interests, forget about it. I'm a big, grown-up girl who knows the vagaries of television, and because I know them so well I can deal with them."

Both women were suddenly aware of attention being paid them by a table of four people, two men and two women. One of the men got up from the table and approached them, said, "My wife and I have enjoyed you for years."

Renée and Maureen looked at each other. The man seemed to be talking to the middle of the table. It wasn't clear to whom he was speaking. He said, "We miss you, Miss Ballantyne. I feel like a fool, but my wife wanted your autograph."

Renée was embarrassed but accommodated him on a piece of paper he placed before her. She glanced up at Maureen and wondered what she was thinking. After the man had returned to the table and everyone had offered their thanks, she said to Maureen, "Never fails to amaze me, the power of the tube. God, what a hot mike and that infernal red eye will do."

Maureen didn't indicate that she was slightly disappointed that it was Renée who received the attention and not she. She waited until the couples had returned to their normal dinner conversation before saying, "Let's get back to what we were talking about. I appreciate your concern about me. Sure, I've thought about the ramifications of it. It means leaving a very secure little pond in which I function as a very big fish to come to this wonderful communications jungle to take my chances. I also know that choosing me bucks a trend. Hell, no matter how hard I try I can't get rid of the wrinkles, and evidently that wonderful male viewing population out there can't stand to have its news delivered by a wrinkled face. But do you know what conclusion I've come to, Renée? I've decided to say, fuck 'em all. I want this anchor spot so bad I can taste it."

Their food was served and they ate in silence, Renée attacking her veal piccata with enthusiasm, Maureen doing little more than shoving chicken in wine sauce around with a fork.

Renée sat back and dabbed at her lips with her napkin. "My eyes are still bigger than my stomach, my father would be pleased to know, rest his soul."

Maureen dropped her fork to the plate and said, "So, do I have it?"

"Probably," Renée replied. She leaned forward and said, "Look, Mo, I'm beating around the bush a little and I'm sorry for that. I've known you a long time and have always liked and admired you."

"The feeling is mutual."

"I know. We also share some things that a lot of people don't. You were there."

Maureen had been waiting for Renée to refer to a specific time in their lives at which an incident had occurred that had brought them very close together.

They'd worked together at a television station in Kansas City, Maureen's hometown, and although it had never been stated, there'd been an intense competition between them.

Renée had known Maureen's husband, a handsome, slick young man who'd broken a ton of hearts in town. There had been a great deal of surprise at Maureen's marrying him, not so much because she'd decided to but because he'd decided to settle down. The skepticism proved itself out when they separated almost immediately after Julie's birth.

While all this was going on, Renée had gotten pregnant by a man she'd been seeing. After weeks of agonizing she called Maureen and met her for a drink, told her she was pregnant and that she intended to abort. Maureen's initial response was negative. She hadn't practiced the Catholic faith into which she'd been born, but there were strong and lingering remnants. The thought of an abortion was abhorrent to her.

"I don't want to be stuck with a child without a husband," Renée had said.

Maureen was hurt by the comment at the time. She was, after all, in precisely that position. But she also understood. It wasn't until much later that she had been able to admit to herself that she'd performed her own style of abortion, not medically but emotionally, by using her mother so that she would not be strapped with a child as she sought success in broadcasting. Was it any different?

Now, sitting in Antolotti's, she was not anxious to rehash the past. The present and future were much more important. She waited until a waiter had confirmed that they were finished eating and had removed the plates before saying, "Renée, what does all this have to do with the anchor job?"

Renée was not as cool and confident as she had been upon her arrival. Her face reflected an inner sadness, and eyes that were always so bright and burning were now dull and directed at the table. Maureen reached across and placed her hand on her arm. "Is something wrong?"

Renée tried to smile but it was strained and transient.

She said softly, "I would give anything, Maureen, to have had that child I gave up. I'd give anything to have a son or daughter. You have a daughter, Maureen, although you don't act like it. Doesn't it ever bother you that you don't see her, that she lives with someone else and isn't part of your daily life?"

Maureen felt a hot flush hit her face. She'd been asked that question before by other people, and always resented the intrusion into what she considered a private and personal matter. But she didn't want to respond with anger, not to this person who'd shared so much with her over the years. She said in a controlled voice, "Yes, of course it bothers me, but we all make decisions in our lives. My goals don't coincide with being an active mother, Renée. Because of that Julie is much better off with my mother in Kansas City than being with me. But I really don't want to discuss this. I have enough trouble dealing with it in my quiet moments alone. Again, what does this have to do with the anchor spot?"

"I think you ought to stay in Washington, cut down your activities a little, and bring Julie to live with you."

Maureen was flabbergasted at the directness of the statement. She started to say something, realized it was the wrong time, and tried again.

"Look, Mo, I know this is none of my business and that I'm projecting me on you, but I also know that life is flying by. How old is Julie now, fifteen? What a difficult time for a young girl, and what a wonderful time for a mother to be involved."

Maureen now didn't try to disguise her anger. She snapped, "I don't want to discuss Julie or Julie's relationship with me, Renée. Let's get back to business. I want the anchor spot. Do I have it or don't I?"

Renée shifted in her chair and crossed one long leg over the other. She placed her arm over the back of the chair and her face returned to its original relaxed state. She said, "All right, Mo, fine, the anchor spot is probably yours. I can't say for certain because I'm not making the final decision, but I've already let Monroe and Schwartz know how I feel. I've cast my vote for you and will do whatever I can to make it happen."

Maureen's face and voice became animated. "That's good news. How did they react?"

"They both like you, recognize what a pro you are and that you would do a hell of a job. There are other considerations, of course. Even though Rachoff has given it to us, Howard still has to deliver better ratings and do it fast. If he feels there's a better way to go, he'll have to take it."

"With one of the others?"

"Maybe, maybe not. He has other options. He can raid another network or go far afield and bring in someone who's made a name elsewhere, in some other medium. All of these things have been discussed, and as far as I know a decision has not been reached by either Carl or Howard. But I want to ask you one more time, Mo, and I'd like you to think about it overnight. Make sure you really want this. Make sure the priority list is in order, because I have a feeling that once this decision is made, it's too late to redo it."

"Yes, I'll give it some hard thought tonight, Renée, I promise."

Maureen insisted on paying the bill. They walked up forty-ninth for a few blocks, then parted on a corner.

"You'll keep me posted all the way, won't you?" Maureen asked.

"Of course I will."

For a second it appeared that they would turn and walk in different directions. Instead, they embraced and held it for a very long time. Then, without saying another word, they parted.

Maureen was charged with excitement as she headed for the hotel. It was looking better all the time, and her only concern was whether she could contain herself untl the final decision was made.

As she walked across town, the other topic of conversation at dinner crossed her mind, but she deliberately pushed it away. She knew she'd have to call her mother when she got back about Julie's disappearance, and tried to formulate what she would say. By the time she entered the lobby of the Inter-Continental she'd made up her mind to tell her mother to come to New York, would also tell her that she was putting into motion from her end a missing-person alert for Julie, and that her mother should do nothing in Kansas City. All she wanted to do was buy some time until the anchor decision was made and the announcement was public record. Then, whatever happened would not have as much impact.

She stopped at the desk to check for messages. There was a note in her box, and the clerk handed it to her. She'd just unfolded it and was about to read it when an assistant manager suddenly appeared from a room behind the desk and said, "Miss O'Dwyer, can I have a word with you?"

Maureen looked up and said, "Of course."

She followed him into the room, which turned out to be a tiny office, and he closed the door behind them. "I trust you won't be upset at what I did, Miss O'Dwyer, but I felt it was appropriate."

"What did you do?" she asked, laughing.

"Your daughter arrived here an hour ago."

Maureen was speechless. Her body froze and she looked blankly at him.

"Had I not been sure it was your daughter, I would never, of course, have allowed her to go to the room. But she had identification and said you were expecting her."

"I wasn't. . . . She's here?"

"Yes." He smiled, more in relief that she was not angry with him than in sharing any joy he assumed she was experiencing.

"I . . . thank you very much," she said coldly. "I appreciate your courtesy with her."

"My pleasure, Miss O'Dwyer."

The ride in the elevator seemed endless. She stepped off and walked with heavy legs toward her room. She stopped outside and tried to muster renewed strength before putting her key in the lock. Finally, she opened the door. Sitting on the bed was Julie, who was engrossed in a television program. She wore dungarees, sandals, and a sweat shirt with writing on it.

Maureen slammed the door and said, "Julie, what are you doing here?"

Julie looked up and smiled. "I came to see you, Mama. I missed you."

_____CHAPTER 22

Cindy Lewis didn't know what time it was, but she knew it was early. She looked toward a tiny sliver of light that sliced through the corner of heavy drapes covering a huge picture window. The light was gray; it was either very early or cloudy.

She was on her back. She closed her eyes as she waited for her head to join the rest of her in the waking process. When it had, she quickly opened her eyes and glanced to her right. She was afraid to move, so she kept straining to see without turning.

The body next to her stirred. There was a cough, an energetic clearing of the sinuses, then a grunt.

"Oh, my God," Cindy said to herself. She gently placed her elbows on the mattress and raised her torso, turned her head, and looked at the sleeping face of Paul Satterfield.

Now it all came back to her in a flood of confusion and visual images. They'd gone to 21 and had a marvelous time. The restaurant was filled with familiar faces and Cindy felt very much as though she'd stepped into a fantasy land. Paul seemed to know everyone and introduced her around. She couldn't believe how expensive items on the menu were, and she'd mentioned it to him. He'd laughed, given her a hug, and said, "When you're anchoring the nightly news, Cindy, no menu will seem that expensive."

There were times during the evening when she wanted to talk about Hal and the children, about her happy life in Amarillo, but she was afraid to break the spell. If he knew she was married he might not want to be with her; she felt shabby and dishonest in withholding such information, but did anyway.

After dinner they went to a noisy country-and-western bar that was packed with people. Paul said he liked that kind of music, which surprised and delighted her. She liked it too, but would never have dreamed that someone so urban and urbane would share that interest. They stayed an hour. He asked her if she wanted to share some cocaine with him. He assured her that it was the finest quality and that she could safely snort a line in the ladies' room. She declined. She'd never tried drugs and, for the first time, felt hopelessly outdated and old-fashioned. He excused himself to go to the men's room, where, she assumed, he would use it. She'd read about cocaine use, particularly in show business, and wondered what the stuff was like. Everybody seemed to think it was a harmless drug, although she'd learned from having been on a substance abuse committee in Amarillo that there was no such thing, and she dreaded the thought of her children ever becoming involved in the drug culture. She could never understand the hypocrisy of parents she knew who shared that fear, yet in an attempt to appear young went out and used drugs themselves.

They left the bar and climbed into a cab where Satterfield put his arm around her and kissed her on the lips, gently at first, then with more force, ran his tongue over her lips until she parted her teeth, then probed deep inside. She didn't push him away. She'd had a lot to drink but the

decision had been made. That was the way it was. He
gave the driver an address.

"Where are we going?" she asked.

"My place. I have a nice view of the city, the best
stereo rig money can buy, a record collection that won't
quit, and a lifetime supply of cognac."

She said nothing during the ride. She wanted to decline
the invitation to his apartment and ask to be taken back to
the hotel, yet she said none of those things, simply sat in
silence, aware of his arm over her shoulder and of the
masculine potency of him that permeated the cab.

He lived on the upper East Side in a high-rise building.
He had the penthouse and hadn't lied to her. The view
from three sides, of the city and across the river, was magnificent. The apartment was ringed by balconies on which
lush plantings were illuminated by spotlights. Inside, it
was spacious and beautifully furnished. A large expanse of
rust rug tied together heavy Spanish furniture. The walls
were white and dotted with what was undoubtedly expensive art. Cindy had taken a sculpture class once in
Amarillo and recognized a valuable piece of Haber sculpture lighted by two pin spots in the ceiling. She also recognized a numbered Remington print that hung over a rococo
desk.

"Well, what do you think?"

"It's beautiful," she said, "out of a magazine."

He laughed as he went to a bar built into the wall and
removed two snifters and a bottle of cognac. "It's been in
a few magazines, Cindy. It was featured in one of the
architectural magazines once, and some ads have been
shot here."

They sat on a couch in the living room and he toasted
her. "Here's to taking New York by storm." They clinked
glasses and sipped. Cindy had never liked cognac, always
ended up with acid indigestion after taking even a sip, but
she didn't want to offend him, again was afraid to demonstrate a lack of the worldliness that obviously played such
a part in big-time television.

"What's on your mind?" he asked. "What are you thinking about?"

She didn't answer honestly. She had been thinking of Hal, how angry he would be that she'd even placed herself in a position of betrayal. They'd pledged to each other before they were married that they would never cheapen their relationship by having affairs. They'd agreed that they would end the marriage before they would ever allow that to happen, would do it honorably and without the sort of shabbiness that both of them believed adultery to represent. Once, she'd allowed herself to get a little close to someone at the newspaper and had ended up in a situation she had to run from to preserve the integrity of her commitment to Hal. She'd been very ashamed of that, had realized it had occurred only because she had given out messages that had been misunderstood. But had they been misunderstood, she had to ask herself after that episode, or had she given messages to the man that he'd read accurately? It didn't matter, she'd decided, and had forgotten the entire affair.

Now, however, she'd gone much further still. She knew why she was there, knew what Satterfield wanted and expected.

"Kick off your shoes," he said, "and get comfortable. I'll put on some music. Feel like some more country?"

"That would be fine," she said, "although I like other music, too."

He eventually came up with an album featuring Tony Bennett and the jazz pianist Bill Evans. The music oozed from four corners and helped establish a cozy, warm mood in the room. He'd lowered most of the lights, which led Cindy to speculate on just how many women had been seduced in this atmosphere by this good-looking and smooth celebrity. Probably hundreds, she decided. What would that make her? she wondered. Would it prove that she was attractive and wanted? She and Hal had had an argument once about that. It involved a friend of theirs who, after a divorce, had gone on a wild sexual fling in which she estimated fifty men had been involved over a two-year period. When she told Hal and Cindy about it, she said she'd never felt more attractive and wanted in her life, to which Hal had replied, "Any woman can get laid, and it's been that way since the beginning of man and woman, for Christ's sake. All any woman who isn't grossly unattractive has to do to get a man into bed is to lead him there. What the hell kind of badge is that to wear?"

Their friend had responded angrily, but eventually calmed down. She and Cindy had discussed it later and it all made Cindy realize how different they were, what gaps in perception they had about life and love, sex and relationships. She knew that if she and Hal ever dissolved the marriage, she could never do what her friend had done. Life might change but she wouldn't. That was the way she was.

She brought her thoughts back to the reality of the place and situation.

"Your husband wouldn't like this, would he?" Satterfield asked casually.

"My husband? I . . ."

"I know you're married, Cindy. I read the reports on you. What kind of guy is he?"

"He's a . . . he's a very good guy, a very good husband and father."

"Glad to hear it. I'm sure you wouldn't be married to anyone less than that."

"That's right."

"Well, I've never aspired to the role of cuckolder. I have codes about women, and one of them is to not mess around with the married ones, unless, of course, they're unhappy."

"Unhappy? Is that all it takes to justify it?"

"I can't think of a better reason. Nobody ever said we were supposed to be unhappy on this earth."

She turned so that she faced him directly. She was glad

a topic had been introduced that she felt strongly about, one she could discuss intelligently. She said, "But everyone is unhappy now and then. No marriage is perfect. There've been many times when Hal made me angry and unhappy, but I never considered the answer being to cheat on him."

"How about him? How does he feel?"

"The same."

He laughed. It was soft and gentle, but there was an edge that Cindy didn't miss. He said, "I'd bet every cent I make for the rest of my life that Hal has had his moments with other women."

"No, he hasn't. I'd bet my *life* on that."

"Have it as you will. Look, I suppose it is silly to even get into a discussion like this. I turned on to you the minute I saw you. We probably come from different viewpoints, but like the song goes, the fundamental things apply as time goes by. Man and woman. You probably think I play this game all the time, use a line on women, lower the lights and serve good brandy and play soft music. Not true. I'm fussy about the women I'm with. I want you to know that more than anything, I want to be with you tonight." He slid closer on the couch until their thighs touched. He touched her hair. She leaned her head back against the couch and closed her eyes as he kissed her. His hand found a breast through her dress and massaged it. She started to say, "No," but the word wouldn't come.

He ran his hand over the front of her, over the tops of her thighs, and to her knee. Then it was beneath her dress and spreading her thighs apart.

She shook her head but maintained the pressure of his kiss. He suddenly stood, pulled her from the couch by her hands, and walked her to the bedroom. In the center of the room was a huge circular bed. An amber light from the ceiling cast an inviting glow over it. The music played through speakers in that room, too.

"I really can't," she said. "I . . ."

"I love you," he said.

The words stunned her.

"I have to love a woman before I'm intimate with her," he said. "Yes, I love you, Cindy Lewis."

Minutes later they were naked on the bed. He kissed her tenderly on the neck and ear, his fingers fluttering over her body. He tugged gently at her pubic hair while running his tongue inside her ear.

She responded, yet there was a stiffness to her. Parallel sensations of pleasure and revulsion took over, which rendered her immobile.

He stopped caressing her for a moment, reached into a drawer at the side of the bed, and held up a small capsule wrapped in multicolored cloth. "Ever try this?" he asked.

"What is it?"

"A popper. Amyl nitrite. Believe me, if you think you've ever come before, this will change your mind."

Her initial thought was that it was something to insert in her, but he said, "Just when you're about to come you break the capsule under your nose. The cloth absorbs the liquid and all you have to do is inhale."

"No, I don't want anything like that."

"Suit yourself. You don't mind if I enjoy it, do you?"

"No."

He placed the capsule on the bed next to them and resumed lovemaking. Eventually he straddled her and offered his erection to her mouth.

"Please, I don't want . . ."

"Don't like oral sex? You don't know what you're missing."

"I'm sorry, I really shouldn't be here, and . . ."

He quickly moved between her legs and entered her. She gasped at the feel of him inside. He began a slow, steady movement until he was ready to climax, then grasped the capsule and held it beneath his nose, crushed it, and took a deep breath as he came. He shuddered, moaned, yelled, "Shit!"

He poured himself cognac and brought it to the bed. They said nothing to each other for a few minutes. Then he said, "I enjoyed it very much. I hope you did."

"Oh, yes, of course I did." In fact, she had not, had been unable to let herself go so that she might share in the pleasure. She glanced over at the crushed capsule and realized how selfish he'd been, more concerned with his own pleasure than with hers. But she also wondered whether that wasn't understandable, that perhaps she had never practiced the sort of self-indulgence in her own sexual life that created maximum enjoyment. Every time she and Hal made love, they each felt a need to satisfy the other, and for Cindy that approach had always made sense. Now, as she thought about what had just occurred in bed and about the questioin of moving to New York, she wondered whether it wasn't time to be more selfish. She'd once heard a lecture by Ayn Rand, who made the point that selfishness was only negative because we gave the word that meaning. In fact, Miss Rand told the women's club that a sense of self is positive, and all good things come out of a selfish act. Cindy had discussed the lecture with Hal that night at dinner. She told him that what Miss Rand had said made sense to her. Hal bought none of it, even after she explained to the best of her ability the underlying philosophy, that a woman does not enter the convent because of a love of God, but, rather, does it to avoid the secular life. But out of that selfish motivation come good works—the lepers are treated, the orphans fed, missions built.

"What are you thinking?" Satterfield asked.

"Nothing, really," she said, which wasn't true. She'd been telling herself that spending this time with another man was not as terrible as what her heart was screaming. She was trying to divorce her intellect from her emotions, to convince herself in a clear and cognitive way that she was entitled to pleasure simply for herself.

"You're a beautiful woman, Cindy," Satterfield said.

"Thank you, but I don't consider myself beautiful."

"You should. If you don't no one else will."

"Then why do you?"

"A natural eye for beauty," he said, chuckling. He dipped his index finger into the cognac and rubbed it on her nipple. His mouth found it and he made sucking sounds of enjoyment.

Cindy fought the feelings inside her. She'd always had sensitive breasts, and the feel of his lips and tongue on her sent a direct message of sexual yearning to her groin. He moved to her other breast, and his hand found her beneath the sheets. She wanted to get out of bed, get dressed, and race back to the hotel, forgetting this night had ever happened, wiping it from her consciousness, denying even the possibility of it, but she did not, could not. She found her body relaxing beneath his caresses and she adjusted herself to better accommodate his exploration. When he'd brought her to a state of intense need for release, he reached into the night table drawer and pulled out another capsule.

"Please, don't use that," she said.

"Why not?"

"Don't use anything."

They fell asleep in each other's arms. Cindy was spent from the intensity of her orgasm. She awoke an hour later and stared at him. He slept soundly, his face contented and relaxed, almost boyish. She almost got up, dressed, and left. Instead, she pulled the covers up to her neck and dozed off.

Now, it was morning. She slipped out of bed and went to the bathroom. She wanted to shower but decided to wait until she returned to the hotel. She brushed her teeth with her finger, ran his comb through her hair, returned to the bedroom, and dressed. By now he was awake and sitting up, grinning.

"I have to go," she said.

"Sure, I know. Have a good day."

When she returned to the hotel the red light on her telephone was flashing. She called the desk and asked who had left a message. "Your husband, Mrs. Lewis," the switchboard operator said. "He left a message informing you that he's catching the nine o'clock flight and will be in New York this afternoon."

"That's all?"

"Yes, ma'am."

"Thank you very much."

Chapter 23

Veronica Frazier was to meet the film crew at seven A.M. in a coffee shop at Lexington Avenue and Ninety-eighth Street. She was early. She sat in a booth and ordered coffee and a toasted English muffin.

She spread that morning's *Daily News* on the stained Formica tabletop and browsed through it. There was little that captured her attention until she reached the entertainment pages. There, on the television page, were photographs of her, Cindy Lewis, and Maureen O'Dwyer. The accompanying story was brief and to the point. The Empire Broadcasting System had announced it would choose a new female anchor for its evening network news. The Brickhouse Award dinner, which was to be held the following night, was mentioned as playing a role in the selection. The item also said that the three candidates would appear that evening on *Lively Five*.

Veronica's reactions were mixed. There was a natural excitement at seeing her photograph in a major New York newspaper. On the other hand, there was a certain resentment of the way things were being handled at EBS. Surely, she reasoned, there should have been extensive discussions with her and the others about the potential for becoming the anchor. She didn't know about the leak that had prompted releasing the news.

There wasn't time to ponder it, however, because as she took her first sip of coffee the film crew arrived, led by a tall, slender, handsome young black man. He immediately came to the table, extended his hand, and said, "Good morning, Veronica, I'm Gregory Oates. All set to go?"

Veronica shook her head and smiled. "I don't know. Where are we going and what am I doing exactly?"

Oates smiled broadly and slid into the booth across from her. Two other crew members joined them and introduced themselves.

"I'll fill you in the best I can," Oates said. "How's the coffee?"

"Not bad."

"You guys hungry?" he asked his crew. One of them nodded. He motioned for a waitress to take their orders, turned to Veronica, and scrutinized her through narrowed eyes. "Boy, oh, boy, you are as beautiful as everybody says. The picture in the *News* doesn't do you justice. Let's just hope the guy you're meeting didn't read the *News* this morning."

Ordinarily, Veronica might have been annoyed at the comment. She wasn't, however. It seemed so genuine from him that she could do nothing but smile and say, "Thank you."

"You're dressed right," he said.

Veronica glanced down at what she was wearing. She'd been told to dress casually but with some style—designer jeans, red silk blouse, a hand-tooled leather vest and boots. Her raincoat was tucked neatly into the corner of the booth.

They chatted about mundane matters until the food was served. Then, Oates said, "We've been working on this story for a month now and I think we're about to see it pay off. I saw the report you did that put you up for the Brickhouse thing and I was impressed. Obviously, you know a lot about drugs, east or west. It doesn't matter, it's all the same, except the thing we have here is a mind-blower. It's bad enough kids can buy shit on any street corner in this city, but when a prime source is one of their teachers, you know how far things have gotten out of hand.''

Veronica's response of incredulity took a little playacting. She thought back to when she was a high school student in Detroit. There had been at least two teachers in that school selling drugs to students, and although it wasn't openly accepted, there was a tacit understanding that it was simply a way of earning extra money, no different from moonlighting in second and third jobs. But she didn't tell Oates that, simply listened carefully as he told her more about the assignment. They'd managed to gain the cooperation of a major drug dealer in the city. Oates was vague about how it was accomplished, and Veronica asked.

"Well, this particular gentleman made a few mistakes and was about to get nailed for a very long stay in the slammer." Oates grinned. "A friend of mine, a narc, rung me in on it and we made a deal. The dealer helps us put together an investigative report and the police look the other way."

"What was in it for the police?" Veronica asked.

Oates sat back in the booth and lowered his chin. "A good question," he said. "What they get out of it is the goods on a string of dealers who work for our friend, including this particular teacher."

"Hands washing hands, backs being scratched," Veronica said sarcastically.

"That's reality, isn't it?" Oates asked. "Anyway, our friend arranged to deliver some shit to the teacher today, only he informed him that he couldn't do it personally and was sending a surrogate."

It took Veronica a moment to realize that the surrogate was she. "Why would he trust me?"

"Because our friend tells a good story. We helped him write it and he delivered it like a spade Richard Burton. He told the teacher that you and he went back years in the drug business, that you were his main lady, and that you were the one person in the entire world he trusted. He also told the teacher what a dynamite-looking chick you were, which didn't hurt. Along with handing out goodies to kids in school, this teacher has been known to boff a few in the supply room."

"A class act."

"Exactly. Shaping the minds and values of American youth. Okay, Veronica, here's what we do. We set up the rented truck we're using across the street from where you meet him. We give you the bag of goodies and you hand it to him in exchange for the money he'll be carrying. All we ask is that you keep him talking as long as you can. Talk about the business, about the quality of the stuff you're giving him, mention what's in the bag so that we get it on tape, and see if you can get him to confirm that he knows what he's buying and the reasons for it. Get him to talk about his customers, the kids, if you can do it without arousing suspicion. Flirt with him a little if you have to, play with his chest hair underneath the gold chain, even make a date to turn on with him later in the day. Just keep it going as long as it's safe and credible."

For the first time Veronica feared the assignment. She wasn't sure she could carry it off without planting a seed of doubt with the teacher. If that happened, there was no telling how he might respond.

Oates asked whether she had any questions.

"I suppose I'm a little surprised at the role I'm playing in this," she said.

"How so?"

"Well, I can understand going underground to *buy* drugs, but being in the role of *selling* them throws me a little."

Oates laughed gently, which only enhanced his appeal. He looked like the singer, Lou Rawls, Veronica decided, and she felt herself naturally warming to him. She thought for a moment, chewing her cheek, as she often did when mulling over a question. Finally, she said, "It almost seems to me that having a reporter sell drugs for a story puts the network in a tenuous legal position."

Oates nodded. "That was all discussed before we went ahead with it. If you were taking the money and the teacher was going to distribute the drugs, it would be a different story, but this whole thing has been choreographed in concert with the police. He'll be arrested before he has a chance to do anything with the stuff. Feel better?"

"I guess so. What time do I meet him?"

He looked at his watch. "In a couple of hours. We should be going and get set up. Ready?"

"I guess so."

They rode uptown until they reached a small grocery store on the northwest corner of a busy intersection. The sign in front of the store was in Spanish. A half-dozen people milled about in front of it, two of them adults, the rest teenagers. The driver stopped the van on the southeast corner and asked Oates where he wanted to position it. Oates looked around, spotted an empty metered space just across the corner, and said, "Let's put it there." He turned and asked the cameraman whether it would provide him an unencumbered shot of the store. The cameraman said it would, and the driver moved to the empty spot.

While the crew readied equipment in the rear of the van, with the camera lens up against a one-way window on the side panel, Oates pulled a paper bag from behind the seat and handed it to Veronica. "Here it is," he said.

"What's in it?" she asked.

"An assortment of goodies, pot, 'ludes, uppers and downers, the usual mixture."

"It's the real stuff?"

"Yup. We considered filling the bag with phony drugs, but were afraid he might take a look and get wise."

She looked out the window toward the store. The bag felt heavy on her lap, and she nervously ran a fingernail up and down it. Oates sensed her anxiety and mentioned it.

"Don't worry about me," Veronica said, "I'll do just fine."

"It's all work, Veronica. Funny, but I have trouble with that name. Are you called anything else?"

"Some people call me Ronnie."

"Can I?"

She laughed. "Of course. By the way, where are the police?"

He pointed to a corner where two Spanish-looking men leaned against a building. They were dressed sloppily, and one wore a battered cowboy hat. "There's two of them," Oates said. "That car parked down the street has a couple, too." He pointed to a battered green sedan parked in front of a hydrant.

"Will they arrest him while I'm there?" Veronica asked.

"No, we don't want you involved in that aspect of it. As soon as you're safely away they'll make their bust. We'll get that on tape, too."

Now it was just a matter of sitting and waiting. Oates filled her in further on the dealer who'd cooperated with them and on the story the teacher had been given about her. He drilled her a few times until she was completely comfortable with it, then asked if she had any last-minute questions."

"I don't think so. I just hope it works."

"It will," he said. He placed his hand on her arm and squeezed. It was a comforting gesture that she appreciated. She turned and looked into his large brown eyes and felt a wave of warmth come over her.

They passed the time making small talk. He asked her how she felt about being considered for the anchor spot.

"Mixed feelings, I suppose," she said. "That's an honest answer."

"Why would you have mixed feelings? It seems to me it would represent the culmination of a dream for anyone in this business."

"I suppose it does, and that's exactly how I felt when I first heard the rumor that there was a possibility of it. But I learned a long time ago that nothing in life is that wonderful. As they say, no such thing as a free lunch."

He smiled. "Nobody would claim, including me, that any situation represents perfection, but being a network anchor ain't bad."

"I know that, and if they offer it to me I can't imagine turning it down. But being here on this assignment raises questions in my mind."

"Why?"

"There's something very real about doing this story. It's the same feeling I had when I did the report in San Francisco. Sitting behind a desk, all the makeup in place, and reading what somebody else has written, isn't very real. I sit there night after night and can't help but realize why I'm there."

"Because you're . . ."

"Because I'm black and beautiful and can read simple words without stumbling over them. I'd rather be respected for what I can do than what I look like, what I represent."

Oates shrugged and lighted a long thin cigar. "Mind if I smoke?" he asked.

"Of course not."

"I know what you mean, Ronnie," he said in reponse to her last remark. "But the older I get, the more of a realist I become."

She laughed.

"What's funny?"

"Talking about getting old. How old are you?"

"A very old thirty."

"Oh."

"That may not seem old to you, but it occurred to me only this year that it's older than I ever thought I'd be." He turned and went over technical details with the crew in the back of the van, checked his watch, then said to her, "I think it's time you got going. I suggest you walk a few blocks north, then take a right and go down to Second Avenue. You have a half-hour before you're supposed to meet him in front of the store. The dealer told him you'd have his description so that you wouldn't have trouble recognizing him. He's a nondescript guy, about thirty-five, a bit of a paunch, and losing his hair prematurely. His glasses have clear rims, and he told our dealer friend he'd be wearing a brown leather jacket."

"Sounds easy enough."

"Comfortable?" Oates asked.

She patted her bosom beneath her raincoat, where a wireless FM microphone had been secured. "I think so."

"Good, let's go. Good luck."

"Thanks."

She walked casually up the street, pausing only once to look back at the van. The bag was securely tucked under her left arm, and she had a fleeting fantasy of being mugged and having the drugs stolen before she could deliver them to the teacher. Something blew into her eye and she paused in front of a store window and blinked until tears washed it away. Two men made suggestive comments to her, which she pointedly ignored as she continued walking. Her mind was flooded with thoughts, none of them directly related to the assignment she was about to fulfill. She tried to push them away but was only partially successful.

She reached Second Avenue and paused before turning right. Two young black boys, one carrying a huge portable radio and cassette player from which disco music blared, looked her up and down. "Hey, baby, where you goin'?" he asked.

She walked away from them and tried to bring her thoughts back to the confrontation she would soon have with the teacher. A flashily dressed young black man sauntered by and smiled. She thought of Roscoe, and the image caused her stomach to turn. Although it was cool, her forehead was suddenly damp. Her mother's face flashed before her, then disappeared in the blare of automobile horns and street noise. She was bombarded by tiny fragments of thought, sailing through her mind like electronic images on an arcade game screen, dots and dashes, annoying bleeps of sound.

As she prepared to turn west and to approach the teacher who would, by now, be standing in front of the store, she considered forgetting the whole thing. She glanced at a wire trash basket on the street and wanted to throw the bag into it and run, get on a plane and fly back to . . . to Detroit, to her mother. It was as though she were there anyway, so familiar were the situation and the feelings. The street. Men making suggestive comments. The mission, always keeping the mission in mind, the goals and dreams of escaping the street and its people and going where everything and everybody was clean and pure, where no one was used by anyone else, where there was perpetual peace.

Four youths approached her, swaggering side by side, taking up the entire sidewalk. They passed a joint back and forth, and as they got closer Veronica could see a glassiness in their eyes, the lack of reality that would rule their lives forever, victims of their birth and of a society in which birth was a role of the dice. She stepped aside to allow them to pass.

"Hey, pussy, what's your name?" one of them yelled, laughing.

"Pretty mama," said another, as he cupped his genitals and thrust his pelvis at her.

All the fears up to that moment were now washed away. She turned and walked with deliberate speed toward her rendezvous in front of the Spanish grocery store. She paused on the other side of Third Avenue. He was there, dressed as promised, looking nervously up and down the street. It appeared that he might turn and walk away at any moment. She stepped out into the street and waited until a bus had passed before crossing against the light.

He spotted her and watched as she approached. When she was within six feet of him, he again looked to his left and right, then moved around to the side of the store. Her final thought before closing the gap between them was the old joke about a monumental biblical scene being shot by Cecil B. De Mille, in which all the cameras malfunctioned except one, and when that cameraman was asked whether he'd gotten the shot he replied, "Ready anytime you are, C.B." She hoped the cameras in the van were rolling.

The first words out of her mouth were those given her by Gregory Oates. It was a code that had been established between the turncoat dealer and the teacher. "Looks like rain," she said.

"Not to me," the teacher said. He was obviously apprehensive about receiving goods from somebody new, and his eyes darted back and forth behind his glasses.

"You look uptight," she said as she stepped closer to him.

"Sure, you bet I am." He looked at the bag. "Is that it?"

"It sure is, baby."

"Let me see."

"Sure you can see, when I see what you have. You show me yours and I'll show you mine." She laughed seductively, which seemed to put him more at ease.

He took a few steps to the side and peered around the corner of the store. Confident that no one was observing them, he returned his attention to her. "Jesus, Martin was right. You are a beauty."

She smiled. "Martin has good taste, always did. Look, I don't like handing stuff over to a stranger any more than you like getting it from one. Martin and I get it on, dig? We'll be doing more of this together from now on, and I'd like to get to know you a little better, but this isn't the time. Let's do what we're supposed to do and meet up later for a cup of coffee. Right now, all I want to do is hand over this shit to you. It's all here, uppers, downers, 'ludes, good pot . . ."

"What about the coke?" he asked.

She felt a twinge of panic. Oates hadn't mentioned cocaine, and she couldn't know whether he'd simply forgotten to tell her or whether it had been inadvertently left out of the deal. She decided to assume there was no cocaine and said, "That's coming later in the day. There was a foul-up, but it got straightened out. When you and I meet up later I'll have it."

"Jesus, I didn't bargain for this. I'm paying for what I ordered, not what I'm going to get later on."

She shrugged and dug her hands deeper into her raincoat, said, "Don't pay me for the coke, then. Pay me for the other stuff and give me the rest when I deliver it to you."

He thought for a moment. "Yeah, I suppose we can do that. Where do you want to meet up?"

"You name it. You live in the neighborhood?"

"Not far."

"Great, I'll come by to see you. Just tell me where and when."

"I don't get out of school today until four. Goddamn faculty meeting. I also have to get this stuff to my runners at school."

"How many do you have?"

"Just two, seniors. I only use the smart ones." He guffawed. "One of them will probably be valedictorian this year. Okay, give me the bag." He reached into his jacket and pulled out an envelope around which two rubber bands were tightly fastened. He removed the bands, opened the envelope, and took out most of the bills in it. They were all large denominations. "I think this is fair. Bring the coke to my apartment and I'll give you the rest."

"Okay." She handed him the bag and took the bills, which she put into her raincoat pocket. "Where do you live?"

He mumbled an address and apartment number. "Make it five. I'll be sure to be there by then."

"You can count on it."

She wanted to continue the conversation but knew that would be pushing it. She turned and walked away, aware that he was watching her, headed south on Third Avenue, pausing at mid-block to turn and see whether he had turned the corner to observe her. He was gone.

As she crossed Third at the next block and doubled back toward the van, she looked up the street on which they'd stood. The two plainclothes cops had the teacher up against the wall, his feet spread wide, his head and hands pressed tightly against the wall. One was frisking him, the other held the bag. She quickly returned to the van and got in.

"Beautiful, Ronnie, absolutely beautiful. We got every bit of it."

It was as though someone had pulled the plug on her. All her energy drained out. She slumped against the seat, closed her eyes, and trembled.

Oates put his arm over her shoulder and pulled her closer to him. "Easy, easy, it's all over. Not only did we get a hell of an ending for this story, but you just helped put out of business a real creep."

She wanted to return to her hotel but Oates insisted they have lunch after delivering the tape to the studio.

They went to a neighborhood Chinese restaurant where, over a variety of dishes, they talked for two hours about their lives. It was at once a rewarding yet upsetting lunch for Veronica. She couldn't remember ever having opened up so freely to another human being, and the more she talked the more relaxed she became. But it frightened her, too, telling things to a stranger who might not be what he seemed, who might hurt her as others had. No matter, she decided. It felt good to be free and easy with him, and when lunch was over she felt a keen disappointment.

"What's on your agenda now?" he asked.

"Back to my hotel, I suppose. I have to be at the studio at four-thirty. I'm being interviewed on *Lively Five*."

"That's right, I forgot. Well, Ronnie, do your best. Fame and fortune might ride in the balance." He laughed.

She started to say something, then simply smiled and slowly shook her head. "Fame and fortune. Frankly, I got more out of this morning."

"I'm glad. Look, I don't know what your plans are for the Brickhouse dinner tomorrow night, but I'd love to sit with you."

"That would be wonderful," she said.

He took her hand and held it for a moment, his eyes searching hers for something she couldn't identify. He said, "I wish I were free tonight. I'd like to have dinner with you."

"I'm sorry you're not, but tomorrow night will be nice. I'll count on it."

She hadn't been back in her room more than twenty minutes when the phone rang. She picked it up and heard a familiar voice say, "Ronnie, baby, this is your uncle Roscoe."

"I don't want to talk to you," she said.

"Oh, you'll always want to talk to your uncle Roscoe. Hey, baby, I read the paper this morning. My little girl is about to become superstar woman, queen of the airwaves. Do you know how proud that makes your uncle Roscoe, Ronnie? Just imagine, I took that skinny little girl livin' in a rattrap in Detroit and launched her on the way to the big time. Damn, I am one proud uncle."

She hung up.

It rang moments later. She let it ring, then picked it up out of desperation.

Now, his voice was changed. He said in slow, measured tones, "Don't you ever hang up a phone on me again, you cunt. There ain't anybody in that whole fuckin' network who'd give you one minute on national TV if they knew what you really were."

She cried silently as he continued talking, threatening that he would go to the network and tell them about her if she didn't get smart and bring him in on her success. "Shit, baby, every superstar needs a manager. That's what's nice about friends, dig? Family's got to take care of each other. Now, don't you pull your bullshit on me again, you bitch. Uncle Roscoe will be waiting for you in the bar of your hotel the minute you get off that interview the paper says you're on tonight, and, baby, you had better be there."

She was incapable of rational thought for the next half-hour. She paced the floor, swore loudly, threw a telephone book across the room. Finally, she picked up the phone, dialed EBS's main number, and asked the operator to put her through to Gregory Oates, in Editing. Someone there told her that he'd gone to another facility. She was transferred and eventually reached him.

"You sound upset," he said after she'd stumbled over her initial words. "What's the matter? This thing this morning getting to you?"

"No, no, it isn't that. Look, I can't explain it now, but I have to talk to you. I know you said you were busy tonight, but if there's any chance of breaking free I'd . . . I'd be very grateful."

"Just name the time and place."

"Thank God," she muttered.

"What did you say?" he asked.

"I said . . . I'll tell you what I said when I see you. Could you be at the studio for the interview? We could leave right from there."

"You're on. I'll see you then. And, Ronnie, calm down. Whatever is getting to you can't be that bad. Hold on tight, knock 'em dead on the interview, and count on me."

"Thank you."

"That's the last time you ever say that to me. See you later."

One of the cohosts of EBS's nightly local newscast, *Lively Five,* looked up from a note he'd made on the script in front of him and waited for a red light on camera three to go on. Then he said into the camera, "Coming up now is an interview that is rather unusual, not only for this program but for television in general. Those of you who read the papers this morning are aware that this network has been committed to finding a new coanchor for the seven o'clock nightly network news. We've looked carefully at the best journalists available in America and, like a baseball team committed to growth from within, have turned to our own news organization from which to make that choice. With us tonight are three outstanding women in our profession, whose achievements in broadcast journalism have brought them to New York for tomorrow night's prestigious Brickhouse Foundation dinner. They're here because their commitment to journalism and their performance has earned them the highest regard of their peers."

Another camera slowly panned the faces of Maureen O'Dwyer, Cindy Lewis, and Veronica Frazier while the host continued to introduce that segment of the program. It came to rest on Renée Ballantyne.

"One of America's finest journalists, Renée Ballantyne,

who for the past year has applied her vast experience to the management of this network's news operations, is here in the studio with us now to talk to these three outstanding television women, one of whom may soon become a familiar and trusted national figure."

The director switched to the camera focused on Renée's face. She smiled and said, "I'm honored to have been chosen to be the one to interview these three vital, talented, and committed women. Each represents the finest example of the American woman taking her place alongside familiar male faces of television journalism. They come from diverse backgrounds and bring into their profession their own particular experiences, education, and dedication to informing the public of the important issues of our time. Let me introduce them to you."

As she recited the names, the camera paused in a close-up of each woman. Howard Monroe and Carl Schwartz stood together in the master control room and watched the monitors. The first to be introduced was Maureen. She did not look at ease, and Monroe commented on it. He said, "I've never seen that tic in her mouth before."

Schwartz wanted to respond but didn't. He watched as the camera shifted to Cindy Lewis, who sat in the middle. There was a pleasant placidity to her face, a look of contentment and wonder.

Then, Veronica's face filled the monitor. There was no denying her natural beauty, but fatigue and worry came through. "She's got a great face," Monroe said, "beautiful and appropriately world-weary."

"Maybe she didn't get much sleep last night," Schwartz said.

"She was up early on that school drug assignment this morning," Monroe said. "I understand it went well."

"Yes, I heard that, too."

Renée shifted in her chair so that she was facing the three women to her right. She said, "Millions of Americans are going to want to know your views on television news. There is a growing cynicism about the quality of news presented on television, and the credibility of those coming into American living rooms every evening will be of great importance. Maureen, what do you feel is most important in this regard?''

Maureen's green eyes had trouble coming to rest on the source of the question. When they did, she said in a voice honed by years of reporting, ''I think the American public is tired of news being treated as show business. Part of the problem, I believe, is that we've so grossly underestimated the public. We assume they want their news delivered in the same fashion as sitcoms and game shows. This world is too complicated and volatile to take that approach. I've been directly involved in many of the most meaningful stories of our time, and we must assure our viewing public that what we report to them is accurate, honest, and more than a quarter-inch deep.''

''Cindy?'' Renée said. ''What do you feel is most important?''

She bit her lip and opened her eyes wide, which caused Carl Schwartz and Howard Monroe to smile as they watched from the control room. They expected her to begin by saying, ''Golly,'' but she didn't. Her expression quickly shifted into one of thought and concern as she said, ''I don't think people believe other people anymore, and that's a shame. Everywhere I go people are cynical about the things that mean a great deal to me.''

''Such as?'' Renée asked.

''Such as government and education and, of course, news. I think people in this very difficult and confusing age need to have faith, and I would like to be able to give them that. I come from a small town, like small towns where most Americans live. I like to think of myself as an honest person who's interested in the world my children are going to inherit. I want to make it a better place for all of us, and I think one of the most important things is to understand it. That's always what I've tried to do in my career as a broadcaster, to understand it myself and to have other people understand the world they live in.''

"Not bad," Schwartz said to Monroe.

"Boiler plate," Monroe said.

"Veronica, you come to us from San Francisco. What do you think is most important in the role of a national television journalist?" Renée asked.

"I have no idea," Veronica said. She hadn't been thinking about the question because her mind had been dwelling upon the events of the day, the assignment that morning, the call from Roscoe, the fact that Gregory Oates stood in a corner of the studio and waited for her. Just before Renée asked the question, Veronica had been pondering whether she could tell Oates everything. Renée's question had snapped her out of her reverie. She gathered her thoughts and said, "I think one of the problems in journalism is too much thought about how it should be done, how an anchor should conduct herself. I just don't know how to answer your question because I spend more time thinking about life and my role in it than about how to be a popular newscaster. Probably most people who watch the news feel the same way. They're trying to make something of their individual lives, and a war in the Middle East, a coup in South America, or a rape and mugging in . . ." She hesitated. ". . . in Detroit doesn't have much relevance to them. People are trying to pay for a house and raise their children decently and keep from becoming a statistic with a failed marriage. I really haven't had time to think about bigger, maybe more important things than my own life. I suppose that's the key to being a good newscaster, to understand that people watching are just the same as the newscaster, have the same problems and dreams."

"Jesus Christ," Monroe said, "is she going to cry?"

"It looks like she's done a little of that already," Schwartz said.

The camera returned to Renée, who said, "I'm sure our viewers would like to know something about each of you on a personal level. Would you mind telling us very briefly who you are?" She smiled warmly.

Since she hadn't directed the question at anyone in particular, the camera pulled back and took in all three. They glanced at one another before Cindy Lewis said, "There isn't much to say about me. I'm married to a wonderful man named Hal. I have wonderful children and a beautiful house in Texas. I love to cook, to take care of my family, and to do my job. I guess you could say I'm a pretty simple person."

Maureen's face broke into a smile that was both understanding and cruel. She said, "From the work I've seen you do, Cindy, I'd say you're anything but simple."

Maureen's comment seemed to fluster Cindy. She managed to say, "Thank you. Coming from someone of your ability it's a real compliment."

"Maureen?" Renée said. "How about your personal background?"

Maureen was tempted to quip that Renée knew full well about her personal life, but she knew it would be inappropriate. She said, "I'm a midwestern girl. I live in Washington and have been reporting news from our nation's capital for a number of years now, as many viewers know. I love theater, the opera, music, the Washington Redskins, but more than anything I like being a reporter. I've devoted most of my adult working life to becoming the best possible journalist I can be, and I want to apply the sum and substance of my years of experience to reporting nationally those things that have a direct impact on everyone who sits in front of a television set in search of answers to our day's perplexing questions."

Veronica didn't wait for Renée to direct the question to her. She said matter-of-factly, "I'm black. I come from Detroit, where my mother supported our family by cleaning other people's houses. I'm proud of my family and proud of what I have been able to accomplish in my life. I don't believe that people should look down on any other group of people. I believe in equality, but I think every person must work hard to earn it, and should not expect it simply because they were fortunate enough to be born in

America. I did what I had to do to make something of my own individual life, and I intend to do just that for the rest of it. I grew up in Detroit, went to school there, and then moved to California, where I received my degree from the University of California at Berkeley. I work at the EBS television station in San Francisco. It's a beautiful city and I've found happiness there. I love to read, I like to listen to jazz because my father was a jazz musician and played records at home when I was growing up. I enjoy being a broadcaster. I like the fact that people know me and respect me for what I do on television, but more than that I want to be respected as a person. If I am, then everything else makes sense.''

Renée glanced at the floor director to see whether she should continue the segment or whether time was running short. He answered by pulling apart with his hands an imaginary string of taffy. The gesture meant to stretch the interview, to continue with it and to fill time that obviously was available, a decision made in the control room and transmitted to the floor director through his headset.

Renée had not expected the interview to go this long. The essence of journalism, it seemed, was to deliver many bits of information but never to allow one thing to extend beyond the viewers' threshold of boredom. She wasn't quite sure what to ask next; then she looked at Cindy Lewis and said, "You're a woman, Cindy, with whom millions of American women can identify. If you become coanchor of our network newscast each evening, what will that do to the quality of your life as a wife and mother? Have you thought about that?''

"Yes, I certainly have. I know that many women would disagree with me, but I believe the most important thing in a woman's life is to establish a strong, loving, and committed relationship with a man, and with a family you create together. It always bothers me that women who believe in that are made to feel guilty about it. I hate it when someone asks what you do and the woman says, apologetically, 'I'm just a housewife.' I can't imagine a more important job than being a wife and mother. There is nobody else in this world more responsible for shaping the kind of citizens my children become than me and my husband. That doesn't mean I don't believe in many things that the feminist leaders believe in. I want to be paid the same for doing the same job as a man, and for doing it as well. I want to have the opportunity to work in a field that interests me. But when all is said and done, my job at the television station in Amarillo, or my job as coanchor of the network newscast, should I be given it, will never even come close to the importance of being a mother to my children and wife to my husband.''

"Maureen?" Renée asked.

Maureen resisted debating Cindy about the role of women in society, so she simply said, "I agree completely. Each of us must make a decision about what we do with our lives, and one person's decision is as valid as the next. I don't happen to be married, so I don't have the same conflict as Cindy. I believe that individuals should be left alone to make their own decisions, to follow their respective hearts, and to create for themselves the most rewarding, fulfilling, and productive lives they can.''

"Veronica, how do you feel about this?" Renée asked.

"I'm not married either. I don't have children. That doesn't mean that I don't believe in those things. My life to this point has followed a career instead of marriage. If, someday, marriage enters into my life, I will happily embrace it and be the best possible wife and mother I can be. In the meantime, I'm sitting here as a professional young woman being considered for a very important position in American broadcasting. I ake things one day at a time, and I don't know any oth r way to approach it.''

Renée glanced up at the floor director, who was waving his index finger in the air, meaning that she should wrap it up. She looked into the camera and said, "I think you'll agree that sitting with me are three very remarkable women. One of them may win an award at the Brickhouse dinner tomorrow night, and one of them will be a nightly fixture on television sets across America. I wish them all well, and know that no matter what occurs, they have already made a positive contribution to the world in which they live. Thanks for being with us tonight, and now back to you, Charles."

Lively Five's cohost took it back from Renée and began reporting on a major dock fire that had been raging all afternoon. The microphones were removed from around the necks of the three women and they followed Renée out of the studio and to the dressing room.

"I've never been so excited in my life," Cindy said.

"Good job," Maureen said to Renée.

"I'm exhausted," was Veronica's comment.

Someone from the production staff came into the dressing room and handed a slip of paper to Cindy. On it was a message taken by an operator at EBS. She beamed and said, "Hal is here, my husband. He flew up just to be with me at the dinner tomorrow night."

"That's wonderful," Maureen said.

Greg Oates entered the dressing room. "What suspense," he said. "Which one will be crowned queen of the network?"

Renée gave him a look indicating her displeasure at his flippancy. He ignored her and said to Veronica, "Ready?"

"Yes." She thanked Renée for the interview, turned, and left the room with him.

"I like her," Cindy said to no one in particular. When she didn't receive any reaction, she excused herself and went to a phone, where she dialed the hotel. Hal answered in her room.

"Honey, how wonderful that you're here. Did you have a good trip?"

"We were delayed because of weather, but it all worked out pretty good. Where are you?"

"Didn't you see me?"

"See you where?"

"On television. I was just interviewed on *Lively Five*."

"I didn't know."

"Of course you didn't, I'm sorry. I'll be there as soon as I can. I'm leaving right now."

"Fine. By the way, there was a phone call for you here in the room."

"Really? who was it?"

"Herb Machlin. He seemed a little upset when I answered."

"Oh, he's the executive I told you about who'll help make the decision about the anchor job. I'll tell you all about it."

"Okay. I'm starved."

"You always are. That's what happens when I leave, you miss my cooking."

He laughed. "Just get here as soon as you can. I miss you, Cindy."

"And I missed you, too."

Maureen and Renée remained in the dressing room. Renée asked how Maureen felt the interview had gone.

"Good, although I could have done without the personal questions. By the way, Julie is here."

Renée's surprise was genuine. She started to ask, but Maureen cut her off. "I think it will all work out. Anything new on the decision?"

"No, Mo. Believe me, if anything does develop I'll let you know immediately."

"Thanks. I think I'd better get back to the hotel. It isn't easy having Julie here, especially under the circumstances."

"Is she here to stay?" Renée asked.

"No, of course not. Just a visit. We'll spend a couple of days together and then she'll go back to Kansas City. You did a good job, Renée, you always do. You probably should have stayed on the air instead of going into management."

"Sometimes I think the same thing. I miss that red light."

"And that hot mike. God, it is seductive, isn't it?"

Renée smiled, walked her to the door, and wished her a good night.

Veronica and Greg Oates went to the Bull & Bear, where they settled in at a table and ordered drinks. After an awkward silence, he leaned across the table and asked, "What's wrong? Boy, lady, when I heard you on the phone this afternoon, I knew I was talking to somebody who was carrying a hell of a weight around with her. Let's not play charades. We don't know each other very well, but I like you, and that's a fact. Lay it out on the table quick and simple so that we don't waste the evening."

Tears welled up in her eyes and she hated herself for it. Her operative philosophy for so long had been that no one, nothing, was worthy of her tears. She'd done her crying as a child and teenager. Now, tears could accomplish nothing. But those convictions had gone down the tube today. She fought her emotions, drew a deep breath, pressed her lips together, and rolled her eyes toward the ceiling. Once she was certain she had control, she leaned forward and said, "This beautiful, talented, and black Berkeley graduate who's up for a Brickhouse Award, and who might become coanchor of a nightly network newscast across America, was a hooker, b-a-b-y. This impressive example of American black womanhood ran drugs in Detroit and put the money in her pocket. This wonderful role model for young black American women did tricks on the street, went down on any white stranger who had the money to pay for it, spread her legs for whatever the market would bear, and proudly brought the loot home to Mama, who was off all day on her hands and knees cleaning vomit and shit off other people's bathroom floors."

It came out in a torrent of words, with hardly a breath in between. She slumped back in the comfortable armchair and stared at the table. Oates said nothing. Finally, she looked up at him. He cocked his head and smiled.

"What the hell are you smiling at?"

"You. It must have been a rotten life. I'm glad you're out of it."

She wasn't quite sure how to respond. She'd expected something else, a lecture, disappointment, perhaps disgust. Instead, he leaned across the table, took her hand, and said, "I'm sorry."

"Sorry for what?" The anger in her voice was intense.

"Sorry that you feel that you have to tell me this. We all do what we must, Ronnie, and even though it might not be the most tasteful of things, we do it nonetheless. Hell, there are five million women out there who do the same thing because they think it's hip, dig? As far as I'm concerned, being an honest whore makes more sense. Don't get me wrong, I'm not letting you off the hook. You take an action and you live with it. What you decided to do to get yourself out of the ghetto is your business, but it will always be with you. The important thing is that you have the ability to come to peace with yourself about it. You know what bothers me?"

She dabbed at her eyes with a napkin and asked, "What?"

"Why this sudden and overwhelming need to tell me? We don't even know each other. This is the kind of thing you tell a shrink if it bothers you. What's to be gained by laying it on me?"

She told him about Roscoe and about his threats, that he was waiting for her in the hotel bar. When she was finished, he nodded that he understood, then said, "And by telling me, who's part of this wonderful EBS world, you figure you've cleansed your soul and taken away from your friend Roscoe any ammunition he had. That sounds pretty calculating to me, a little bit of the whore coming through again."

His statement shocked her. She sat straight and said, "What do you mean by that? Do you think I'm trying to clear the decks of my past so that it won't get in the way of being named coanchor? Goddamn it, you're no different than the rest."

"Maybe I am. Calm down, stop yelling. Maybe I'm as cynical as you are, and if you want me to understand what you've done, you'd better start understanding me a little. Look, I think the best thing you could possibly have done was to tell me this. You're right, the creep waiting for you at the hotel has lost his edge, even though I have nothing to do with that job. You've still managed to get rid of the fear and shame and that's good news for you. You should have done it a long time ago. Tell you what, let's finish the drinks and go on over to the hotel. Maybe I can talk a little sense into him."

"I'm afraid."

"That's the trouble, Ronnie, you've been afraid all your life. Now you don't have to be. Come on, let's wrap this up the right way. Believe me, I'm your friend. I'm in your corner. It'll be over and you'll never have to spend another second of your life worrying about whether somebody from your past is going to screw up your future."

They took a cab to the hotel and stepped inside the lobby. Roscoe was sitting at a table next to a railing that separated the main lobby from the cocktail area. He wore a gray vested suit, a bright blue silk tie, and a white-on-white shirt with an unusually high collar. Two things were on the table: a tall, exotic drink and a pearl-gray felt hat with a wide brim. He spotted them immediately, and his expression gave testimony to his displeasure that she was with someone.

"That him?" Oates asked.

"Yes."

"Remember what we decided on the way over."

"I will."

As they approached the table, Oates smiled and extended his hand. Roscoe ignored the gesture and glared at Veronica. She said, "Roscoe, this is my executive producer, Gregory Oates."

Roscoe looked at Oates and said, "No need for you to be here. What I've got to say is between the lady and me."

Oates guided Veronica to a chair and sat in another, ran his tongue over his lips, narrowed his eyes, and said, "Everything you have to say to 'the lady' has already been said to me. But I thought it might make you happy to have the chance to lay your blackmailing shit on me personally. Go ahead, brother, I'm all ears."

The directness of his approach had its intended effect. Roscoe was visibly upset and obviously unsure what to say next.

"If you're having trouble getting it together, my friend," Oates said, smiling, "maybe I can help you." He looked at Veronica, then said to Roscoe, "The lady has put her act together. Whatever business you had with her before is all over, my friend. I suggest we toast her success and let it go at that."

Roscoe tucked in his chin and scrutinized Oates's face. He slowly broke into a wide, toothy grin and said, "Maybe the lady hasn't been honest with you, *my friend.*"

"Along with many things, the lady is very honest. You can take my word for it."

Roscoe leaned forward on the table. "Is that so?" he asked. "Did she tell you that she was a teenage hustler, turned tricks in the alley behind her house?"

Veronica winced at the directness of the statement. She glanced at Oates to see whether he'd been stunned by it. Obviously he hadn't. He said quietly, firmly, "I know all about that, along with everything else. You've got nothing to sell, buddy, and I suggest that you look for a living someplace else."

It now occurred to Roscoe that perhaps Oates was not everything he represented himself to be. He squinted and asked, "Are you sure you're the big man in her life? What did she say you were, her executive producer?"

"That's right. Her success is in my hands. Now, why don't you finish your drink and get lost? I'm getting tired of this conversation."

Roscoe's hand shot across the table and grabbed Oates's wrist.

"Get your hand off me, brother, before you leave here without it."

Roscoe sat back, drained his drink, and again smiled, said, "Boys like you are likely to get cut."

"Are you threatening me?" Oates asked.

"Call it what you will, brother."

"You threaten me again and you'll never cut another human being in your life. Now, get out of here and out of her life. Your days with her are over."

Roscoe stood, carefully adjusted his hat on his head, and stepped away from the table. He turned, smiled more broadly than ever, and said, "Thanks for the drink. I'll make sure to even up with you real soon."

CHAPTER 25

"Isn't it beautiful?" Maureen asked her daughter as they stood at Rockefeller Plaza.

"I've seen pictures of it, especially at Christmas," Julie said. "It's the biggest tree."

"Yes, it is." She put her arm around her daughter's shoulders and they walked up Fifth Avenue. "That's St. Patrick's Cathedral. Want to go in?"

Julie giggled. "I haven't been in a church for as long as I can remember."

"Neither have I," Maureen said. "We are Catholic, you know."

"What does that mean? Being something doesn't matter if you don't believe in it."

"Don't you believe in God?" Maureen asked.

"No, do you?"

"Sometimes."

Julie looked up at her mother, her eyes a mixture of scorn and love. The latter took over and she hugged her, then said, "Let's go inside."

They walked around the perimeter of the church, looking at artifacts on the walls, observing a handful of people praying in pews. Eventually they, too, entered a pew and sat down.

"What do you think?" Maureen whispered.

"I think it's too big."

They slid forward and knelt on the padded rails. Julie was the first to regain her seat. When her mother did, she asked her, "Did you pray?"

"Yes, I did. Did you?"

"I guess so."

"What did you pray for?" Maureen asked.

"I can't tell you because then it wouldn't come true, like blowing out the candles on a cake."

"Do you really believe that if you tell your wish it won't come true?"

"Uh, huh."

"I'll tell you what I prayed for."

"Okay."

"I prayed that you will always be healthy and will grow up to be a beautiful, successful, and happy woman."

Maureen expected Julie to be pleased with what she'd said. Instead, the girl abruptly stood and walked from the pew. Maureen followed her, tempted to pursue the matter but realizing it wouldn't accomplish anything.

"Hungry?" Maureen asked as they continued up Fifth Avenue.

"I sure am."

"What do you feel like?"

Julie shrugged. "Anything, I guess. I don't like Mexican food."

Maureen laughed heartily. "Neither do I."

A couple standing next to them as they waited to cross an intersection recognized Maureen. The woman said, "Maureen O'Dwyer?"

"Yes."

"We love you on television. We saw you tonight. I hope you get it; you deserve it."

"Thank you very much," Maureen said. Then, as an afterthought, she said, "This is my daughter, Julie."

"She's beautiful. She should have been on with you today."

"Well, she was back in the hotel watching me."

The light changed and everyone crossed the street. After they'd progressed another half-block, Julie stopped. Maureen stopped a few paces later, turned, and asked, "What's wrong?"

"Are you proud of me, Mama?"

"Of course I am. I'm not happy with what you did by running away from Grandma's house, but I'm very proud of you. You're my daughter."

"Then why don't you act like I'm your daughter? Why don't you live with me and be my mother?"

Maureen slapped her hands against her thighs and let out a sigh of exasperation. "Julie, you know the situation. You said once that you understood it."

"But I don't understand it now. I hate living with Grandma. I have a mother, and I want to be with her."

A lump formed in Maureen's throat. She tried to continue the conversation but gave it up, simply slipped her hand under Julie's arm and continued walking.

They ended up in Knickers, on Second Avenue. The bar crowd was lively and Maureen considered not staying, but an attractive Oriental hostess approached and asked if they wanted a table for dinner. They followed her to a far corner of the back room. After Julie chose a cheeseburger platter and Maureen a chef's salad, Julie said, "You were very good on television tonight."

Maureen smiled broadly. "I'm glad you saw it and think so. Do you remember Renée Ballantyne?"

Julie shook her head and drank most of the water in her glass.

"What did you think of the others?"

"I guess they're okay. Are you going to get the big job?"

"I don't know. I'd like it. Would that make you proud of me?"

"No."

"Why not?"

"Because having a mother on television isn't important

240

to me. Having a mother as my mother would make me happy."

Maureen knew the conversation was inevitable but couldn't deal with the emotional impact. It again was a matter of focusing her attention on what had taken priority in her life, success in her chosen field. It wasn't as though she'd abandoned her daughter. She sent money every month, enough to totally support her mother and Julie. The house in Kansas City was warm and secure. Julie had lots of clothes and could always look forward to a package of gifts from Washington. But Maureen also knew that it all represented her own rationalization. The girl was reaching out to her as a daughter, and the fact that she could not respond in a way that would please her filled Maureen with self-loathing. *Focus.* The decision had been made years ago and it was too late to change it now.

Their food was served and they ate in silence, Julie frequently glancing up at her mother, which made Maureen uncomfortable.

"Nice place," Maureen finally said.

"I guess so. Do you know what I prayed for in church?"

"No, what?"

"I prayed that you wouldn't get the job."

"Julie, that's terrible."

"Why? Why is it so bad that I don't want my mother to be a big shot on television? My friends don't have big-shot mothers and fathers on television. They work in factories and make meals and are together every night at dinner. What's so great about being on television, anyway?"

Maureen desperately groped for an answer that would be palatable to her. She finally said, "You have to make the best of yourself in this life. That's why I want you to do well in school and to go to college and learn something, so that you can be successful, too. This is a very difficult world, Julie, and you have to be your own person, to have something worthwhile to sell so that you can take care of yourself. The thing I want most is for you to be self-sufficient and to not have to answer to anybody else. I know it may be difficult for you to understand right now at your age, but you'll thank me for it later. You're a very special young woman, and the whole world is at your feet if you do the right things. I miss you, and I know that you miss me, but I work very hard to provide a life for myself and to support you and Grandma. I wish you could understand and appreciate that.''

"Could I have another Coke?"

Maureen reached across the table and patted her hand. "Of course you can. Have all the Coke you want.''

As they exited Knickers, Maureen recognized someone from EBS at the bar. She quickly turned her back so that he wouldn't see her and went through the door. The night air was invigorating, and Maureen had never been happier leaving a place in her life.

"What are we going to do now?" Julie asked.

"Well, we can get some ice cream if you'd like, or go to a movie. Your choice.''

"I'd just as soon go back to the hotel and watch television.''

"Television? You're visiting New York for the first time. There's plenty of time to watch television back in Kansas City.''

"I'm not going back to Kansas City, Mama.''

Maureen laughed. "Of course you are. Where else would you go?''

"I don't know, maybe to California.''

"That's absurd. You belong at home.''

"That's right, Mama, and Kansas City and Grandma's house isn't my home. If I can't be with you, I'll make my own life, just as you have. You seem so fucking proud of what you've done in television that you should be proud of me if I go out and make something of myself.''

"I don't want to talk about this. You're young and mixed up, Julie. Come on, let's get some ice cream.''

"Take your ice cream and shove it, Mama. I don't want

ice cream. I don't want to go back to Kansas City. I want
to be with my mother."

They walked across town to the hotel.

"Are we going upstairs?" Julie asked.

"Yes, I'm very tired. I have a busy day tomorrow."

"Am I coming to that dinner with you?"

"If you'd like."

"I guess there's nothing else to do."

"Oh, yes, there is, Julie. You come to the dinner with
me, and then the next day you get on a plane back to
Kansas City. Do you understand?"

The girl said nothing, simply turned and entered the
lobby. Maureen followed her and they rode the elevator to
their floor. Julie flicked on the television set and plopped
on the bed. Maureen went into the bathroom, where she
brushed her teeth, undressed, and slipped into her robe.
She returned and reclined on the bed. The program was
Love Boat, which Maureen found insufferable. She didn't
express it to Julie, however, even forced herself to laugh
when the laugh track indicated that something funny had
happened.

They watched the entire program without saying a word
to each other. During that time Maureen thought a great
deal about the circumstances of her life and having Julie in
New York. She went through every mental gymnastic she
could come up with to justify changing her mind at this
stage in her life, to dismiss the notion of climbing higher
on the ladder of success and becoming, instead, a mother
to this teenage creature who was the product of her love
for a man, no matter how brief and ill conceived it might
have been. But as hard as she tried, she kept reaching the
same conclusion, that she'd come too far to back off now.

"Want to order something up?" Maureen asked when
the show had ended and the news came on.

"If you want something. I'm not hungry."

"Neither am I." Maureen slid to the edge of her bed
and said, "Julie, I wish you could understand. I love you

as much as any mother has ever loved a child, want the same things for you as every other mother. I wish our lives were such that we could spend every minute together, but that isn't reality. I know you feel deprived and neglected, but if you look around you'll realize that it isn't true. You're a very fortunate young woman, and I'm getting a little tired of your self-pity. If things work out the way I hope they will, it might be possible for us to be together someday, but not now. Believe me, honey, your life is so much better back in Kansas City than if you were living with me. I don't have the time to be a mother the way you perceive a mother should be. Grandma is there all the time and loves you, does everything she can to make you happy. You have to begin understanding that and stop treating her so badly. She's a fine person who loves you very much and is doing something that most people in her position are not called upon to do. Please, Julie, try to understand me. I need you to understand and approve of me."

Julie leaped off the bed and slammed her hand against the on-off knob of the television set. She turned and glared at Maureen. "I don't care whether Grandma is there all the time. I don't care whether you wouldn't be home much. Damn it, Mama, I would be happy if you were home ten minutes every day, just as long as you were there and you were my mother and we were together. Can't you understand that? I love you and don't want to be in Kansas City while you're in Washington, or New York, or Hong Kong, or any other place. I love you, and if I can't be with you I don't want to live."

The intensity and sincerity of her words hit Maureen like a knife in the ribs. She leaned back against the headboard and tried to collect her thoughts. Was Julie threatening suicide? Should that kind of talk be taken seriously? Would she put her on a plane to Kansas City only to receive a call from her mother informing her that Julie had put her head in the oven, or had slashed her wrists and bled to death in a bathtub? Would she wake up in the morning to find the window open and the curtains blowing freely into the hotel room, get out of bed and look down at a body sprawled many floors below on the streets of Manhattan? Had she misjudged, assumed too much of Julie, missed the point?

"Julie, do you want to come live with me?"

"Yes."

"Fine, then that's what will be. Will it make you happy if I turn down this job in New York and go home to Washington?"

"I don't care where we live, Mama, as long as we live together."

"Fine. I have the inside track on the coanchor job, but I love you more than the job, Julie, and if it makes you happy, I'll tell everyone in the morning that I don't want it, that I want to go back to Washington and live with my daughter." She hesitated. "Are you sure that's what you want, Julie?"

"Yes, of course. We could have a wonderful life there. Grandma could come live with us too, so that you wouldn't feel that you had to be home for me. You could do all the things you wanted to do, but at least when you did come home I'd be there."

Maureen looked down at her lap and bit her lip, then stood, extended her arms, and accepted her daughter into them. They embraced for a long time. When they disengaged, Julie was smiling from ear to ear. She asked, "Do you mean it, Mama?"

She said, "Yes," hoping the pause wasn't telling.

"We can call Grandma and tell her to ship everything right now."

Maureen shook her head. "No, no sense in doing that. It will take a while to make the plans. Here's what we'll do. You and I will have a nice day together tomorrow and go to the dinner. The next day you can go back to Kansas City and tell Grandma. She'll have to make lots of arrangements to sell the house and to pack everything. In the meantime, I'll go back to Washington and start getting things ready on that end. I know it might seem a long time to you, but it really won't be. The time will fly right by. Please, understand the need to do it right. If we do, everyone will benefit from it. How does that sound to you?''

The smile was even broader. ''It sounds terrific, Mama. I love you very much.''

They embraced again. ''And I love you, too, Julie.'' She stepped back and held Julie at arm's length. ''Hungry now?''

''I'd love some ice cream.''

Maureen dialed room service and ordered up two hot fudge sundaes. She hung up and said, ''My figure doesn't need it, but this is a special occasion.

It was the largest crowd in the history of the annual Brickhouse Awards dinner. The ballroom of the Waldorf-Astoria was packed to capacity. A society orchestra played light, danceable tunes during the cocktail hour. Although it was billed as a black-tie affair, only about a third of those attending were in formal wear.

Cindy Lewis stood with Hal near one of three bars. She drank a whiskey sour, he bourbon on the rocks. They looked out over the crowd. "Isn't it exciting?" she said.

"Lots of people, that's for sure," He looked at her and said, "This has been a wonderful experience for you, hasn't it?"

"Oh, yes, it really has, Hal. I know it probably doesn't mean anything to you, but it's been fun being with so many important people in television." She thought of the night with Paul Satterfield and her stomach twisted into a tight knot. She'd seen him as they entered the hotel. He was with a striking blond. He noticed her, too, but didn't acknowledge her, for which she was grateful.

That night weighed heavily on her. She wanted to tell Hal what had happened and to have him understand, but she was afraid. Their rules of marriage prohibited any sort of outside involvement, and they'd lived comfortably within that code all their years together. She couldn't imagine a more devastating emotional blow to anyone than infidelity. Sometimes she wondered whether Hal had always been faithful to her. It seemed that most men had their affairs, some more serious than others, some simply one-night flings on business trips. Somehow, she could not conceive of Hal ever cheating on her, and that conviction had always provided her with immense comfort. Now *she'd* broken the code and felt hopelessly shabby and cheap.

Herb Machlin approached them. On his arm was a woman Cindy assumed was his wife.

"Hello there," Machlin said. "Cindy Lewis, this is my wife, Marcie."

Cindy extended her hand to Machlin's wife and said, "This is my husband, Hal, who's come all the way from Amarillo for tonight."

Machlin and Hal shook hands.

"Having a good time?" Machlin asked.

"Yes, we certainly are," Cindy said. She glanced at Hal to see whether his face confirmed it. He smiled broadly and nodded, which made her feel good.

"Do you think you'll win?" Marcie asked Cindy.

"I have no idea, and I really don't care. Just being nominated and attending the dinner is enough for me." She grasped Hal's arm and squeezed.

"I think you'll walk off with it, Cindy," Machlin said. "By the way, you have heard that I'm no longer involved with the anchor project?"

Cindy hadn't heard it and it took her a moment to process what he'd said. When she did, she said, "I'm sorry."

Her comment caused Machlin to laugh. "Nothing to be sorry about. That's the way this business goes. By the way, heard a great joke today. This couple goes out to celebrate their twentieth anniversary. They have a wonderful dinner and they go dancing, and all the while the wife notices a little bulge in his jacket pocket. When they get home they go to the bedroom and he takes out a beautifully wrapped package, tells her it's a gift. She asks him whether it's earrings she'd liked in a store, or a necklace she'd admired, and he tells her it's neither of those things. He tells her to open the box. She does and inside are two aspirin. She says to him, 'Aspirin? I don't have a headache.' And he says, 'Great, let's fuck.'"

Marcie laughed and shook her head. Cindy laughed, too; Hal managed a smile.

"Well, so much for levity," Machlin said. "Have a good time and good luck. You deserve it."

"Thank you," Cindy said. As Hal and Cindy watched them walk away, Hal said, "Strange fellow."

"Not really, Hal. He's pretty nice. I know he wants me to win and to get the job."

Hal drained his glass, turned, and placed it on the bar for a refill. He said, "About this job, Cindy. It would mean moving to New York, wouldn't it?"

She avoided his eyes. "Yes," she said softly.

"It would mean uprooting our entire lives. The kids would have to go to school here, and I'd have to give up my business. Have you thought of all those things?"

"Yes, I have. I realize it would be the biggest decision of our lives."

He chewed on his cheek and stepped back to allow other people to approach the bar. Cindy looked at him and was overcome with love and respect. He was a fine man, totally dedicated to her and to his family, honorable and decent. She'd decided a little earlier in the evening that he was more handsome than most men in the room, and felt pride at having him at her side, at being loved by him.

"Cindy, how real is this opportunity for you?"

"What do you mean?"

"Have they offered you the job?"

She sighed and sipped her drink. "No, it isn't definite, but I understand from some people that it's likely that I will be offered it. I guess it has to do with a lot of things, including the award tonight. But what's important, Hal, is that we decide what we want to do in case it is offered. That would be too late to think about it. I'd like to know now. I know this isn't the best time to talk about it. I wish you'd come up earlier in the week."

"I couldn't get away, Cindy. Johnson was out sick and . . ."

She touched his arm and smiled. "Hal, I'm sorry, I wasn't complaining. I was just explaining how I feel about the need to talk this over."

Veronica Frazier and Gregory Oates approached the bar. She smiled at Cindy and said, "You look beautiful."

Cindy blushed and said, "Veronica, please meet my husband, Hal."

After introductions were completed, Veronica and Greg walked away. Hal asked, "She's also being considered for the job?"

"Absolutely," Cindy said. "Isn't she beautiful?"

"Yes, she is, but not as beautiful as you."

She pressed against him and ran her hand around his waist. "Hal, I love you very much. Thank you for being here."

"Let's get back to the job, Cindy. You really think you'll be given it?"

"I think it's a good possibility, honey. If I am, what do you think about it?"

He paused, then took her arm and said, "Come on, let's find a little breathing room." They went to a corner of the ballroom where they sat on chairs, their knees touching. He took her hands and leaned forward. "Cindy, I've thought a lot about this since you told me on the phone that it was a possibility. I don't want to leave Amarillo. I've built my entire life around my business. All my friends are there, the children are happy in school, and the quality of life is a hell of a lot better, I think, than here in New York. I don't know whether I could adjust to living here. I don't like big cities, as you know. When we had that opportunity to move to Dallas, I turned it down because Dallas was too big, too busy. I'm a small-town guy."

Cindy knew what was coming, and her face reflected it. She'd hoped that he would be more open to the idea of making the move if it meant an important achievement in her life. At the same time she was committed to not doing something that was disruptive to what they had. She forced a smile and said, "Hal, I understand completely. Life is too short to cause trouble between two people who love each other very much. Yes, if they offered me the job I would like to take it. I suppose it's ego. How many women get to do such a thing in their lives? But there's nothing in this world more important than you and the children, and if a decision has to be made then that's the thing that will determine it. Do you understand that? Do you believe it?"

He leaned even closer and kissed her lightly on the lips. He sat back, crossed his legs, and said, "I've thought a lot about this, Cindy, and I've decided that if this opportunity is given to you, you should take it. Hell, we've lived our entire lives in Amarillo, Texas. A change might be good for everybody. If you get the job we'll pack up and leave. It will cause problems, of course, but you've always thrown your total support behind me in everything I've tried to do with my life. I think it's time that I reciprocated."

She didn't know what to say. Her eyes filled and she swallowed a large lump in her throat. Finally, after looking everywhere but at him, she said, "Hal, you're a remarkable man. I thank God for you every day, for the fact that you chose me to love. I don't know what else to say except thank you."

He stood, twisted a little finger in his ear, and said, "Let's dance."

• • •

Maureen O'Dwyer and her daughter stood with a group of Maureen's friends near the bandstand. Julie wore a pretty flowered dress they'd bought that afternoon for the dinner. Maureen had had trouble deciding what to wear, and finally settled on a kelly-green cocktail dress scooped low at the neck. It was a dress she often turned to when faced with a dilemma. It complemented her red hair and made her feel, she thought, more feminine than did most of her other clothing.

Her friends made a big fuss over Julie, which seemed to please the teenager. Her Kansas City upbringing set her apart from other young people Maureen had met in New York and Washington. It pleased her that Julie was appropriately her age, and as the evening progressed she experienced a warmth and pleasure she hadn't felt in a very long time.

"You must be very proud of your mother," someone said to Julie.

"Yes, I am, I always have been."

"Not nearly as proud as I am of her," Maureen said.

The orchestra launched into a medley of Cole Porter tunes. Carl Schwartz, who was in the group surrounding Maureen and Julie, extended his hand to Julie and asked, "Care to dance?"

Julie's nervous reaction delighted Maureen and she laughed loudly. "Go ahead," she said. "It isn't rock 'n' roll, but you'll manage."

Schwartz led her to the dance floor and Maureen watched with pleasure. A young man who stood near her asked, "How about Mama?"

"Sure, why not?" Maureen said. As they danced she thought of Jack Maitland. He'd sent her a telegram that day wishing her luck, telling her to break a leg, and claiming he missed her. He'd signed it "love," which had touched her. She considered calling him but hadn't. The plan to bring Julie and her mother to Washington was linked, she felt, in some way, to Maitland. There had been many men in her life, but Maitland, no matter what problems they had, loomed as the one who might play the most lasting role. There were many things about him she didn't like. He was aggressive, ambitious, often cruel, and there were times when she wondered whether a sensitive bone existed in his entire body. But he excited her at the same time, and if she wanted to be completely truthful she had to admit that the traits that bothered her about him actually paralleled many of her own unattractive qualities.

The cocktail hour ended and the guests found their tables. Veronica and Greg Oates sat with Howard Monroe, his wife, and two junior staff members and their wives.

Maureen and Julie joined Schwartz and his wife and an assortment of people from News at a table close to the podium.

Cindy and Hal sat with Renée Ballantyne and her date for the evening, a handsome Italian fashion designer named Carlos who punctuated most of what he said with Italian phrases even though he'd been in the United States for forty years. Others at the table included a leading television gossip columnist and her husband, and two TV writers, one with his wife, the other with a high-energy blond who wore a leopard-skin jump suit with buttons opened to her navel and enough makeup to cover Kate Smith.

Dinner consisted of London broil, peas, cheese potatoes, salad, and rolls. The band played throughout dinner, which made conversation difficult. The columnist focused on Cindy and asked many questions in anticipation of her winning the award and, as she said, "becoming America's most familiar female television face." Cindy kept shifting the subject back to her personal life. She bragged to everyone about Hal's success in the insurance business, about her children and her home in Amarillo. At one point she pulled out her wallet and passed pictures of her children around the table.

"You're real, aren't you?" the columnist said as she looked at the photographs.

"I hope so," Cindy said.

The band played a succession of popular show tunes and the dance floor became crowded. Cindy and Hal danced. She saw Maureen sitting at the table with her daughter and it struck her that if anyone deserved the award and anchor spot it was Maureen O'Dwyer. They danced past Renée and Carlos. Renée smiled and wished her luck. Cindy thanked her and started to again express her appreciation for the interview, but the music swept the couples away from each other.

The orchestra stopped playing and they all returned to their tables. S. Carlton Borg, chairman of the board of the Brickhouse Foundation, stepped to the podium. He spent a few minutes extolling the virtues of the foundation, pointed to historic moments in its past, and proudly listed the goals for the future. He then turned the evening over to the master of ceremonies, Phil Morgan, host of a popular nationally syndicated television talk show that devoted itself to behavioral topics, especially sex. Morgan bounded to the stage, announced that in his entire career he had never been more honored than to be chosen for that evening's MC chore, and introduced the first presenter.

The early awards dealt with technical achievements, then moved on to programming concepts. The presenters and winners now included more familiar faces.

"I think we're last," Cindy said to Hal.

"They always save the best for the end," he said. He squirmed in his chair, which meant his back was bothering him.

Morgan paused for dramatic effect before saying, "Our final award of the evening is for excellence in investigative journalism. There is no higher calling in the field than this category, and it is appropriate that it's been saved for last. Presenting it is a gentleman whose columns have enlightened readers across the nation for many years. He's considered one of the finest investigative journalists of our day, and it gives me great pleasure to introduce Mr. Roger Quale.''

Quale, who wrote a syndicated column and did daily reports on a network morning program, stepped to the podium and held up his hands to silence the audience. He adjusted half-glasses on his nose and looked down at papers he'd brought with him. "There is something especially rewarding about tonight's investigative journalism award. Obviously, the feminist movement has had considerable impact on our society, because half of the nominees in this category are female. I also am aware that one of them might well become one of America's most familiar faces and voices on television. That aspect doesn't concern me, however. What is important is that each of these six people has contributed something of significance to the American public. Each of them has worked hard to develop stories that enhance our understanding of our fellow man and the world in which we live. No matter who wins, even if it is a man, I congratulate each of them for making television a more respected and trusted medium.''

He coughed, picked up another piece of paper, and introduced the six nominees. He paused, cleared his throat, and said, "And the winner is . . ." He squinted at the paper that was contained in the winner's envelope, looked up, smiled, and said, "The winner is Veronica Frazier of San Francisco.''

There was a spontaneous outburst of applause as Veronica stood, leaned over and kissed Greg, then moved gracefully toward the podium, stopping twice to acknowledge congratulations from well-wishers. She joined Quale and accepted his kiss on her cheek.

She held the statue he handed her as she stood in front of the microphone and composed herself, glanced around the room, and broke into a broad grin. The applause started up again, and she waited patiently until it subsided. Then she said, "Thank you. I did not expect this, and you can believe that. I won't bore you with a speech, but I do want to say that in order to do good investigative work you must, of necessity, be cynical about the world in which you live. That's been the story of my life, but it won't be anymore. Until recently I have not been happy with my world. That has changed for me, and tonight plays a part in that change. I just want to assure those people who have had faith in me that this award does not represent something I've done in the past. Instead, it represents my future, and I will do everything in my power to live up to it."

She accepted another kiss from Quale as she left the podium and returned to her table, where Oates embraced her.

"I'm so happy for her," Cindy Lewis said, hugging Hal.

Julie kissed Maureen on the cheek and said, "Don't feel bad, Mama."

Maureen continued to applaud as she said to her daughter, "I'm delighted for her." She turned her head slightly to the left to hide a wet glaze that had come over her eyes.

The orchestra came to life and people danced. A group gathered around Veronica's table to congratulate her. Included were Cindy and Hal, Renée Ballantyne and her date, Howard Monroe and his wife, and Herb and Marcie Machlin. Suggestions were made to get together at another place later in the evening, but Veronica begged off. "I'm exhausted," she said. "Please understand, and thank you."

Renée went to where Maureen sat with Julie. She grinned, grabbed her friend's hand, and said, "No big deal. You'll get it anyway."

Maureen nervously looked over her shoulder to see whether Julie had heard. She evidently hadn't. The expression on Maureen's face told Renée that she didn't want the girl to be party to the conversation, and Renée dropped it. She said, "How about a nightcap?"

"Yes, I'd love that," Maureen said. She turned to Julie and asked, "Would you mind if I joined some of my friends later?"

Julie shook her head. "Of course not."

Maureen and Renée agreed to meet in the lounge of the Inter-Continental in two hours. Renée and Carlos went to the dance floor. Veronica, her arm looped through Greg Oates's arm, came to the table and said, "I'm surprised you didn't get it, Maureen. You are the best."

Maureen looked up and winked. "Thanks, but you deserved it. I'm proud to be in the same business with you."

Cindy and Hal accepted an invitation to join a group of people for cocktails at the Carlyle. Cindy almost declined when she thought Satterfield and his date would be in the party, but he said they had a previous engagement. Cindy introduced him to Hal, and the two men shook hands. She hoped Paul wouldn't, with some expression or gesture, arouse Hal's suspicion. He didn't, simply said good night and left.

Hal turned and whispered in her ear, "I'm very proud of you, Cindy. I hope you know that."

She put her arm around his waist and pulled him close. "I know that, Hal, and it's all I ever need in my life. We won't stay long. I know you're tired."

"Just my back acting up a little. Come on, we'll have a good time. I should get used to New York nightlife."

Veronica and Gregory Oates went to his apartment, where he made coffee. They sat on the couch, shoes off, their fingers laced together.

"Happy?" he asked.

"More numb than happy," she said. "I'm glad it's over."

"The award or Roscoe?"

"Both. I don't think I've ever dreaded anything more than walking into that bar last night."

Oates laughed. "I think it worked. He backed off, the son of a bitch."

She stood and went to the window. He came up behind and put his arms around her waist. "What's the matter?"

She said it so softly he had trouble hearing her. "He

didn't back off completely, Greg. He called Mr. Monroe this afternoon and told him everything.''

Oates released his grip and muttered, "That bastard. What did Monroe say?''

Veronica turned and touched his cheek with her fingers. "It doesn't matter. Monroe asked me whether what Roscoe told him was true, and I said it was, every word of it. I told him it didn't matter to me, that I was glad it was out in the open so that it could be put to rest.''

"What was Monroe's reaction?''

"He said he was in my corner where the anchor job was concerned, but this situation might cause a problem. I told him I didn't care.''

"You've been through a lot, Ronnie. I'm sorry.''

She stepped closer and put her arms around his neck, her lips lightly touching his. "Don't be sorry, Greg. I'm not. I feel as though I've just woken up from a bad dream, and I don't think I've ever been happier.'' She ran her tongue over his lips and explored the surfaces of his teeth. She experienced a desperate warmth in her loins, more than passion, bound up in the comfort and security of having entered a new world from which the past had truly been exorcised. She pressed as hard as she could against him as she continued to explore his mouth, her hands gripping the back of his shirt. The hard bones of his pelvis pushed against her, thighs fused, her breasts flattened by his chest. Yet, in the midst of her intense arousal, there was something noticeably lacking, that familiar male hardness that was inevitable under the circumstances.

He pulled his head back, and she looked up into a serious, troubled face.

"What's the matter?'' she asked.

"I think we should talk.''

"All right.''

They sat on the couch and he stared across the room before turning and saying, "I don't want to lead you along, Ronnie.''

She laughed. "What makes you feel that I *have* been led along?"

"I'm talking about the personal *us*. You're very beautiful and very warm. I'm like any other man, in a sense. I respond to you on a lot of levels, but maybe the response on one of them isn't what you'd expect it to be."

Veronica said nothing. She knew what he was saying, yet could not accept it. He said it quickly, flatly. "It's true, Ronnie, I'm gay."

She turned, cocked her head, and managed a thin smile. "I'm not shocked at that, you know. It's just that . . ."

"Just that you're disappointed." His smile was filled with understanding. "I know how you feel. Frankly, if there were ever a time in my life that I wished I didn't feel this way, it's now that I've met you. The fact is, Ms. Frazier, I happen to respond to members of my own sex more than I do those of your gender. I've had sexual experiences with women, but those were a while ago. I have a lover, a male, and we share something very beautiful. I don't talk about this with many people, as you can understand. I'm not happy in the closet, but the closet seems to be the most secure place for me."

Veronica was filled with conflicting reactions. She was angry. This wonderful specimen of masculinity had excited her, and she had looked forward to extending what they had into the physical arena. She was disappointed, of course, and even had a fleeting feeling of failure for not being enough of a woman to bring out his normal male instincts.

"I can't read you," he said, touching her arm. "I've avoided situations like this for a long time because it's embarrassing for me to have to admit it, but things just developed, didn't they, between us?"

"Yes, they did, Greg," she said. She looked into his eyes and said, "You must be very strong to handle this."

"Strong? No, just human. I believe in love between people, and look for it in my own life. I don't kid myself.

Being homosexual, or bisexual, as I suppose I am, isn't something to brag about. But it represents *me,* and I want to be true to me."

He touched her hair, then wrapped his fingers in it and pulled her to him. They embraced. He ran his hand up and down her back as she nuzzled her face into his neck. They remained that way for a long time. Then she said, "It doesn't matter to me that we won't make love, but I would like to go to bed with you, Greg, just to hold and be held by somebody who means something to me."

They went to the bedroom, where they undressed and slipped into bed. He became partially aroused and she thought, for a moment, that things might magically change, but he became flaccid as quickly as he'd grown semierect. He had a beautiful body, lean and hard, the muscles of his arm and shoulders clearly defined beneath copper skin, legs long and slender. She was filled with desire, yet knew it would not be satisfied that night.

"Do you want to come to work for the special investigative unit?" he asked.

"Yes."

"What about the anchor job? It still might be offered to you, no matter what Monroe says."

"I don't want it. I have a feeling that to do that job right, you have to give up more of your life than I'm willing to, at least for now. I've sold myself every inch of the way, Greg, and I never want to sell myself again."

He sat up against the headboard and laughed gently.

"What's funny?"

"You, the situation. Here you are in bed with someone who's offering you a career opportunity, yet you're not giving up what you've been used to giving up, your body, your sex. You're in bed with a man who can't appreciate that exchange. It's ironic, if you think about it."

She did think about it and joined his laughter. "You're right. And you know what?"

"What?"

"I love you for it."

"For what?"

"For giving and not taking, even though it's because you can't."

"If I could, I would."

"I doubt that."

They fell asleep in each other's arms. In the morning, over breakfast, he asked her whether getting loose from her contract with Stanton in San Francisco would be a problem.

"I don't think so."

"Why not?" he asked.

"Because I won't let it be a problem. Is that good enough?"

"It is for me."

Cindy and Hal returned to the Inter-Continental after spending an hour at the Carlyle with people from the awards dinner. It had been a pleasant gathering, but both became anxious to leave shortly after arriving. Someone in the group had suggested going back to his apartment, where he had what he termed "prime pot and coke." A few of the others agreed, but Hal and Cindy said they were tired and wanted to get a good night's sleep.

Now, alone in the hotel, they got into pajamas and sat in bed watching an old movie on television.

"What are you thinking?" she asked.

"About nothing, really. Oh, that isn't true. I was thinking about moving to New York, about how different life will be here for us."

"Have you changed your mind?" she asked. Before he could answer she added, "It's all right if you have, Hal. I want you to believe that. I think I would like the job, but it isn't nearly as important as you and the kids. Any decision we make has to be based upon that."

He turned on his side and placed his hand on her thigh. He looked up into her eyes and said, "It's one of those situations, Cindy, that can't be ruled by emotions. Sure, I don't want to move to New York. I like Amarillo and the life we have there, and if I went with how I felt, that would be my decision. But I also realize there's more to it than that. Every decision we make can't be based upon my professional needs. You might say I've been influenced by the feminist movement, even though I don't often show it.''

She smiled softly and ran her fingers through his hair. "I don't think movements matter, Hal. What matters is what we have between us, and that's very precious."

He unbuttoned her pajama top, slid his hand through the opening, and cupped her breast. A pulse of pleasure shot through her body. She purred. More than anything she wanted to make love with him, but there was a rigidity to her body that she knew resulted from the night with Satterfield. She felt dishonorable at having betrayed the one person in her life who meant something to her, and wanted to immediately tell him everything, to get rid of it, to cleanse herself, but the words wouldn't come.

"What's the matter?" he asked.

"I'm just tense, that's all." She suddenly embraced him and said, "Oh, my God, how much I love you."

They removed their pajamas and he kissed the length of her body, his hands exploring every crevice as his lips found her most intimate parts. He mounted and entered her, but held himself away from her with stiff arms. He looked down and said, "I'm glad to be here. It feels so good being in you."

"Yes, it does."

They remained naked as they prepared to sleep, she on her left side, he snuggled in close behind her.

"I love you," he said.

"I love you, too, Hal." She paused, then turned and said, "There's something we have to talk about."

"The job? I thought that was settled."

"No, there . . . there's something else."

"Can't it wait until morning?"

"I suppose so."

"Then let's save it for breakfast. I'm beat."

"I know, I know." She kissed his forehead and turned once again on her side, listening for hours to the heavy breathing that accompanied his sleep.

Maureen had been waiting a half-hour in the lounge of the hotel before Renée arrived. She apologized, claiming she'd had to get rid of Carlos, which wasn't easy.

"How's Julie?" Renée asked.

"Fine. She's upstairs watching television. She's an addict."

Renée laughed, ordered a cognac, and slipped her shoes off beneath the table.

"So, Renée, tell me about the comment you made at dinner, about my getting it anyway. Is that firm?"

"Nothing is firm in this world, Mo, which you know. But I think it looks pretty good. Howard has ruled out Veronica Frazier."

Maureen's eyes opened wide. "Why?" she asked. "The girl just won an award tonight."

"Well, it's a long story that I'd just as soon not get into. The important thing is that Frazier is out of the running."

"What about Cindy Lewis?"

"She still has her fans within the department, but I have a funny feeling about her."

"Which is?"

"That she wouldn't take it if it were offered to her."

"Which leaves me. Should I be flattered or feel I'm winning by default?"

Renée shook her head and rolled up her eyes. "There you go, Maureen, finding the negative in everything. No, the one who deserves it is you. We all know that. We're having a meeting tomorrow to resolve this. I'll call you the moment a decision has been reached."

They spent the next half-hour discussing the awards dinner and the people who'd attended. Maureen ended the evening by saying, "I have to get to bed, Renée. I'm taking Julie to the airport first thing in the morning. She's going back to Kansas City."

"Give her my love."

"I will." They stood and shook hands. "Thanks for everything."

"No thanks necessary. Frankly, we'll all be glad when this circus is over and we can get back to the business of running a news department."

"Amen."

Maureen went to her room, where Julie had fallen asleep on the bed, the television blaring. She tiptoed across the room and went to the desk, took a piece of hotel stationery, pulled a pen from her purse, and began to write:

My Dearest Julie,

I don't know whether you will ever understand me or the things I do in my life, and perhaps it's asking too much for you to understand at your age. Having you with me in New York these few days has provided the happiest moments of my life, and you must believe that.

I hope and pray that someday you will gain the maturity and wisdom to look back and realize that what I am about to do does not define the love I have for you as a mother. Love is an individual thing, and each person responds to it, and demonstrates it, in different ways. I don't wish to come off a martyr with you, but I do feel very deeply that the decision I've made as I write this letter is in your best interest.

I meant it when I agreed to have you come live with me in Washington. But sometimes our hearts get in the way of our heads and we have to look at a situation with more than pure emotion. I am about to be offered the job as anchor of the evening network news. I've spent my entire life trying to achieve that sort of success in my business, and now that I am at the threshold I cannot, will not walk away from it. It is a decision that I dread, and yet I know it must be made. Were I to return to Washington there would be no debate about having you come live with me, but being in New York and working under the pressure of that job is not compatible with being a mother to a teenager in New York.

I want you to stay in Kansas City with Grandma, at least until things change in my life that would make it more sensible for you to live with me. In the meantime, I can only ask that you try to understand, that you respect me as an individual and human being and that you realize that I love you, love you more than anything in the world. It may not seem that way. It probably appears to you that I love this new job more than I love my daughter, but if you stop to really think about it, this decision doesn't have to mean that. I need the peace of mind of knowing that you are safe and secure with Grandma so that I can devote my full energy to fulfilling the faith people are showing me by giving me such an important job in television.

I have to admit that I don't have the courage to say these things to you face to face. You'll be getting on the plane in the morning and going back having been lied to by me, and I am not proud of that. But there are many things in life that we are not proud of and yet must live with, and I must live with this.

I've spent my adult life in a field of communications, and yet I'm not able to communicate directly with the one person in this world whom I truly love.

I'm sorry, Julie, but this is the way it must be.

Love,
Mother

She carefully folded the sheets of paper, slipped them

into an envelope, and addressed it to Julie in Kansas City. There were two other letters on the desk she'd intended to mail. She put the three together in her purse, closed it, and went to the bed where Julie was asleep. She touched her daughter's shoulder. "Wake up, honeybunch, get undressed and let's go to bed."

Julie yawned, stretched, and opened her eyes. She smiled.

"You fell asleep," Maureen said.

"I know. I'm glad you're back." She stood on the bed, which made her taller than her mother, and gave her a hug.

Maureen disengaged and went to the bathroom, turning as she was about to close the door and saying, "Come on, get changed. That plane leaves early in the morning."

The meeting took place in Howard Monroe's personal conference room. Attending were Monroe, Carl Schwartz, Renée Ballantyne, Jenkins Drew, who'd been invited more as a courtesy than for any other reason, Jim Hanratty, and two representatives of the Corsan Group, the organization retained by EBS to study audience reaction to the anchor candidates.

Monroe introduced the Corsan people. They went to the front of the room, where an easel held a series of charts and graphs. One of the men, small and slender and wearing a tweed suit and red bow tie, unveiled the first chart and began the presentation. It was highly technical and was based on a series of measured reactions of people who had volunteered to view pieces of tape and film and to allow their physical and chemical reactions to be qualitatively determined and plotted.

It took a half-hour for the Corsan scientists to present their findings. When they were through they invited questions.

Carl Schwartz shifted in his chair and asked, "Are you saying that none of the candidates tested out positively? Is that what you're telling us with all these numbers and pretty pictures?"

"Exactly," the professional Corsan scientist said. "We established what we felt were reasonable minimums in terms of reaction. None of the candidates met those minimums."

"Because enough saliva didn't flow?" Schwartz asked, unable to disguise the scorn in his voice.

The Corsan scientist did not seem offended by the tone of his question. The other man at the easel, a rotund gentleman with a cherubic face and perpetual smile, said, "We also collected subjective reactions from the people tested. Their comments were codified and included in the overall findings. Chart number seven dealt with that. If the decision were to be made purely on the basis of those subjective reactions, there's no doubt that Miss O'Dwyer should be chosen. But reactions like those are not to be trusted. People often say things that they think you want to hear, which is why the scientific testing is invariably more accurate. Although Miss O'Dwyer scored highest on the subjective comments, the visceral response to her as measured was lowest of the three."

Monroe asked, "What was the breakdown of men and women in the study?"

The one with the bow tie went back to a previous chart and said, "Here are the demographics. Perhaps I went over them too fast."

Monroe waved his hand. "No, I just forgot, that's all."

There were a few more questions, then Monroe thanked the Corsan representatives for their presentation. They left the room, and Monroe looked at those who remained. "Well," he said, "the boys in the lab say we don't have an anchor out of the three. How do you feel about it?"

"You know how I feel," Schwartz said. "I think it's all a lot of goddamn nonsense. I think we should ignore it and make our choice right now based upon our professional judgment."

Monroe drummed his fingers on the conference table and bit his lip. "I'm not sure we can simply ignore a study like this. Hell, we commissioned it, and if we're going to ignore it we've wasted a hell of a lot of money.''

"Maybe we should simply take from it the results of the viewer comments,'' Renée said. "You know I'm in Maureen's corner, and I think Carl is, too. If the viewers they used in the study decided they liked her best, that's good enough for me.''

"But not for me,'' Monroe said. "Besides, there are other considerations.'' He looked at Jenkins Drew, who'd said nothing so far. He was immaculately dressed in a three-piece suit and looked very much like a model in a clothing ad. "Even though Entertainment has been taken out of this decision-making process, I don't want to ignore input from you, Jenkins, or from your people. What do you feel about it?''

Drew looked around the table, then said, "Of the three, the last one I would choose is Maureen O'Dwyer. She's too hard, too much the professional journalist. No matter what you think, ladies and gentlemen of News, viewers don't respond to professional excellence in journalism. They respond to something more intangible, a face, a smile, a manner on camera. Frankly, I agree with Corsan. None of them really hits me hard, and I think we'd have a hell of a time promoting one of them into a position that would significantly boost ratings. Simply having a new face would probably bring us up a point or two, but that isn't good enough, and I think we all know Mr. Rachoff won't stand for a temporary, short-lived success.''

Jim Hanratty, vice-president of public relations, chimed in. "Jenkins is right, of course. The only one of the three that I would be comfortable with as a promotional vehicle is the black gal from San Francisco, Frazier, but Howard tells me that circumstances have arisen that could rule her out. Maureen O'Dwyer is exactly what Jenkins said. She's a pro, and we all know that, but she's not what a top-rated anchorperson is made of. I'd hate to be in the position of having to hype her to a point where Rachoff and the stock-holders are satisfied. As for the Lewis gal from Amarillo, I don't see her at all. She's cute and there might be an initial *pleasant* reaction to her, but it wouldn't last very long. Frankly, I think we ought to drop all three and go after somebody else. I know that delays things, but I also know that Rachoff would be happier with that than seeing us try to make something out of nothing.''

Monroe nodded. ''I agree. I don't see anything else we can do but look elsewhere.''

Schwartz stood. ''If that's the decision, I'd just as soon end the meeting. I have other things to do.''

''Is it decided, then?'' Monroe asked. ''Do we drop the idea of using one of these three women as anchor and find her somewhere else?'' When no one responded, he said, ''Fine. I'll tell Mr. Rachoff the decision, explain it to him fully, and let you know what's been decided. Thanks for being here this morning. Maybe we can meet this after-noon after I get more input.''

Five minutes after the meeting broke up, Monroe came to Renée Ballatyne's office. He closed the door and said, ''I want to bounce something off you.''

''What is it?''

''Have you considered getting out of management and going back on the air?''

''No.''

''Would you? If I were to suggest to Rachoff that we tap you for the anchor spot, would you do it?''

''Absolutely not.''

''That firm?''

She smiled. She'd been thinking for the last five min-utes about breaking the news to Maureen. She didn't look forward to it but she intended to place a call to the hotel later in the morning and invite her to lunch.

''Why not?'' Monroe asked. ''The comments after you did the interview with them were a good indication, I think, that it would work. You're beautiful, bright, tal-ented, and a familiar face. You combine all O'Dwyer's professional qualities with a softness that she doesn't have."

"My goodness, Howard, I haven't received such flattery from a man in a long time. Are you sure you aren't responding personally to me and suspending professional judgment?"

"No, I'm not. Think about it, Renée. That's all I ask. Frankly, I'm not champing at the bit to tell Rachoff that after all this time and money we came up a cropper. I'd like to suggest you to him because he might buy it."

She said nothing, just stared at him blankly.

"Well, will you at least allow me to suggest it to him and promise that you'll think it over?"

She closed her eyes, leaned back, nodded, and said, "Sure, Howard. Go ahead and suggest it. But be warned. I don't want it."

_____CHAPTER 28

"Well?" Hal asked Cindy after they'd finished breakfast in the hotel coffee shop. "What was it you wanted to talk to me about last night?"

Cindy dreaded reaching the point where she'd actually be called upon to tell him she'd been unfaithful. As much as she wanted to admit it and get it out in the open, the contemplation of actually having to look into his eyes when she did was excruciating. She buttered another piece of toast and dipped it into a cup of lukewarm coffee.

"Cindy," Hal said, "what was it you wanted to tell me?"

"Just a silly thought I had, Hal, that's all. Nothing that can't wait until we get back to Amarillo."

"I don't like that, you know."

She smiled.

"Remember years ago when we agreed that we would never say we had something to talk about and then put off the actual conversation until another day? It's so damn frustrating. Remember that promise we made?"

She nodded and finished the toast. "I'd love some fresh coffee. Would you?"

"I've had enough." He leaned across the table and took her hand said, "No games. You're driving me crazy."

Her laughter was forced. She lifted his hand and kissed the back of it, then said, "I told you it was nothing, silly. I'm sorry I even brought it up. Please, let's just forget the whole thing."

A waitress refilled her cup and Cindy added cream and sugar with exaggerated flourish, aware all the while that Hal was watching her from across the table. She lifted the cup to her lips, smacked them, and said, "Ummmmmmmm, good coffee. Sure you don't want more?"

He couldn't help but smile now that he knew she was deliberately avoiding the issue. He said, "Positive. Frankly, the coffee you make back home is a hell of a lot better than this. Come on, Cindy, tell me what's on your mind and let's get it over with."

She knew it was no use. He wouldn't let go of it for the rest of the day, and if she hoped to have any sort of relaxed time with him she would have to tell him something. She considered making up a story, but none of the things she came up with made sense. She reasoned, of course, that it would be more pleasant simply to avoid telling him anything than to face his reaction to her admission that she'd been, after all these years, unfaithful, had betrayed the trust he'd placed in her. Had she the power, she would have erased the night with Paul Satterfield that had represented neither pleasure nor fulfillment. *How stupid, how utterly, damnably stupid and impetuous,* she said to herself. She felt what someone in prison must feel for having had a momentary lapse in judgment and paying for it for many years behind bars. She was behind her own bars at that moment, and groped for a way to be free.

"Well?" Hal asked.

She stood, wrapped a scarf around her neck, and said, "It's so hot in here. I need some air." She looked at him. He hadn't moved. "Please, Hal, I don't feel well."

They stood in front of the hotel for a few minutes and watched a passing stream of people on the sidewalk.

"Are you okay?" he asked.

"Yes, much better. It was so stuffy in there."

He took her hand and they walked up the avenue, pausing to peer into shop windows.

"It's an amazing city, isn't it?" she said.

"Big, that's for sure. It'd take me a long time to get used to it."

"Maybe we won't have to. After all, they haven't offered me the job."

"But you think they will?"

"That's what I've been told, but who ever knows?"

They said nothing else for blocks. It felt good to have her hand in his, to have him there with her, and she appreciated the fact that he had not pressed again for an explanation of what was on her mind. As they continued walking an acute fright gripped her. She had an overwhelming need to run. It didn't matter where, as long as it was away from New York, away from the realization that it was in this city that something she'd always considered sacred had become shabby and cheap. Hal sensed the change in her and put his arm around her. He asked, "Cold?"

"No, just anxious to get on a plane and go home."

He placed both hands on her arms and intently surveyed her face. "Cindy, enough of this. It doesn't matter what it is you want to tell me, but if you don't, it's going to create a gap between us that neither of us needs. Did something happen here before I arrived?"

She guffawed. "Of course not. What could have happened?"

"Was there another man?"

She drew her lips into a thin line and vehemently shook her head. "Of course not. Why would you even think such a thing?"

She started to walk away but he gripped her tightly and said, "Tell me, damn it. Was it that Machlin character?"

Her legs shook and her heart beat so fast and loudly that she wondered whether he heard it. "God, no. Do you really think I could betray you for someone like him?"

Now it was Hal's turn to be angry. He snapped, "I

don't want to be in the business of making judgments about the relative worth of a man, whether he's handsome or smooth enough to entice you into an affair. Don't play games with me, Cindy. I've come all the way up here to be with you and to support you. It's taken a lot for me to do it, and now I feel as though I'm being toyed with. Was there someone at the awards dinner who you'd slept with? If there was and you didn't tell me, I'm not sure I'll ever stop hating you. It's one thing to betray a marriage, but it's another to make me look like a fool."

A few people stopped to observe their conversation. It had become animated and had all the trappings of a public fight, which always seemed to capture interest on the street.

"Let's walk," she said.

He continued to hold her hand as they turned west. They walked to the river and stood on a decrepit abandoned pier. Across the river were rows of high-rise apartment buildings. Cindy said, "All those people living there, each of them with their own lives and problems."

"Would you like to live there?" Hal asked.

"No."

"I mean when we move to New York."

She turned and buried her face against his chest. The crying started as a series of hesitant shudders, then erupted into uncontrollable sobbing. He held her closer and said over and over, "Cindy, what's wrong, what's wrong?"

She pulled away from him and went to a rotted piling. She leaned against it and looked down into river water slick with shimmering multicolored oil and pollution. "I slept with another man," she said.

Hal had not reached her yet, hadn't quite heard what she'd said. "What was that?" he asked.

She spun around and pressed her hand against her face, her fingers spread across her nose and cheeks. She said into her hand, "I slept with another man."

It looked to her as though Hal had been rammed in the back with a lance. He stiffened, and his face turned to granite. It was obvious he wanted to say something but was incapable of it. A strong breeze came off the river and blew his hair into a salt-and-pepper beehive. She wanted to reach out to him but was afraid.

"Hal, I'm so sorry."

He turned and walked with deliberate, wooden strides across the pier, stopping at the opposite edge. He peered into the water, and for a moment she wondered whether he might jump. She started to run toward him but stopped halfway and said in a voice loud enough to carry over the wind, "Hal, I love you so much. I know how you feel and I would do anything if it hadn't happened. You must believe me. There is no man or thing in this world that means more to me than you. Please, please, oh, God, please try to understand and forgive me."

He kicked an empty fast-food box into the water and tapped his toe on the spot where the box had stood, then turned to his right and slowly walked toward the street.

"Hal," she cried.

He stopped, looked up into a pristine blue sky, and said over his shoulder, "We have a reservation back to Amarillo in the morning, Cindy. It's TWA and leaves from Kennedy Airport at nine-forty-five. I assume you'll be there."

"Where are you going now?"

"Does it matter?"

She looked down at the silver planks of the pier and said into the wind, "I suppose it doesn't." When she looked up he was gone.

She walked for hours, stopping neither to look in shop windows nor to observe the rich tapestry of Manhattan street life. It was as though she had been struck deaf and blind, a person in a void incapable of input from things or people around her. Eventually, she went into a Greek coffee shop, where she ordered a large lunch and barely touched it. The waitress asked whether there was something wrong with the food. "No, it was fine, thank you," Cindy said as she put money on the table.

"You pay up front."

Cindy left the shop and continued her aimless walking. She had no idea where Hal might have gone, whether he'd returned to the hotel or perhaps had even gone to the airport and taken the first available flight home. She secretly hoped that it was the latter. The thought of again facing him filled her with dread.

She arrived at the hotel at four and approached her room with trepidation. She knocked. There was no response, so she used her key. In the center of the room was a pile of cartons, each bearing a label that read "Bryce Audio." She got to her knees and read the black printing on them. Hal had purchased an expensive and elaborate stereo system and she couldn't help smiling. He'd wanted a new system for years but was reluctant to spend the money. All she could think of was a distraught woman buying a new hat. "I love you, Hal," she said as she began to shake. She leaned her forehead against one of the cartons and allowed the tears to flow freely. When there were no more to come she got to her feet and went to the phone, dialed a number, and waited for someone to answer. "Hello, may I speak with Mr. Machlin, please?" she said.

"You can dial him directly," the operator said. "His extension is three one nine five."

"Can't you connect me?" Cindy asked.

"Yes, but please make note of his extension for future reference."

"Yes, I'm doing that right now." She wrote the number in the air, with her thumb and index finger pressed together as though they contained a pencil. She waited. Another female voice said, "Mr. Machlin's office."

"This is Cindy Lewis. May I speak with him?"

"He's busy in a conference right now. Can he call you back?"

"Please, it's very urgent. I must speak with him."

"Just a moment," the secretary said. A few seconds later Machlin came on the phone.

"Hello, Cindy," he said. "What can I do for you?"

"I don't want the job."

"Pardon?"

"I don't want the job. I don't want to be an anchor of anything except my family. Please, I'm sorry if this causes any problems, but I wasn't cut out for this. I just wish to return home, where I understand things."

It was obvious that he felt awkward discussing it with her, that there must have been other people in the office. He said, "I told you I'm no longer a part of this decision. Why don't you call Howard Monroe?"

"Call him?"

"Yes. Tell him what you told me. He's the one who's handling this now."

"Thank you." She hung up, dialed EBS's number again, and when her call was answered asked to be connected with Mr. Monroe's office. The operator gave her his direct extension, and Cindy went through the charade of pretending to write it down. The connection was made and Monroe's secretary answered. Mr. Monroe was out of the office and would not return for an hour.

"Is there anyone else I could talk to?"

Her question amused the secretary. She said through a stifled giggle, "Lots of people, I suppose. What is it in reference to?"

"Nothing. Thank you, I'll call back later."

She considered asking the desk to send up a typewriter. She wanted to write Hal a long letter explaining her feelings; perhaps through the permanence of type she would be able to secure his understanding and forgiveness. But she realized it would be a silly exercise. Her fear of facing him was now a thing of the past. She wanted to be with him, to touch him and look into his eyes and tell him everything that was inside her, explain that fateful evening and what led up to it, her thoughts and feelings during it. She would tell him she thought only of him and of the family, that she hated every second of the night in bed with Satterfield, and that she would gladly give both arms if she could cancel those hours of her life.

After a half-hour of thought and anxiety, she placed a call to her home in Amarillo. Maria answered. Never before had she been so happy to hear a familiar voice. "Maria, how are you?"

"Good, *Señora*. Everything is good here. How are you?"

"Fine. Just fine. Are the children there?"

"*Sí*. Just a moment." She called out one of the children's names. Cindy's oldest son came on the line. They talked for a few minutes before he turned the phone over to one of the other kids. Cindy had all she could do to keep from crying, but she managed to maintain her composure. When the conversation was over she picked up her purse, left the room and went to the bar, ordered a double bourbon on the rocks, and nursed it until she realized it was dinner time. She walked to the lobby, picked up a hotel phone, and dialed her room number.

"Hello," Hal said.

"Hal, it's Cindy."

"I figured that. Where are you?"

"Downstairs, in the bar."

"We have some talking to do, Cindy."

"I know. Please come down and join me."

"In a few minutes."

_____CHAPTER 29

Maureen O'Dwyer walked quickly up Lexington Avenue on the way to her luncheon date with Renée at Antolotti's. She crossed the avenue, entered the post office, fished in her handbag, pulled out envelopes, and shoved them into a slot. The moment they were gone she felt weak and leaned against the wall. A few deep breaths later she was back outside and heading for Forty-ninth Street.

She was warmly greeted as she came through the door, and she accepted the offer of a complimentary drink while she waited for Renée. She sat on the single barstool and took a fast swig of a Bloody Mary that had been set in front of her.

"I saw you on the news the other night," the tuxedoed bartender said.

"Did you?" Maureen asked.

"Yes, you should come back to New York."

Maureen smiled. "I might just do that. You might be seeing a lot more of me."

"That would be wonderful, Miss O'Dwyer."

Renée's call suggesting lunch had not come as a complete surprise. Maureen was sure this was it, that she would be offered the job as anchor, and no matter how hard she tried she could not keep her hand from trembling as she lifted her glass. A glow of satisfaction gently washed over her. She thought of her father and his constant admonition never to give up on something if you wanted it badly enough. Being given the anchor slot certainly proved that adage. She tried not to think of Julie, who, by now, was at thirty thousand feet and winging home to Kansas City. She was momentarily annoyed at herself for how she'd handled the situation with Julie. Sending a letter so quickly wasn't necessary. She should have allowed the girl to settle in at her mother's house before breaking the news. She also wondered whether it really would be necessary to renege on the promise to bring her east. Once she was established in her new anchor spot, she could probably arrange things so that Julie could join her. But it would have to be further in the future, after she was secure and things had settled down.

She didn't have much time to think about it, however, because Renée came through the door and tapped her on the shoulder. Maureen swung around on the stool and they embraced.

Once at their table, and after Renée had ordered a drink to "catch up," she asked how the trip to the airport had gone.

"Fine. She's a lovely girl, isn't she?"

Renée nodded enthusiastically. "She certainly is, someone to be proud of. Did she have a good time here?"

"Not as good as I did. We had fun, took long walks, bought some things, and had some interesting talks. I think an understanding is developing between us that we've never had before. It's been a rocky road and probably will be for a while, but she's getting old enough to understand things that she couldn't before. I guess I never was much of a kid person. I'll probably be much happier as a mother when my kid is no longer a kid."

"So you can apply the grandmother concept?"

"What's that?"

"Love them, spend time with them, but know you can walk away."

Maureen wondered what Renée was really thinking, whether her thoughts were on the child she'd never had. She buttered a roll and said, "So, tell me what's new in the swinging, swirling world of big-time television entertainment."

"Lots."

Maureen sensed discomfort in Renée and it concerned her. She started to ask a direct question about the anchor choice, but a waiter came to the table and asked if they were ready to order. Renée requested menus, and they made their choices. Then Renée cleared her throat, glanced around the room, and said, "I would just as soon hold off the discussion about the anchor job, Mo, until the end of lunch, but I know that isn't fair."

Maureen sat in stunned silence. The news could be nothing but bad, judging from the way Renée had broached the subject. She was afraid to ask, afraid to have the words spoken.

She didn't have to. Renée said, "You're not getting it, Maureen. That's the bottom line."

"I see," Maureen said, trying desperately not to lose control of her voice. "Why not?"

Renée slowly shook her head and fiddled with a gold bracelet on her left wrist as she formed the words in her mind.

"Why?" Maureen asked again. The anxious tremor was gone from her voice. Now there was O'Dwyer anger. "Why, damn it?" She leaned closer and clenched her fist over the table.

Renée looked up. "Maureen, it was a committee decision, and not just those of us in News management. They'd brought in outside consultants, a think-tank operation with charts and graphs and scientific measurement of audience response to you and the others. It's the rage these days, I suppose. The ad agencies are all using them. They measure saliva flow and eye twitches and . . ."

Renée hadn't intended to make Maureen laugh, but that was the result. It was not, however, a happy, mirthful laugh. It dripped with irony and anger. She said, "Saliva flow and eye twitches? Are you telling me that I've been denied a job because a bunch of slobs didn't drool on cue?"

Renée was very aware of the growing hostility across the table and tried to soften it. "It wasn't just that, Maureen. I don't think anybody wanted to put faith in studies like those, but the stakes are so big that they pulled out every stop. If it makes you feel better, the subjective comments from viewers who were tested were all favorable to you."

"But subjective judgments don't count, do they? Who got it, Renée, Betty Boop from Amarillo"—she pronounced the word with an exaggerated southern drawl—"or the black cat from Frisco?"

"Neither. All three of you were ruled out."

Maureen was silent because there was so much to say. All she managed was, "Jesus."

"I know, I know. Look, Mo, sometimes these things end up for the better."

"Bullshit. Don't give me that Pollyanna crap, Renée. My pins have been kicked out from under me because of . . . because of . . . oh, shit, I can't believe it, can't accept it. What about Carl Schwartz? Did he sit still for this?"

"He's part of the army, Mo, that's all. If you mean was he in your corner, of course he was, one hundred percent. So was I. But EBS has been floundering too long, and the order is out, boost the news ratings and do it goddamn fast."

Their food was served and they ate halfheartedly. Halfway through the meal Maureen asked, "What happens now? Are you going after Barbara Walters or Jane Pauley? How about Supreme Court Justice O'Connor? She'd make a hell of an anchor, would probably get the spit flowing when the saliva tests were taken."

Renée placed her fork on the plate with surprising force. She sat up straight and said in low, measured tones,

"Knock it off, Maureen. You're a big girl and you've known from the minute you set foot into this business that you were rolling dice. You had an opportunity, you gave it your best shot, and it didn't work. Where does that leave you? It leaves you a respected journalist on television and radio in the nation's capital. You make more money than most women would ever hope to see in a career. You're healthy, you have a lovely daughter, and you didn't have to give up anything in order to take a shot at the next rung. You stay right where you are, firmly entrenched on the rung below, and I really think you ought to start looking at it that way and stop feeling sorry for yourself."

"How charming to have lunch with you, Renée. You deliver the bad news and then give me a lecture on how to react."

"Maybe you've needed a lecture for a long time, Maureen. Maybe if you'd had one a long time ago, things might have worked out differently. This shell you wrap yourself in, the tough-broad facade, doesn't do you justice." The words had an effect. Maureen visibly relaxed and Renée sipped her wine. After moments of silence, Renée said, "Feel better. It's not the end of the world."

Maureen smiled sardonically. "You said before that I didn't have to give up anything in order to reach for the next rung. That's not true."

Renée raised her eyebrows. "What did you give up, Mo? You still have everything you had before in Washington."

"I gave up Julie."

"How?"

"I promised her that she could come live with me in Washington. I told her I wasn't going to take the anchor job in New York."

Renée broke into a broad smile. "How wonderful. Now your promise can come true."

Maureen told her about the letter she'd written. Renée suggested that a simple phone call to Kansas City would square that away, but Maureen disagreed. The fact that she'd made those promises knowing all the while that she would write such a letter and cancel them could do nothing but set up a serious lack of trust between them.

"You will have her come to Washington to live with you?" Renée asked.

"I'll try."

They left the restaurant and stood together on the street. Renée extended her hand and Maureen took it. Renée said, "Things do work out sometimes for the better, Mo. I think what's happened this past week is very positive for everyone."

Maureen pursed her lips and squeezed Renée's hand. "Thanks for everything, Renée. We'll be in touch."

"Yes, we will."

Veronica sat across the desk from Howard Monroe. They'd discussed the call from Roscoe, and Monroe had assured her that it really didn't matter to him. What was left unsaid was that she was not being offered the anchor job for that reason. It didn't matter. She'd told him how anxious she was to join the special investigative unit and to work with Greg Oates, and he assured her that she had his complete blessing.

He sat impassively, the phone held to his ear as he waited for Craig Stanton in San Francisco to come on the line. When Stanton did, Monroe said, "Craig, every time I talk to somebody in San Francisco I have this little twinge of envy."

"Don't," Stanton said. "It's raining here, and there's always the threat of imminent destruction from earthquakes, tidal waves, and other acts of nature. What's new?"

"Lots, but that's the advantage of working here in Big Town, USA. Look, Craig, I'm sitting here with Veronica Frazier."

"Say hello for me."

Monroe looked at Veronica and said, "He says hello." She waved her fingers in the air to return the greeting.

"She says hello, too, Craig. Look, Ms. Frazier had been offered a slot with the special investigative unit out of Chicago. She wants it, and I think she should have it."

There was silence on the other end. Finally, Stanton said, "That's fine for her and for you, but what about me? She's built a reputation here. Besides, she has a contract. I was reluctant to let her come to New York because I figured something like this would come out of it. No, Howard, sorry, but I'm not letting her go."

Monroe looked across the desk at Veronica and said, "He's not letting you go."

She leaned forward and asked, "Can he do that?"

Monroe smiled and said into the phone, "Craig, the investigative unit is network, and you know that the network can break any contract with an affiliate. I would prefer not to have to go through that procedure, but I will if you force the issue. I think we all could benefit from having someone of Ms. Frazier's talents on that investigative unit, and I'll do whatever I have to to make it a reality. Let's not hassle each other over it. The decision has been made and that's it."

Again, silence. Stanton said, "Who am I to argue with somebody in New York?"

"No need for sarcasm."

"No sarcasm intended, Howard. If you think it's the right move, go ahead. Like you say, I'm a loser no matter how I view it. Let me talk to her."

Monroe handed her the phone. She said, "Hello Craig."

"Hello, Ronnie. I knew this was going to happen, and so did you." She started to say something, but he cut her off. "I'm mad as hell, feel betrayed, have the distinct impression that I have been used by a consummate user, but I'm also a realist. Congratulations. I hope you take from it what you want, what you need. I won't press the issue, but when you come back here to pack up your things I'd enjoy dinner and a chance to wrap things up."

"All right, Craig. Thank you."

"Thank me for what? I've just been mugged by the powers that be. See you when you get back."

"Good-bye."

Greg Oates was waiting for her in the newsroom when she left Monroe's office. She told him what had happened. He said, "Congratulations."

"Thank you, Greg, thank you for everything. It's amazing how a week can change a person's life. I hated coming to New York, but I think it was the best thing that's ever happened to me, and it's because of you."

"What are you doing for dinner?"

"It depends on you. I thought I might fly back to California tonight. I have lots of packing to do, things to square away, friends to say good-bye to."

"Can't you go tomorrow?"

"Of course I can."

"I thought we might have dinner together and catch some sounds. There are good people appearing around town."

"I'd love it, but I have to call my mother in Detroit to tell her about my new job."

"She'll be happy, won't she?"

"She's a mother, Greg. She's been happy with me no matter what I've done, good or bad. I guess that's what mothers are all about."

"Exactly. Come on, I'll walk you back to the hotel."

CHAPTER 31

It was early the next morning, four A.M. Cindy Lewis lay awake in the Inter-Continental. She looked over at Hal, who hugged the far edge of the bed. He seemed to be sleeping but she asked, "Hal, are you asleep?"

He said without moving, "No. Obviously you aren't either."

He turned on his back and sat up.

"We didn't make much sense in the bar, honey," she said. "If we don't talk about it there'll never be a way to make it right."

"I'm not sure all the talk in the world will ever accomplish that, Cindy. You know what we've always told the kids, that one of the worst things that can happen between people is a loss of trust. We've hammered that home because we believed in it. In fact, I thought we believed in many things together, but it seems I was wrong."

"That's not true, Hal. I believe just as strongly as ever in the values we've shared all these years. What I did doesn't change how I feel. I don't know if you can ever understand that, but it's true."

He suddenly shook with rage, swung his legs off the side of the bed, and sent the telephone flying from the night table. "Goddamn it, why, Cindy? Did you feel that you missed something being married all these years to the same man? Have all the goddamn gurus gotten to you, convinced you that the rules can be changed without other people being hurt?'' He stood, walked to the pile of stereo cartons and slapped his hand against them, turned, and said, ''Was he better in the sack, Cindy, was he younger, firmer, did he bring a little bag of tricks with him to give you a bigger and better orgasm?''

She started to cry but managed to say through the tears, ''Oh, Hal, no, no, no. There's only been you, I only want you for the rest of my life. Please, I understand how you feel, but all I can ask is that you try to forgive me. I beg you for that.'' She got up from the bed and buried her face in his chest. ''We can work it out, I know we can. I wanted this week in New York so much and it's turned out to be the most miserable experience of my life. It's gotten in the way of the one thing in the world that's important to me, and that's you. Do you know how cheap and dirty I've felt ever since it happened, how miserable it made me feel when you told me you would change your whole life to accommodate me if I were offered the job?''

''Look, Cindy, intellectually I think I can understand and accept, but emotionally it's another story. There'll never be a time watching television when both of us won't be reminded of what happened. When people have talked about the tremendous influence of television I always thought I knew what they were saying. Now it hits home, and I can't promise anything. Can you understand *that?*''

''We both can try, that's all.''

They stayed up, packing their things in preparation for their flight back to Amarillo that morning. They said little, kept their distance, and treated each other with courtesy that bordered on silliness. They had breakfast at the hotel, checked out, and took a cab to Kennedy Airport. As they approached it, Hal turned to her and said, ''I love you.''

''And I love you, Hal.''

''It might not be enough.''

''Let's just hope it is.''

Maureen O'Dwyer ended her telephone conversation with
Joe Coughlin in Washington by saying, "I'll be back this
afternoon, Joe. How are things there?"

"Just waiting for you to return, sweetheart. Maurice
filled in nicely on the radio show. The TV people are talking about generating a nightly interview segment and your
name came up as a possible hostess, but more on that
when you're back."

"Thanks, Joe. See you later."

She hung up and placed a call to Kansas City. The line
was busy. So she took a few minutes to put things in a
suitcase. She'd rehearsed a speech to Julie ever since waking up that morning, then realized that the letter had certainly not arrived yet, and that she could head off its
delivery by making sure her mother understood the situation. She tried the number again and, to her relief, her
mother answered. "Mama, how are you?"

"All right," her mother said rather coldly.

"How's Julie?"

"She's fine. She told me we're all moving to Washington. It's a fine thing, not telling me and having the child
come home with the news."

"Everything's been happening so fast, Mama, that I

didn't have a chance. Look, I want you and Julie to join me in Washington. How do you feel about that?''

''I don't like leaving here. This is my home.''

''You don't have to, but I want Julie with me. Why would you want to stay there alone?''

''Because I don't trust politicians.''

Maureen laughed and thought of Jack Maitland. ''Living in Washington doesn't have anything to do with politicians, Mama. You don't have to have anything to do with them. The point is, I need you here. I'm still going to be very busy, and Julie needs someone at home. Please, think about it.''

''I will.''

Maureen carefully formed the words in her mind before she said, ''Mama, I mailed a letter to Julie that I don't want her to receive.''

''Why?''

''It doesn't matter. I know I've made lots of mistakes in my life and I'd like to stop making them. I'm sure you'd like me to stop making them, too.''

There was a hint of a smile in her mother's voice as she said, ''Yes, that would be nice.''

''Please, when the mailman delivers the letter from me to Julie, tear it up immediately, burn it, just don't let her see it.''

''All right.''

''And, Mama, I *would* like you and Julie with me in Washington. Please, don't make it difficult for me to catch up with my life, with my mistakes. I need both of you very much.''

''I suppose it wouldn't be too bad. We'll see.''

''That's all I can ask. Is Julie there?''

''No.''

''Tell her I love her and that I'll call her tomorrow.''

''I will.''

''Mama, I love *you* very much. Thank you for everything you've done.''

''You take care of yourself. The girl needs you.''

"And I need you. Good-bye."

Minutes after she'd hung up, the phone rang. It was Congressman Jack Maitland. He said, "Hello, stranger, when are you coming back?"

"Today. Why are you calling?"

"I wanted to let you know that I was going to be out of town for a few days."

"Where are you going?"

"Florida. Joe Paley offered me his condominium in Lauderdale for a few days and I thought I'd take him up on it. It's been a bitch of a week here and I need to get away."

"Are you taking somebody with you?"

"Who would I take?"

"I don't know, some nubile young thing with stringy blond hair and cute tits and ass."

"Funny, Mo, but I figured you probably latched on to some adorable young flower child with curly black hair and a beard up in New York."

"As a matter of fact, I did, and I intended to invite you to the wedding, but I figured you'd be tied up in weighty matters of state. Why don't you invite me to Florida with you?"

"Good idea. Can you get away?"

"Probably not, but I will. I'd like to have a serious talk with you, Congressman."

"About what?"

"About a potential piece of important legislation."

They worked out plans for meeting in Florida. Maureen would take a flight directly from Kennedy Airport to Fort Lauderdale. There was an awkward pause before the conversation ended.

"I've missed you, Mo," Maitland said.

"I've missed you, too, Jack. There have been some interesting changes in my life that I'm anxious to tell you about."

"Well, we'll have some quiet time for me to hear them. Have a safe trip."

"You, too."

Veronica had just checked in at the ticket counter and was about to go to the coffee shop when she saw Cindy and Hal Lewis come through the front doors of the terminal, preceded by a skycap. They got in line and Veronica went over to them.

"Hi," Cindy said. "How are you?"

"Just fine, Cindy," Veronica said. "Looks like the week is over."

Hal said gruffly, "Yes, looks like it."

There seemed little more to say, so Veronica said, "I really enjoyed meeting you, Cindy. I wish you all the best in the world."

"And the same to you, Veronica. It's been quite a week."

Veronica laughed. "In more ways than one. Have a nice flight."

"You, too."

As Veronica was about to turn and leave, Maureen O'Dwyer approached them. She spotted Cindy and Veronica and waved.

"Have a nice flight," Cindy yelled to her.

"Same to you," Maureen yelled, not breaking stride as she headed for her airline's ticket counter.

"I really admire her," Cindy said.

"So do I," Veronica said. "I hope we all meet up again."

"We will," Cindy said. "If you're ever in Amarillo, please visit us." She glanced up at Hal, who smiled and nodded.

Cindy and Hal watched Veronica walk away from them and enter a coffee shop at the far end of the terminal. Cindy said, "So many people, so many different lives, so many problems."

Hal started to say something, but the passenger in front moved away. Hal stepped up to the ticket counter and said to the young woman in uniform, "Mr. and Mrs. Lewis to Amarillo."

Bestselling Books

☐ 16663-3	DRAGON STAR Olivia O'Neill	$2.95
☐ 34232-9	THE HOLLOW MEN Sean Flannery	$3.50
☐ 46895-0	LADY JADE Leslie O'Grady	$3.25
☐ 55258-7	THE MYRMIDON PROJECT Chuck Scarborough & William Murray	$3.25
☐ 65366-9	THE PATRIARCH Chaim Bermant	$3.25
☐ 70885-4	REBEL IN HIS ARMS Francine Rivers	$3.50
☐ 78374-0	STAR STRUCK Linda Palmer	$3.25
☐ 02572-2	APOCALYPSE BRIGADE Alfred Coppel	$3.50
☐ 83288-1	TWILIGHT'S BURNING Diane Guest	$3.25
☐ 65219-0	PASSAGE TO GLORY Robin Leigh Smith	$3.50
☐ 75887-8	SENSEI David Charney	$3.50
☐ 05285-1	BED REST Rita Kashner	$3.25
☐ 62674-2	ON ANY GIVEN SUNDAY Ben Elisco	$3.25

Available wherever paperbacks are sold or use this coupon.

CHARTER BOOKS
Book Mailing Service
P.O. Box 690, Rockville Centre, NY 11571

Please send me the titles checked above. I enclose _____
Include $1.00 for postage and handling if one book is ordered; 50¢ per book for
two or more. California, Illinois, New York and Tennessee residents please add
sales tax.

NAME _____

ADDRESS _____

CITY _____ STATE/ZIP _____

(allow six weeks for delivery)

A-4

Bestsellers you've been hearing about—and want to read

____ **GOD EMPEROR OF DUNE**   06233-3–$3.95
    Frank Herbert
____ **INFAMY: PEARL HARBOR AND ITS AFTERMATH**   05991-X–$3.95
    John Toland
____ **DEATH BEAM**   05655-4–$3.50
    Robert Moss
____ **FOR RICHER, FOR POORER**   05397-0–$3.50
    Edwin Stewart
____ **DINNER AT THE HOMESICK RESTAURANT**   05999-5–$3.50
    Anne Tyler
____ **LAID BACK IN WASHINGTON**   05779-8–$3.25
    Art Buchwald
____ **THE KEEP**   06440-9–$3.95
    F. Paul Wilson
____ **HERS THE KINGDOM**   06147-7–$3.95
    Shirley Streshinsky
____ **THE THIRD DEADLY SIN**   05465-9–$3.95
    Lawrence Sanders
____ **NAM**   06000-4–$3.50
    Mark Baker
____ **FOR SPECIAL SERVICES**   05860-3–$3.50
    John Gardner
____ **200 HUNDRED CALORIE SOLUTION: HOW TO**   06065-9–$3.50
    BURN AN EXTRA 200 CALORIES A DAY AND LOSE WEIGHT
    Martin Katahn, Ph.D.

Available at your local bookstore or return this form to:

 BERKLEY
Book Mailing Service
P.O. Box 690, Rockville Centre, NY 11571

Please send me the titles checked above. I enclose _____
Include $1.00 for postage and handling if one book is ordered; 50¢ per book for two or more. California, Illinois, New York and Tennessee residents please add sales tax.

NAME _____

ADDRESS _____

CITY _____ STATE/ZIP _____

(allow six weeks for delivery)

1D